STEPHEN EDGER

Stephen is the author of eleven books and five short stories and has been writing since 2010. He was born in Darlington and raised in London, but has lived in Southampton since studying law at University over a decade ago.

Stephen has worked in financial services for more than a decade and it is his detailed understanding of this industry that adds authenticity to his work.

Stephen regularly tweets about his work on Twitter.com and can be followed as @StephenEdger.

Learn more by visiting www.stephenedger.com

STEPHEN EDGER

Downfall

Lindsey,

Nice to meet you! Thanks for coming to see us!

Stephen

×

THANK YOU

This is my opportunity to say a big 'Thank You' to those who have helped / inspired me to write and have given helpful ideas and feedback on this story.

Special thanks as always to Tim Ford and Jo Taylor for proof-reading my final draft. Also, thanks to Sue Dewis, Claire Knight, Jo Robertson, Karen Ratcliffe, Jo Sugden, Sue Wallace, Val Spencer, Sebella O'Donovan, Jackie Roche, and Selina Trafford, for providing valuable feedback prior to publication. Thanks also to Noelle Holten for her valuable insights into the UK prison system.

Final thanks should go to everyone who has downloaded or purchased a paperback copy of Integration, Remorse, Redemption, Snatched, Shadow Line, Trespass, Crosshairs, Complicit, Double Cross or Fragments. It has truly inspired me to continue writing and to tell the stories that run through my imagination every day.

Until the next time, keep reading.

WEDNESDAY

1

Johnson Carmichael tightened his grip around the older man's throat and forced him back towards the balcony doors.

The man gasped. 'Please, surely we can reach an understanding?'

An understanding? Who did he think he was dealing with, one of his members' club cohorts?

Carmichael's eyes bulged, the whites contrasting with the darkness of the skin around them. 'Tell me what you gave her!' They crashed into the apartment's closed balcony doors.

There was a moment of recognition on the man's face. 'You saw that?'

'I see *everything*!'

He'd been tailing the man for days, ever since the man's jealous wife visited the office and offered five grand for photographic evidence. She was fifty, if a day, but the years of expensive treatments had left her skin smooth and ageless. The deep maroon hair was treated, but the roots offered no indication of their natural tone. She was attractive, sure, but he'd vowed never to become romantically involved with a client. Not again.

'What has your husband done?' He knew the answer before she offered it. It was always the same.

She kept her shoulders straight, her chin slightly raised. What was it with the jilted middle class and their need to maintain decent posture? 'He's seeing someone behind my back.'

'You're after a divorce?'

She nodded.

'Do you want me to catch him in the act?'

She bit her lip to keep the tears in check. 'Whatever it takes.'

'Where will I find him?'

She handed him a business card.

Carmichael turned it over in his hands. 'He's a barrister?' He shouldn't have been surprised. They were always barristers, or accountants, or company owners. He was bored of philanderers, but the money was decent. 'How many women is he seeing?'

A sharp intake of breath. 'Well, one…I mean…I think he's only seeing -'

'Who is she? Friend of yours?'

'A neighbour.'

'What makes you suspect?' He was amazed at how varied the answers to this question inevitably were. Some said they'd found text messages or emails. Some said they'd found a stray pair of knickers. Others claimed it was just instinct. Regardless, ninety-nine per cent of the time, they were right.

'A friend told me.'

That was a new one. 'And you believe this friend?'

'She has no reason to lie to me.'

'How does she know? Has she seen them together?'

The client looked away, taking a deep breath. 'She…she was seeing him until he…he broke it off with her.'

His hatred of the man was growing by the second. 'So his former lover has confessed everything to you? That's pretty cold.'

She fixed him with a determined look. 'Can you help me or not?'

He sucked the air through his teeth. 'I'll need more details. I need to know the hours he spends at the office or in court, who the woman is, and when he sees her. It could be expensive.'

'Money isn't a problem.'

'There's a daily rate, an evening rate and a weekend rate. The rate is hourly and non-negotiable. Usually my assistant handles...' His words tailed off, as she placed a large white envelope on the desk between them.

'Whatever it takes, Mr Carmichael.'

The philanderer had been easy to track. Every morning he drove from their luxury beachside house in Sandbanks to Poole station, where he boarded a train to Southampton. He was a creature of habit: the same large macchiato and almond croissant for the journey, and The Daily Telegraph read via his tablet. He ignored the other commuters, not even offering a smile or a greeting. At Southampton, he walked the half mile to the court, unless it was raining, in which case he caught a taxi; it's not like he pays for it.

The first five days of surveillance were a waste of time. Carmichael wanted to call the client and tell her she'd made a mistake, but then, earlier today, a breakthrough. The jury returned its verdict, and the defence team went out to celebrate. Wearing a pinstripe suit and a blank expression, Carmichael passed unnoticed, as the champagne flowed and the pats on the back continued into the late evening. He felt like a voyeur watching them congratulate each other. Sharp stumbled from the party in the arms of a redheaded waitress, young enough to be his daughter.

In the waitress's Ocean Village apartment, the older man was still trying to wriggle free of the vice-like grip around his neck.

Carmichael dug his fingernails further. 'I saw you drop something into her drink. Tell me what the fuck it is or I'm going to squash your face into this wall.'

The man's eyes widened. 'I don't know what it's called…it's something I get online…please, I can't breathe.'

'Is it Rohypnol? Rufies?'

The red face nodded eagerly. Beads of sweat shimmered below his grey hairline.

Carmichael loosened his grip and turned back to check on the girl. She was still face down on the bed, naked. He checked for a pulse: it was slow, but there. He moved her into the recovery position. He pulled out his phone, and saw he'd missed a dozen calls from his assistant Melissa. He ignored them and dialled for an ambulance.

The older man reached out a hand. 'Please, there's no need to call for backup. I'll pay…whatever you want. Please? I'm begging you.'

Carmichael ran a hand over his close-cropped afro and spoke into the phone. He described the girl's condition before giving the address. His shirt collar was damp. He disconnected the call and opened the white PVC doors, stepping onto the balcony. Ten floors up, there was a decent view of the marina. How a waitress could afford a place like this was beyond him. The sun hung like an orange ball on the horizon. He closed his eyes and raised his head, allowing the light breeze to cool him.

The man was putting on his shirt when Carmichael stepped back into the room. 'I can get you a thousand pounds now, and a further thousand tomorrow. Will that do it? Will that make this all go away?' The man offered a hand to close the deal.

An extra two grand on top of what the client had already paid was tempting, and he'd be able to keep it off the books, but he turned his back instead.

The man placed his hand on Carmichael's arm. 'Okay, okay, an extra two thousand tomorrow. You can't say fairer than that. Man, you *do* drive a hard bargain. Can we shake on three thousand? It's not like she'll remember anything about this anyway.'

Carmichael's eyes bulged once more in the mirror's reflection. The red mist descended. He span round and threw a right hook. It connected with the man's left cheek. The man yelped, as he stumbled backwards.

'Wait…you can't,' the man sputtered.

Carmichael pulled him up by his shirt collar, and growled. 'I can do whatever the fuck I like. I'm not the police.'

'Who the hell are you then?'

'I'm the detective your wife hired to catch you cheating. Your marriage is over.' He hit him again, and again, driving the older man onto the balcony.

'What the hell is wrong with you? She's just some whore.'

Carmichael coiled his fingers around the exposed

neck once again, bending him back over the balcony rail. The older man's limbs flailed against his attacker to no effect. It would be so easy to keep pushing, to let gravity do the rest. Carmichael ground his teeth. The man's knuckles were white from gripping the edge of the balcony, as he tried to pull himself back up.

The door to the apartment burst open. 'Johnson, no!' Melissa raced across the room and pulled on Carmichael's arm. 'You can't. Let him go. Not like this.'

The older man glanced from Carmichael to the woman who was coming to his rescue, and then back again. Carmichael pushed a little further, and then pulled him forward, and flung him into the room. The man crashed into the side of the bed, and remained on his knees as he got his breath back.

Melissa waved a finger in Carmichael's face. 'What the hell do you think you're doing?'

'I'm working the case. What do you think I'm doing?'

'You weren't supposed to be working today. When I didn't see you this morning, I assumed you were going to your daughter's funeral.'

Carmichael walked back into the room and checked on the waitress's condition.

'I've been phoning you. Why didn't you go to the funeral, Johnson? You need to say -'

'You've no idea what I need!'

'I know *this* isn't healthy. Taking out your grief on some worthless scumbag isn't the answer.'

'What do you know about it? Have you ever lost a child?' She didn't answer. 'Exactly, so you cannot even imagine what I'm going through.'

She raised her hands in mock surrender. 'You're right, I don't know what it's like, but, Johnson, I'm your friend. In fact, I may be your only friend, and that gives me the right to worry about you. You're not the same since she passed away. You can't keep blaming yourself for what happened. It isn't your fault you weren't a donor match.'

He turned his back on her and pulled a small plastic packet out of his trouser pocket.

'And don't think I haven't seen you taking those things. What are they anyway?'

He threw two pills into his mouth and swallowed them dry. He turned back to face her. 'Don't forget you work for *me*, Melissa, not the other way around. You need to mind your own business.'

'Um, actually, I think you'll find we agreed to be partners when I came back to work for the firm. Don't forget that once I've got my licence, I'll be as qualified as you.'

The man clambered to his feet, before Carmichael knocked him back down.

Melissa dragged Carmichael to the kitchen. 'He'd have every right to press charges against you,' she whispered. 'It isn't your job to be judge, jury, and executioner. You were hired to take photographs. That was all! You shouldn't even be here.'

'He spiked her drink. He needs to be taught a lesson!'

'Then let the police handle it. You've got to stop taking things so personally. You need to relax more. I've not seen you go to the pub in months. Why don't we go out for a drink now? We could talk and -'

'Then I *would* be a walking cliché, wouldn't I? Not all private detectives need alcohol to get through the day.'

'Right now, alcohol would be safer than whatever else you're on, and it would be safer than threatening to push people over balconies. I'm warning you, Johnson, you're on a dangerous road. Next stop is self-destruction. Don't throw it all away.'

2

Kelly walks across the room and perches on the edge of the bed. She gazes longingly at the man still handcuffed to the bedframe. Blood covers the restraints around his wrists. She can't believe this is how their night together has ended. She still has butterflies in her stomach. Going to bed with a man she barely knows is not like her, but she isn't ashamed. If anything, she feels a sense of freedom greater than any she has ever known.

Everyone warns you about the perils of internet dating, but without it, she wouldn't have met Todd. She rubs her hand over his hairy chest. He flinches. He isn't even her usual type: he has a noticeable paunch, a second chin, and is thinning on top. She's always pictured herself with someone so much more rugged and dangerous.

They had met earlier that evening in a small café in Totton. She was nervous at first. With her upbringing that was understandable. He seemed anxious too. He kept glancing at the door, like he wanted to bolt at any minute. She put that down to nerves. She promised she wouldn't bite, and was only seeking companionship. He relaxed a bit, and ordered them both a coffee. He seemed so chivalrous.

She didn't tell him too much about her background. He worked for a bank. He said he was the branch manager, but his body language suggested he wasn't being honest. Not necessarily lying, more exaggerating the importance of his role. She can forgive that. After all, she wasn't entirely honest in her online profile either.

The restraints clatter against the headboard as he pulls on them again. She places a finger to her lips to quieten him.

She has been looking for love for some time. It hasn't been easy. She's spent hours in bars and clubs, waiting to be chatted up, but to no avail. She hasn't been able to figure out why that is. She's only thirty-four, isn't overweight, and her long blonde curls flow down her back. She doesn't have any female friends she can talk to about it. Her brother does, but it isn't right to discuss such matters with them.

Her brother is four years older, and they now live together in Southampton. Growing up wasn't easy for either of them, but they are closer now; at least she thinks they are. Even after all that has happened to them, she's still able to wrap him around her finger. He wouldn't approve of her seeing Todd, and he will go ballistic if he ever finds out she's slept with him.

Her date with Todd had been going so well. They ordered a second coffee, but his nerves returned and he suddenly said he needed to leave. She walked back to the car park with him. She told him she enjoyed their date, and would like to get to know him better. She leaned in for a kiss, but he thrust out a hand instead, promising he would call her soon.

She watched him walk away, a sadness in her heart. Something about his demeanour told her he wouldn't call. She had to know why. What had she done wrong? She'd been funny, sophisticated even. She hated that he judged their potential together after one short date.

She waited for him to exit the car park before following him back here. She watched him go inside the small block of flats, before finding his name and flat number. She snuck in and caught the lift to the third floor, as her feet were aching. She isn't used to wearing heels.

He was surprised to see her at his door, but she made it impossible for him to close it. She told him exactly what she was going to do with him. He offered little resistance when she removed the six inch blade from her handbag.

She leans over and kisses his cheek. There is resignation in his eyes, as if he senses what is to follow. She puts her dress back on and fixes her hair in the bathroom mirror. She applies her favourite cherry red lipstick and admires her reflection. She skips back into the bedroom, and pulls her phone out. She takes a picture of him. He begins to cry.

'Hush there, my big bear,' she soothes. 'We had fun, but now it's time for me to go. You should know I'll never forget our night together. It was…' She sighs. 'It was perfect.'

She checks her watch. Her brother will be expecting her home by midnight, so she doesn't have long. She opens Todd's wardrobe and uses one of his work shirts as a makeshift apron. He is sobbing beneath the tape that covers his lips.

She tilts her head and makes a sad face. 'There, there, my love. It will all be over soon enough.' She bends and kisses him, pushing her tongue against the tape so he can feel it. She admires the mark her lipstick has left on the tape. 'That's something to remember me by.'

His eyes widen with panic, and he mumbles.

'I know what you're going to say, that I can let you live, and you won't tell anyone what happened, but I can't take that risk. If my brother ever…well, he'd go into meltdown. I don't have any other choice. If it's any consolation, this isn't the first time I've done this.'

It's been years since she's felt the urge to kill. That pounding in her heart, the giddy excitement as the adrenalin courses through her veins. It is an urge she has tried to suppress, but tonight it's back with a vengeance. If she can't have him, nobody will.

He sees the knife in her hand, and desperately shakes his head as she firmly presses the blade against his left wrist. She runs the blade down his forearm, before repeating the gesture on his other arm. He is howling beneath the tape.

'All done. It won't be long now, my love. The angels are coming for you.' She picks up her shoes and opens the bedroom door. His groaning catches her attention and she turns back to look at him. Her heart is heavy. She frowns and considers him for a moment. 'As you were so good to me, I'll return the favour.'

There is a flicker of hope in his eyes, as she reaches for the restraints, but she is just checking they are firm. She pushes the blade beneath his right ear. He groans louder now, his eyes begging her. She leans in so he can hear her whisper. 'You don't have to thank me, my darling.' She straightens and draws the blade across his neck. There is a choking sound as bubbles pop along the red opening. She rips the tape from his lips and puts in her handbag.

'Here they come, Todd. Can you see them? The angels are coming.'

THURSDAY

3

Melissa was already flitting around the office when he arrived. The last thing he wanted was another confrontation about the fact he'd missed his daughter's funeral. He was switching on his laptop when Melissa poked her head through his door. 'Cup of tea or coffee?'

'Coffee. Black. Two sugars.'

She left the door ajar, returning moments later with his mug. She placed it on his desk, and sat in the chair across from him. She remained silent.

This was one of her things. She'd told him before how powerful an awkward silence can be. The secret to using it is to resist the urge to say something. It's like a Jedi mind trick. Essentially, the first person to speak, yields the power to the other party, and it's almost impossible to reclaim control of the dynamic. He stared back at her, determined not to crack.

Her return to the firm had brought about an upturn in business. She returned only when he agreed to make her a full-time partner, on the basis she would apply for her own investigator's licence. She was young, and had lots of ideas about how to drag the business into the modern age. She had arranged for a website to be created, set up social media accounts for advertising purposes and it had also been her idea to spruce up the office. He'd been renting the space for several years from a former client who still gave him a reduced monthly rate. The space was let as an office with a small flat above the premises. Melissa lived in the flat until a year ago, but since then the space had been vacant. Rather than wasting it, she suggested they convert the flat into two offices and a small kitchen space for making tea and coffee. It enabled them to have an office each, rather than being crammed into the tiny space on the floor below them, which was now a small waiting room with half a dozen chairs and some magazines. He had to admit, the operation was more professional now, and he liked having his own area where he could work in silence, apart from when she invaded it, as she was now doing.

'Can I help you with something?' he finally asked.

She tried to hide her look of satisfaction. 'I thought we should take a look at what new work has come in, so we can divide up who's doing what. There's no time like the present.'

His head had been aching since he'd woken, but he'd run out of the mild amphetamines he'd been taking for the last two weeks. He'd already knocked back four paracetamol, but they hadn't come close to taking the edge off. The fluorescent light overhead was making him squint. He turned it off. Semi-darkness brought slight relief.

'You had an answerphone message from someone called Tom Dewis.'

'I don't know anyone by that name. What does he want?'

She couldn't help but smile. 'He wants you to help him appeal his mother's conviction for murder. It sounds interesting.'

'Doesn't sound like the usual thing we'd take on.'

'Exactly! I googled him.'

'And?'

'And if it's the same guy, he lives in Bassett, near the municipal golf course.'

'Still doesn't ring any bells.'

'Well, I did find something else…there was a news article involving a Tom Dewis sixteen years ago. It involved his father, rather than him, but his name was mentioned in the story.'

'What was the story about?'

'Well, his father was murdered in the family home in Highfield. He was stabbed with a kitchen knife, and bled out before the emergency services arrived. Sue Dewis, Tom's mother, was charged and convicted of his murder, and has been behind bars ever since. Tom was seven at the time.'

'You think it's the guy?

She shrugged. 'Maybe. You'll find out soon enough. I made you an appointment to go and see him on Saturday.'

He screwed up his face. 'Saturday? You know I don't like working over the weekend.'

'When you're self-employed, you have to work when the work's there. Besides, he said he wasn't free until Saturday, so you'll have to lump it.'

'So be it, what else is there?'

'I telephoned our last client. I delicately explained what happened yesterday. She's going to stop by this afternoon to collect the photographs you took. I thought it best not to mention the scrape you got into with her husband.'

'How did she sound?'

'To be honest, she sounded disappointed her suspicions were right.'

'Is that it? Nothing else on the books for this week?'

Melissa sipped her coffee. 'Your next appointment's waiting for you downstairs in reception. You want me to show her up?'

'Who is she? What does she want?'

'Beats me. She made the appointment online. All I know is her name's Mrs Barlow.'

'Very well. Maybe you should sit in on this one. Maybe it'll be something you can handle with me overseeing.'

Melissa returned a few minutes later with a frail-looking silver haired woman. She helped the woman into the chair across from Carmichael. 'Mrs Barlow, this is Johnson Carmichael.'

The old lady held out her hand, which he shook. 'Thank you for agreeing to meet with me, Mr Carmichael. You don't know how much I appreciate it.'

'It's my pleasure. How can I help you?'

She opened her handbag and placed a photograph on the table in front of him. 'This is my daughter. Pretty, isn't she? A real chip off the old block.' She snickered to herself.

He looked at the photograph. The woman in it had platinum blonde hair, which fell beneath her shoulders. She was attractive, maybe in her late thirties or early forties. She was wearing a cocktail dress, and was pouting at the camera. It looked like the sort of profile shot taken on board cruise ships. He passed the photograph to Melissa.

'She was an only child. My husband passed shortly after her birth; heart attack. I raised her single-handedly, and we were very close. Even during her time at university, she would call me almost every day and would visit once a fortnight. Such a good girl.'

'I see. So how can I help?'

She pulled out a tissue and wiped her nose. 'I want you to prosecute the man who killed her.'

He shot a glance at Melissa, before turning back. 'Your daughter is dead?'

Mrs Barlow nodded. 'Dead at thirty-seven. Too young to die.'

'I agree. Can you tell me what happened?'

'She was brainwashed and murdered.'

4

D.S. Beth Taylor changed the radio station as she drove the Ford Focus through Millbrook towards Totton. She was listening out for anything that wasn't an advert for a local business. She finally found a song she recognised and sang along. It was ten a.m., and the morning's rush-hour traffic had long since dissipated. The sun was shining in the cloudless sky, and she lowered the windows for fresh air.

She'd been eagerly tucking into a bacon sandwich when she'd received the call. 'Murder' wasn't a term commonly used in Southampton, which is why there was always a buzz around the office when it was uttered. She was part of the Hampshire Major Investigation Team (H.M.I.T.), based out of the purpose-built headquarters building on the edge of the city. Beth had only had her stripes for four months, but with her D.I. out of the country, it had fallen to her to tackle the investigation. For now, at least. D.C.I. Naomi Payne wanted regular updates of progress. The ivory-coloured blouse Beth had spilt ketchup on was now covered by her buttoned-up jacket.

Beth weaved the Focus through the Millbrook streets, lined with council properties. She spotted truant children messing about in the park, but resisted the urge to argue with them and continued on her way. She pulled onto the kerb-edge when she spotted the police cordon and the uniformed officer protecting the scene. She flashed him her warrant card, and he lifted the tape to allow her under. She put on a pair of latex gloves and shoe protectors from a box outside of the property and headed in. She climbed the staircase, heading towards the noise of chatter at the top. She ducked beneath the tape covering the entrance and stepped into Todd Francis' flat.

She found Dr Neil Spinks in the victim's bedroom. The pathologist was in his mid-fifties, and his pale skin clung to his bones for dear life. He had a full head of light grey hair, and looked like he belonged on a morgue slab himself. He nodded towards her as she entered the room.

'Good morning, detective,' he said cheerily. 'No White today?'

'He's on leave. D.C.I. Payne said I should take the lead. You're stuck with me, I'm afraid.'

'Don't apologise, dear, you're much prettier than that old Geordie.'

'What can you tell me?'

'The victim's name was Todd Francis. Looks like he's been here since late last night. Body temperature at point of discovery would suggest a time of death between ten and midnight. As you can see, somebody restrained him to the headboard, before running a small blade against the length of both arms. There is bruising around the wrists, suggesting he wasn't bound voluntarily. He would have bled out from these wounds alone, but his throat was then cut open, with presumably the same implement.'

'Any ideas what type of knife we should be looking for?'

'I'll need to examine the wounds closer in the lab, but I would guess a six inch blade. There aren't any knives missing from the block in the kitchen, which may suggest whoever did this brought the weapon with them.'

'So you think it was premeditated?'

'It would surprise me if it wasn't.'

'What do you think: sex game taken too far?'

Spinks considered the question. 'The restraints do suggest a bondage fascination. It's not clear whether the handcuffs belonged to the victim or his attacker.'

'Is there anything else you can tell me?'

He passed her a small plastic wallet. 'There's this.'

She lifted the wallet into the light. 'A strand of long blonde hair. You think our suspect is a woman?'

'Maybe, but whether she is or not, that's not real hair.'

'The killer was wearing a wig?'

'A wig or hair extensions. I should be able to confirm more back at the lab.'

She passed the wallet back. 'Do you know if the SOCOs have found any usable prints yet?'

'They're still searching I believe. I've only been here for half an hour. You'll have to check with forensics.'

'Are you finished with your preliminary examination?'

'Oh no, dear. I'll be a little while longer yet.'

'When do you think you'll have finished the post mortem?'

'Assuming I can get the body to my lab in the next

two hours, I should have a verbal report ready for you by mid-afternoon. The paperwork won't be completed before morning.'

She thanked him and headed over to the officer who was coordinating the SOCOs. 'Morning, Dave.'

'Oh hi, Beth. How are you?'

'I'm fine. How are you guys getting on? Any sign of the murder weapon yet?'

'No, not yet. Spinks said he thinks it was a six inch knife with a plain, non-serrated edge. We've bagged the knives we found in the kitchen in case it was cleaned after use. Have you seen the victim yet? It's pretty messy in there.'

She nodded. 'We're on the fifth floor, so point of entry must have been the front door. I didn't notice any signs of obvious forced entry when I came through the door.'

'No there isn't. Either the attacker had a key, or the victim knew his attacker and welcomed them in.'

'What else do we know about the victim?'

'We found a staff security pass for General Financial bank. We've put a call out to the local branches, to see if he worked at any of them. It looks like he lived alone. We've only found one set of clothes, one toothbrush, et cetera. There was a receipt for a café in his wallet. He ordered two coffees there at half past eight last night. We'll see if they have security footage of who he met.'

'Have you spoken to the neighbours yet?'

'Officers are canvassing as we speak.'

'What's your best guess for motive?'

'It doesn't look like anything was taken. We found his wallet on the kitchen countertop, and there's plenty of cash in it. The flat's a bit messy, but given the age of the victim, and the fact he lived alone, that's not surprising. I think it's too early to say. If you pushed me I'd say he invited the wrong person home.'

She thanked him and was about to leave when a thought struck her. 'Who called it in?'

'Sorry?'

'The crime: who called it in? How did we hear about it?'

'I think it was an anonymous tip. You'll have to check with the First Officer Attending.'

She ducked beneath the tape back out to the corridor. She saw one of the forensics team dusting for prints in the lift, so took the stairs.

The victim had lived alone, and there were no obvious signs of a burglary. The bank where he worked hadn't reported him missing. He hadn't been dead long enough for anyone to suspect anything sinister beyond the door of the flat. Yet, somebody had known he was dead and had reported it. The body wouldn't have been discovered for days, so why would the killer risk getting caught? It was a question that troubled her all the way back to the station.

5

Carmichael nearly spat out his coffee. 'I'm sorry? She was…brainwashed?'

The old lady nodded vehemently. 'She joined one of those hippy New Age churches. They're the ones who did it.'

'I'm sorry, Mrs Barlow, you said your daughter was murdered?'

'She's been gone a month now.'

'What have the police concluded?'

She wrinkled her nose. 'They're no use. Accidental death is how they described it. I mean, please, how could she *accidentally* overdose on heroin?'

He could hear the bitterness in her voice, and didn't want to antagonise her further. 'Perhaps you could start at the beginning, Mrs Barlow. Help me understand why you believe this…this church caused your daughter's death.'

'I suppose the first thing you should know is she didn't have an easy upbringing. With her father not around, I had to be both parents and it was a struggle at times. I didn't have any other family to support me. I had some savings to pay the rent on our home, but not much else. That said, I showed her the love of two parents.'

Carmichael checked his watch. It was nearly ten, and his stomach was rumbling from a lack of breakfast.

'She was always easily led. When she was fifteen, she fell in with a bad crowd. She would go out until late at the weekends and wouldn't tell me where she was going, what she was doing, or who she was seeing. I became concerned, but when I challenged her about it…it only drove a greater wedge between us. I still remember the night the police phoned me to say she'd been arrested. I was disappointed with her, but angrier at myself. She'd been found in the back of a stolen car in possession of cocaine. She was formally cautioned, but that was the end of it. The officer who'd arrested her was a member of the church I attended, and put in a good word for her. I don't think she appreciated how lucky she was at the time. I brought her home and we talked for a long time. She showed remorse and promised to stop seeing the group she'd been found with. I insisted she come to church with me again every Sunday. I knew she wasn't keen, but at least I'd be able to keep an eye on her. Despite what she'd told me, she continued to see her old friends.

She removed her glasses, and cleaned them with a corner of her cardigan. 'One night I was contacted by the hospital, telling me she was in a bad way. She'd been found comatose, having ingested a dangerous substance. I learned she had been regularly using drugs for months. She'd even been stealing things from me to pay for her habit. I blamed myself, as all mothers do. This time I told her she had to get clean, or I'd have no choice but to have her locked up. She agreed to attend a rehabilitation clinic, and gradually she got her act together. She went to university, and trained to become a teacher. I was so proud to see her turn her life around, Mr Carmichael. Anyway, last year she went through a messy divorce, and I was worried she might return to her old ways, but I was amazed when she told me she'd found something better. She'd joined a group calling themselves the Church of Eternal Light. Have you heard of them?'

He glanced at Melissa again, but all she offered was a blank expression and a shrug of the shoulders.

'Well, I hadn't either. She told me they were a group of like-minded individuals searching for greater meaning. They are not formally recognised by any denomination as far as I'm aware. I couldn't understand why she couldn't find what she was looking for in the Catholic Church. She told me this group is less judgemental, and focus more on God's words than church-defined doctrine. I agreed to attend one of their services with her, though I use the term "service" loosely. Don't get me wrong, everyone seemed friendly and welcoming, but the service didn't seem to follow any formal structure. It started with the preacher reading from the Lord's book, and inviting the congregation to share their problems and concerns. Each member took a turn to announce something that was troubling them, and then the preacher would reply with a quote from the Bible. It was all a bit too modern for me: lots of clapping and people shouting "Amen". She introduced me to the preacher before we left. He was polite and charming, but there was something in his eyes…I don't know, I can't say why, but I didn't trust him. I kept my opinion to myself, because I'd never seen her as happy as she was. She would phone me almost every day to tell me what she'd been up to. She'd come around and take me out to lunch almost weekly as well. It was great to have my little girl back.' She paused, looking for support.

Melissa nodded encouragingly.

'Something changed in her shortly after Christmas. Her phone calls became less frequent, as did her visits. When I did speak to her, the conversations were far shorter. I knew something was wrong. As a parent you just know.'

Carmichael nodded. 'She was back on the drugs?'

'No, no, no, Mr Carmichael. Quite the opposite. She was clean, at least I think she was.'

'So, what changed?'

'You'll probably think I'm crazy, but they'd indoctrinated her into their cult.'

He nearly spat out his coffee. 'A cult? You're kidding, right?'

She fixed him with a cold stare. '*I am not!* That's how these cults operate. They welcome their members in, offering a better life, and once they've got their claws into you, they isolate you from your family. I've seen documentaries about it.'

'What documentaries?'

'Charles Manson, Jim Jones. Why, you can't read the newspaper without some other loon joining the Church of Scientology.'

'Do you have any evidence your daughter was being manipulated?'

'The way she spoke, the way she dressed: it all changed. When I did catch up with her all she would talk about was God's plan for her. She kept saying that God had spoken to her, and now she knew what her purpose was. She had always been a reluctant churchgoer, and suddenly God was all she spoke about.'

'She dressed differently?'

'Her formal school attire was suddenly gone, and she started wearing these long dresses. They were loose fitting, with sleeves down to the wrist, and the hem just above the ankles. She stopped wearing a bra as well. The school warned her about her sudden appearance change, but she didn't care.'

'A change of identity doesn't necessarily mean -'

'It wasn't just her appearance that changed! I found out she was giving them all of her disposable income. She said God wanted her to help fund the church's activities. That was when I first contacted the police. I told them what was going on, but they didn't take me seriously. They said they wouldn't intervene unless my daughter made a complaint against the church. I begged them to go and speak to her, which they reluctantly agreed to do. But when they got to her house, she made up a bagful of lies about me. She told them I had threatened her, and she was seeking shelter within the church. That's what they do, Mr Carmichael: they persuaded her to turn her back on her family so she would willingly do whatever that crazy preacher wanted. You can imagine, the police treated it as a family issue and dismissed my concerns. They even had the cheek to warn me about my behaviour! As if a seventy-five year-old could be a danger!'

He chose his words carefully. 'What makes you think the Church of Eternal Light caused her death?'

'The last time I spoke to her was six weeks ago. I found out from a family friend that the school had asked her to leave. Allegedly, she started encouraging her secondary school class to come along to the church, and her lessons strayed from the curriculum. Several of the parents made complaints, and despite a number of warnings, she continued to preach in classes. I went to her house, and waited until she eventually arrived home. She was stumbling down the road, and her speech was slurred, so I was certain she had taken something, but she outright denied it, and told me to mind my own business. I told her she needed help and that I was worried about her. I followed her into the house, and the place was a state. There were dirty plates and bowls stacked up all over the kitchen, and the living room looked like it had been ransacked. I thought she'd been burgled, but she told me to stop fussing. She passed out on the sofa, and…I'm not proud of what I did…but I found her diary on the floor and I read it. She'd kept a diary since her days at the clinic. It was mostly filled with drawings and, what I assumed were, quotes from the Bible. Then I found a passage she'd written a week earlier. She sounded scared. She'd seen a side to the preacher that had made her question his motives. It was vague, and I can't remember the exact words, but I knew instinctively she was in danger. I went back to the police, but they again dismissed my fears. Two weeks later the same detective knocked on my door and told me her body had been discovered in a gutter. They found needle marks in her arms and feet, and the medical examiner found heroin in her system. They investigated it for a few days, but the preacher told them she'd fallen into her old ways and hadn't been at the church for several days. They concluded that she was a drug user who had relapsed.'

He knew better than most what it was to lose an adult child, and his heart ached for her. 'I'm sorry for your loss, Mrs Barlow. You have my sincerest sympathy. The thing is, I'm not sure what you think I can do to help. If the police have ruled her death as an accident, then that's the end of it. I'm not sure what else I can do.'

'I want you to investigate the Church of Eternal Light. I want you to prove that the preacher manipulated my daughter and then caused her death.'

'I'm not sure I -'

'The church is in Freemantle, and the preacher's name is Paul Sanza. I'm certain once you've met him, you'll understand why he is a menace. It's too late for my daughter, but he needs to be stopped. No parent should go through what I have. Paul Sanza is a dangerous man, Mr Carmichael. You mark my words.'

6

Why would Todd's killer report the crime?

D.S. Beth Taylor looked at the burger on the napkin in front of her, and removed the sesame seed top. She'd asked them not to add gherkin, but there, staring up at her, was the limp, and squashed pale green mess. She pinched it between her fingers and discarded it on the napkin. She sucked the remnants of onion from her fingertips, and then reached for the plastic pot of ketchup. She peeled the lid off, and gave it a lick, before discarding it in the small bin next to her desk. Only a handful of officers were in the office, most having the sense to eat out. Although the air conditioning was on full blast, it was still sweltering.

I should have opted for the salad.

She emptied the pot of ketchup onto the cheeseburger, and returned the bun. It was only a couple of hours since she'd eaten a bacon sandwich for breakfast, but she was ravenous. She took a large bite out of the burger, when she recognised the voice over her shoulder.

'I'll eat that if you don't want it.' D.C. Oliver Capshaw reached over her shoulder and snatched up the gherkin, and popped it into his mouth. 'Lovely!'

She watched him lick his fingers clean, before sitting down at the desk next to hers. Even though his shift was just beginning, his shirt was creased, his tie pulled down into a tight knot, and his hair looked like it hadn't been brushed in days, rather than hours.

She'd never had a lot of time for Capshaw. He was ten years older than her, not that you would know it to hear them both speak. Here was a man who had made it to detective and decided he was comfortable. He lacked drive and ambition. The moment he'd discovered a bald patch forming on the crown of his head, he'd shaved it all off. He always chose the easy path, rather than tackling a challenge. If Beth had her way, he'd be busted back to uniform, but the D.I. had a soft spot for him.

'What's on then, Sarge?' he asked, leaning back in his chair.

Beth lowered the burger. Although she hated gherkins, she was annoyed that he'd helped himself. For all he knew, she might have been saving it until the end. There was no point in saying anything, as he'd assume she was overreacting.

'Picked up a banker found dead in his flat in Totton overnight. Payne wants me to lead it.'

'A murder? No way.'

'Could be a sex game gone wrong. The victim was found naked and tied to his bed. If it *was* murder, I'm not sure why the killer would report it.'

'So you're thinking accidental death?'

She scrunched up her nose. 'I would have said yes, but the victim's throat was cut.'

'What do you want me to start on?'

'I'm waiting on the M.E.s preliminary report. That should confirm likely cause of death. Time of death is estimated at between ten and midnight last night.

SOCOs found a receipt in the victim's wallet for a café in Totton. He bought drinks sometime around eight. Can you take his photograph to the café and see if anyone remembers if he was drinking with someone? Check their security camera footage too.'

Capshaw smirked. 'What you thinking? He took his killer out for a drink first?'

She didn't return the gesture. 'Why not? Most murder victims know their killer: friend, family, or whatever. Also, find out who his friends were. I want to know who he was close to, what he was like. Did any of his friends have motive to want him dead? I'll go through his bank statements and see if he was in any financial difficulty.'

Capshaw stood. 'Have you heard from the D.I.?'

She shook her head. D.I. Tony White was on leave, though why he'd chosen Majorca was beyond her. It was hardly where she would have expected her fifty-eight year-old boss to head.

Capshaw held up his phone. 'He sent me this last night. Looks like he's having a good time.'

Beth looked closer at the image on the phone. There was White, a broad grin on his face, wearing an unbuttoned Hawaiian shirt, holding up a coconut with a large neon straw in it. There were two women in their twenties hanging from each arm. She rolled her eyes again, and returned to her burger. Capshaw put his phone away and headed for the door.

There was something about this morning's crime scene that seemed so familiar, but she couldn't place what. She had been part of four murder investigations since becoming a detective, but this was the first one she had taken the lead on. She unlocked the computer screen and searched for the four victims' names; names she would never forget.

The last time she'd been involved in a murder investigation was just before Christmas, six months before. An abducted schoolgirl, Freya Coleman was discovered in a village park. Gaunt and badly beaten, she barely survived her ordeal. The discovery of Freya's body led the Major Investigation Team to uncover a seedy ring involved in people trafficking and prostitution, and a host of other girls who had been abducted and killed. Eventually, the team found the man responsible. But as she reviewed the photographs of the crime scenes, there was nothing similar to this morning's one.

She finished the burger and discarded the napkin in the small bin. She reviewed the remaining three cases, each of which had been brought to a satisfactory conclusion, with the perpetrator identified and serving time. She leant back in her chair and rubbed her eyes. What was it that was nagging at her?

She pictured herself back at Todd Francis' flat, and walked through the scene again. He was on the top floor. His neighbours below hadn't heard any banging or crashing, but hadn't been home. There were no signs of forced entry at the front door, so the victim had to know his killer, or at least believed that the killer wasn't a threat. There were no obvious signs of a struggle or ambush inside. In the bedroom, his wrists were still cuffed to the bed frame by his head. A sharp knife had been run along both arms, which would have eventually killed him, but then the killer had slit his throat, meaning the victim bled out in seconds rather than hours. Why?

Why slit the wrists and then the throat? To be doubly sure of death?

No, that didn't make sense. It was almost as if the killer had empathised with the victim, and decided to end his misery. She scrunched up her nose at the theory. There was more to it than that, she was certain.

7

Carmichael jogged across the road towards the old church, before circling around the back. The sun had long since set, and the dark clouds in the sky were foreboding. Beneath a broken street light, two men in dark clothing watched him. Carmichael knew the one in the baseball cap to be a wise-talking Yank, hailing from Detroit. He was wearing a navy blue denim jacket. The larger man to his left, chewing the tip of a matchstick, was unfamiliar. Carmichael nodded at the American, as he approached.

Baseball cap, looked him up and down, before embracing him. 'Yo, brother, you back so soon? You wanna watch your back, my man, you gettin' dangerously close to developin' yourself a habit.'

He was in no mood for the usual theatrics. 'Just give me what I want.'

'Ah, that's where you got this thing all wrong, my friend. You see, what it is, right, you're like the customer, and I'm like your service provider. You see, I got the goods you want, but you got to pay me to get it. You hear what I'm sayin'?'

Carmichael checked nobody else was watching them before showing him the roll of twenties in his hand. 'Good enough?'

Baseball cap put his arm around Carmichael but

spoke to his friend. 'That's what I love about this guy: he's so serious all the time. It's always about gettin' the job done.'

Carmichael shook free of the embrace. 'Come on, man, give me the gear.'

Baseball cap pulled a hurt expression. 'Hey, I'm all for efficiency, but I gotta feel like I'm delivering good customer service. You know what I'm sayin'? And I don't get that vibe from you, my man. You see, service is important to me. I got to know that my customers are gonna stay loyal to me, and not go seeking their supply from another supplier.' He spat out his gum and put a fresh piece in his mouth. 'Now, are you gonna show me and my friend here a bit of love? No love, no gear.'

Carmichael ground his teeth, and forced a smile. 'You want my money or not? I haven't got time for this shit.'

Baseball cap grinned. 'Shit, brother, there's that fuckin' efficiency again. You know if I didn't know better, I'd say you don't like me.'

Carmichael fought the desire to tell him what he really thought. He'd dealt with lowlifes like this his whole life. First, as a teenager in Camden, he'd had to deal with the wide boys who'd thought they were something special. Next, he'd taken pleasure in chasing down small-time dealers when he'd joined the Met. He hated that he was now forced to satisfy his need in this way. He tried to remain calm. 'What do you want?'

'How about you start with your name, and we go from there?'

He looked over both shoulders again. 'It's Seb.'

'Seb who?'

'Seb Carter. Good enough?'

'Tell me, Seb Carter, what's a fine, upstanding citizen like you doing in a shithole like St Mary's? In that fancy suit and tie of yours, you don't look like you belong in this neighbourhood. Tell me why I shouldn't kick your black ass down the sidewalk.'

'Please, I'm sorry if you've got the wrong idea about me. Look, I've got the money, have you got the gear or not. I don't like having my time wasted like this.'

The larger man stepped forward, but Baseball cap waved him back. 'As well as customer service, I got to know I can trust the people I conduct my business with, and Seb, the truth is, I don't trust you. You see, after the last time you bought from me, I sent my man here to check you out. He tells me you're not to be trusted and your fucking name ain't Seb. Tell me, Johnson, what's a black P.I. doin' sniff' around these parts?'

Carmichael pocketed the money and turned to walk away. He stopped when a hand touched his shoulder.

'Where you think you goin', brother? I ain't finished with you yet.'

Carmichael grabbed the hand and yanked the fingers, before twisting the American's wrist behind his back. Baseball cap yelped in pain. His friend's fist connected with Carmichael's jaw and he was forced to let go.

Baseball cap rubbed his hand gingerly. 'Teach this fuckin' prick a lesson.'

The larger man charged at Carmichael again,

sending him crashing into a hedge. Carmichael wriggled his arm free and then brought his elbow down hard onto the larger man's back. The man's grip loosened, and Carmichael took advantage slamming a knee into his ribs, and then his face. With his assailant floored, he lunged towards Baseball cap, who was retreating slowly.

All the bravado and wise cracks were gone. 'Yo, brother, ease up, right. I was just playin' with you. There's no need to go all Rambo on me. I got what you want.' He reached into his pocket, but instead of pulling out pills, he grasped a flick-knife. The moon reflected as he pointed it forward. 'Ha, you weren't expecting that shit were you? You come at me, and I'll stick you.'

Carmichael stalked forward. Baseball cap waved the knife desperately. Carmichael waited for it to pass, before grabbing the extended wrist with his left hand, and the elbow with his right. He slammed the arm into the street light. It cracked audibly.

Baseball cap screamed out in agony as the knife clattered to the floor. 'You broke my fuckin' arm. What the fuck is wrong with you, bro?'

Carmichael released his grip and kicked the knife into the gutter. He straightened his tie. 'First of all, just because we have the same skin colour, it doesn't make us brothers. All this could have been avoided if you'd just given me what I wanted. Instead, you had to show off in front of your girlfriend here. If you had any idea what kind of day I've had, you'd have thought twice about messing around.'

'Fuck you,' he spat.

Carmichael checked they were still alone before

driving his knee into the side of Baseball cap's head. The cap flew off as the wearer slumped unconscious to the floor. He bent over and checked the guy's pockets. He found a bag of twenty pills and pocketed them. So there was no ill feeling, he put the roll of notes in the pocket of the denim jacket.

He jogged back along the street. As soon as he was out of sight he bent over and took a deep breath. His heart was racing. He glanced back around the corner to make sure they weren't following him, before continuing back to where he'd parked. The old church loomed into sight. He stopped and stared at the large cross on the roof. He shook his head, and turned to walk away when he had a better idea. He climbed the steps leading to the large double doors. He unzipped his trousers and urinated.

8

Kelly sashays to the middle of the dancefloor. She raises her arms above her head and her wrists roll as the beat of the music embraces her. She bends her knees slightly as her hips sway in time to the music. She closes her eyes, and for a moment she is no longer in the club. She is freefalling in a tunnel of darkness, but she isn't scared. She is being held aloft by the music, and she is all alone. She is in her happy place. She no longer hears the music being pumped out of the club speakers. She is lost in her own vacuum. She is in her cave.

She continues to move to her own vibe. She doesn't care if anyone can see; they are nothing to her.

A stray elbow connects with her back. An apologetic hand rests on her shoulder and a voice in her ear is sorry for the collision. Then the warm breath and hand are gone, but so is the cave. Her surroundings are all too familiar again. She hears ABBA filling the room. She tries to clear her mind of everything, but she suddenly feels awkward. Her hips can't connect with the music. She lowers her arms to her sides and opens her eyes. The dancefloor is gloomy, save for the red and green bulbs spinning overhead. She is surrounded by drunk couples and groups.

Her breath catches in her throat. Her face is warm and she is woozy. She no longer wants to be here. She can just about see the lights behind the bar in the distance. Her feet are aching in the new stilettos. She knows she shouldn't have bought them, but they look so pretty. She stumbles through the gyrating crowd colliding with each group as she goes. They don't notice.

She peels the sequined dress from her lower back. Her hands are clammy and she doesn't want to think about the state of her armpits. She has no idea how long she spent in her cave, but now she needs a drink. She catches the barman's eye and orders a bottle of water. He brings it over and she pays him. There's nothing she'd prefer to do than tip the bottle over her head, but she knows that won't do. She sips it instead, leaning her elbow on the bar for support.

She's being watched. She hadn't noticed it on the dancefloor, but now that her mind is regaining control, she can sense it. The hairs on the back of her neck lift. She looks to her left and then allows her eyes to wander across the club, past the dancefloor until she sees him. He is standing at the far side of the bar, maybe fifteen feet away. He is with two other lads. The three of them are laughing and joking with each other. His two friends are eyeing girls on the dancefloor, but he isn't. He is staring at her. He looks away every now and again, but those eyes keep returning to where she is standing.

Kelly checks there is nobody behind her he's focusing on, but it is just her. She looks away, her cheeks warming.

Why is he staring? Do I know him?

She dares to look over once more. Her view is blocked by two big lads who have come to the bar to order shots. When they move away he sees her looking for him. She looks away, embarrassed. She silently curses herself for yielding power. She sneaks a second quick glance. He's younger than her. He can't be much older than twenty. He and his two friends look like university students. It's highly likely, the city's clubs are always packed with students. The club is so dark it's difficult to make out his facial features. He looks in good shape. He is wearing a tight-fitting t-shirt and his biceps fill the sleeve. This is a lad who takes care of himself.

She can feel his eyes on her still. She's not used to men staring at her.

Should I go over? Do I wait for him to approach?

She sips her water.

Suddenly, he was next to her. 'Hi, I'm Josh.'

He's leaning in close so she can hear him over the noise of the dancefloor. His lips are an inch from her ear. She can smell his cologne. Her knees are weak. She acknowledges him with a smile.

'What's your name?'

She swallows her water. 'I'm Kelly.'

He extends his hand. 'It's nice to meet you, Kelly. Are you here alone?'

She nods.

What's wrong with me? Why do I feel so self-conscious?

His hand brushes her arm. 'Can I buy you a drink?'

She lifts her water bottle. 'I've got one thanks.'

He turns and orders two shots of Sambuca. He passes her one of the glasses. 'Come on, have a drink with me.'

She puts her bottle on the bar and accepts the drink. They clink the glasses and down the shots. She grimaces, and he grins.

'See, that wasn't so bad, was it?'

He tells her about his friends, but she struggles to understand what he is saying. She catches the odd word, but the music drowns out the rest. He stops, and she realises he has asked a question, but she has no idea what it is. She puts a hand to her ear. 'I couldn't hear.'

He leans in close again. She can smell the Sambuca on his breath. 'I said, do you want to go somewhere a bit quieter so we can talk?'

She bites her lip. Up close, he's cute. He has curly fair hair, and close-cropped stubble. She nods nervously, and allows him to take her hand and lead her across the dancefloor, and up the stairs. He nods at the bouncers as they leave the club and head into the public car park at the rear.

He pulls her close and kisses her neck. 'You're so fit.'

Does he think I'm going to have sex in a car park?

She pushes him back. 'I thought you wanted to talk.'

He tilts his head. 'We both know why we're out here.' He lunges forwards again, but she rebuffs his attempt. 'What the fuck is wrong with you? Stop messing about.'

She slaps his cheek. He slaps hers back, and then punches her in the gut. She bends forward, temporarily winded.

'I'm gonna get what I came for one way or another.' He pushes her back towards the cover of large rubbish containers. 'Behind here will be fine.' He rubs his hands over her bottom, and lifts the back of her dress.

She knows what he wants, but he's underestimated her. She steadies her breathing, and quickly straightens, crashing the back of her head into the bridge of his nose.

He yelps out in pain and covers his face. He lowers his hand and his eyes widen when he sees the blood on his hands. 'Oh you're gonna pay for that, you bitch.'

He stumbles forward, but she is too quick for him, and drives the palm of her hand into his nose again. He clatters back against the rubbish container. Before he can gather his composure, she kicks him in the groin, and then, as he drops to his knees, she grabs his curly hair and repeatedly slams his head into the container.

She releases his hair, and he sinks to the floor. He won't give her any more trouble tonight. But what about next time? She doubts this is the first time he has forced himself onto a girl, and she can't be certain he has learned his lesson. She pokes her head up from behind the container. There is nobody in the car park. She looks at him. He is groaning. It won't be long until he regains consciousness. There is only one thing she can do: she must do it for all of her kind

She gently places her foot on his temple, and rests the stiletto heel in his ear. She slowly counts to three in her head, and then shifts all her weight onto her heel, puncturing the ear drum. He makes a gurgling noise and then there is silence. She slips her foot out of the stiletto, and balances on the other foot while she yanks the shoe out. She is surprised at how tightly it's wedged in. She wiggles, until eventually it squelches out. She wipes the heel with his t-shirt, before slipping the stiletto back on. She walks away from Josh's lifeless body, and exits the car park.

Across the road she sees a rugged man urinating at the door of a church. Did he see what happened? Before she can catch up with him, he has disappeared.

FRIDAY

9

Carmichael's heart felt like it was going to burst through his chest. He was running for his life. The darkness around him was suffocating. Only the occasional street lamp reflecting in the puddles under foot provided any kind of light. He knew he'd have to stop running at any moment. He was out of shape, and had already run further than ever before. Spotting a vacant warehouse, he turned off and headed in. The warehouse was empty, save for a stack of blue barrels at the far side. The moon was shining brightly through the glass windows in one half of the roof. He dived behind the barrels, hoping his pursuer would run on past. He tried to steady his breathing, but his panting was echoing around the room. He covered his mouth and tried to limit the breaths through his nose. His entire body was dripping with sweat.

A noise at the far side of the building. His eyes widened. He dared to poke his face around the edge of the barrels. The dark figure stood in the entrance of the warehouse, his shadow framed by the moonlight outside. Carmichael's heart found an extra gear. He pulled his head back. He was trapped. There was no way he could get out without being seen. It wasn't fair. This wasn't the way it was supposed to end. He'd always imagined he'd live into old age. He didn't deserve this.

He poked his head around the barrels again. The figure was no longer standing in the entrance. The doorway beckoned to him. There was light at the end of the tunnel. His pursuer must have passed on by. He clambered to his feet, his breathing suddenly calmer. He stepped out and walked tentatively across the warehouse, looking left and right as he went. He'd survived. All that fear had been for nothing. He felt ridiculous. He giggled at his own silliness. The illuminated doorway grew as he approached it.

Chains clattered behind him. He froze. He didn't want to turn around. He already knew what he'd see. He needed to run, but his feet wouldn't budge. The doorway beyond him shrank. He stretched out a hand, desperately clawing for the light. Heavy footsteps thudded over his shoulder. He looked at his feet, but it was like they were glued to the floor. Is that what had happened? Had he walked into a trap?

The chains clattered again. He gulped and turned his head. The large-framed shadow came into view. He was carrying a large chain, on the end of which were wrist manacles.

'Are…are they for me?' he whispered.

The figure nodded slowly.

Carmichael accepted his fate, and pushed his wrists out behind his back. The figure fastened the manacles in place, and pulled on the chain to check they were secure.

He dropped to his knees. 'What happens next?'

The figure pointed to a large wooden door to their left. Carmichael watched the door open, and a new shadowy figure emerge. He knew who it was even before he had stepped into the moon's glow.

'Janus, you're alive? I thought you…'

Janus Stratovsky put a finger to his lips while slowly shaking his head. He continued to approach until he was standing directly in front of Carmichael.

'I'm sorry, Janus. I didn't mean for you to die…it was an accident. You were trying to kill me. We both had our hands on the gun. I'm not even sure it was me who squeezed the trigger. I didn't have a choice afterwards. I didn't deserve to be found with your body. I had to get rid of you. You understand that, right? A man in your position knows that. You must have disposed of countless bodies in your time. You don't make it to the second throne of the Russian mafia without getting your hands dirty.'

Stratovsky was still watching him. A small smile broke out across his face.

'Are you here to kill me? Is that what this is? Revenge? Go ahead. I deserve it.'

Stratovsky shook his head, and pointed at a door to Carmichael's right. The detective craned his neck round to look. The door opened and an overweight man stepped through. He slowly crossed the floor, and joined Stratovsky in the light.

'Lennon? I watched you fall. You died. How are you here now?'

Lennon leaned in and sneered, drool hanging from his lips.

'I'm not going to apologise to you. You're a child snatcher, rapist and killer. You had it coming. If I hadn't let you die, you'd have done it again. You told me you were going to beat the system. I couldn't let that happen.'

Lennon tilted his head.

'Do what you like to me now. I know I did the right thing.'

The two men stepped apart and a new figure appeared in the doorway ahead of him. He couldn't make out who it was at first. The figure was smaller, slimmer. She stepped into the light.

'Anita?'

She bent and stroked his face with her hand. She was crying. He wanted to embrace her, to protect her, but his hands couldn't break free of the manacles. He pulled and tugged, but they were stuck fast.

'It'll be okay, my love. I'll get us out of here. I'll protect you.'

She shook her head gently, kissed his forehead, before standing. Stratovsky grabbed her right arm in his hands, and Lennon grabbed the left.

'No, you can't take her,' he screamed out. 'She's my little girl. Take me instead. Please? You need to leave her alone. I'm the one you want revenge on. Please? I'm begging you. Don't take Anita.'

They walked backwards with her. He pulled at the manacles again, but the figure behind him continued to grip them tightly.

'Anita!' he yelled out as she sunk further away. 'I'll come for you. They won't get away with this. Please! Leave her alone. Punish me, not her!'

Carmichael shot bolt upright in bed. His bedsheets were soaking wet. He was panting, and at first he couldn't work out where he was. He remembered seeing Anita being led away, and he raced from his room to the front door of his flat but it was still locked and the security chain was still in place. He checked the spare room and kitchen, but he was alone. He returned to his bedroom and checked the clock. It was half past three. He sat on the edge of his bed.

It had been a nightmare. It had been so vivid. The faces of Lennon and Stratovsky had been so clear. Anita had looked as she had the first time he'd met her. He pushed the damp sheet onto the floor, and grabbed a fresh one from the basket under the bed. He laid back down, and closed his eyes. Sleep wouldn't come. He kept seeing Anita's crying face being pulled away from him, and being unable to do anything about it. He reached for the small plastic bottle on the bedside table. He unscrewed the lid and dropped two pills onto his tongue. He took a gulp of water and swallowed the pills. He was about to replace the lid, but thought better of it and put two further pills on his tongue. He chased them back with a second gulp of water, before lying back down. He prayed sleep would come for him again soon.

10

The Medical Examiner smiled, as Beth approached. 'We must stop meeting like this, dear. People will think you've started killing strangers in order to spend more time with me.'

'No disrespect intended, doc, but I'd rather not be seeing you so soon. What have we got?'

Spinks pulled the thin white sheet from the body. The young man was lying flat on his front, his head tilted to one side. A large patch of red covered the concrete beneath him. He was wearing a pair of brown cotton trousers, and what was once a cream-coloured t-shirt, though it was now stained beyond repair.

Spinks crouched on one knee. 'Male in his early twenties beaten, and evidently stabbed through the ear with a long, blunt implement of some sort.' He circled the exposed ear with his gloved finger. 'The blood here indicates the entry point. Whatever was forced in was at least three inches long. I haven't been able to assess exact depth yet, but will know once I've examined the brain.'

'Any idea what could have been used?'

'A skewer of some sort? There's a kebab shop along the road. That might be a good starting point.

You're looking for something with a diameter no bigger than a five pence piece.'

Beth grimaced. 'Was the stabbing the cause of death?'

'On initial examination, I'd say so. The bruising around the face appears to have been made before death occurred, but I wouldn't have thought that alone was enough to kill him.'

'Time of death?'

Spinks checked his watch. 'It's eight a.m. now. Victim has been dead for approximately nine hours, so you're looking at about eleven o'clock last night.'

'He's not wearing a jacket.'

'Indeed he isn't. It was mild last night. Based on his clothing, it wouldn't surprise me if he was in the club that backs on to this car park.'

'Yet he wasn't discovered until a couple of hours ago.'

'In fairness, these large rubbish containers did a good job of concealing the body from view. In the dead of night, unless you happened to walk behind the bins, there's no reason you would notice him back here.'

Beth bent to examine the entry wound. A trail of dried blood covered the lobe and had flowed down the victim's neck onto the floor. 'It must have been something sharp, right? I mean, to puncture the skull, must take some force.'

'The right tool with the right amount of applied force would do it. It might point to pre-meditation. I would guess the killer brought the murder weapon with them.'

'What else can you tell me about the victim?'

'The SOCOs are on site. I must get on.'

'Sure, doc. I understand. I appreciate your time. What time should I send someone for your findings?'

'I'm still finishing my write-up of yesterday's victim, but I should be able to confirm something verbally after lunch.'

Beth walked the perimeter of the car park, looking for lines of sight. There were two security cameras on high poles either side of where the victim had been discovered, but both were angled away from the body and towards the car park. There were over three hundred cameras across the city spanning car parks and public areas. The feeds are monitored by a team of staff, 24 hours a day, and 365 days a year. She would put a call in to them when she got back to the office to request access to the area's footage. If Spinks was right, and the crime was pre-meditated, there was a chance they might see the killer leaving the car park. If they were lucky, their killer might even have been stupid enough to drive to the crime.

'Morning, Sarge,' said a voice over her shoulder. She turned and saw D.C. Oliver Capshaw approaching. He was yawning and rubbing his eyes.

'Late night last night, was it?'

'Sorry, Sarge, the little one's teething at the moment. He had us up every hour on the hour.' He yawned again. 'I'll be fine with a few cups of coffee.'

She rolled her eyes. 'Tell me what you see, Capshaw.'

'Sarge?'

'Look around us. What do you see?'

He scratched his head. 'A car park…a church…a night club. You want me to start door-to-door enquiries?'

'No, well, yes, but not yet. What isn't right about this scene?'

He looked around again and then pulled a face. 'It's St. Mary's, Sarge. Nothing's right about this place.'

She closed her eyes. 'Look beyond all that. Stop seeing what's straight in front of you and look for what you can't see.'

He rolled his eyes. He disliked people that told him to think outside the box. There was no box! 'I don't know what you're driving at, Sarge. Can you save us both time, and just tell me?'

She opened her eyes. 'Fine,' she sighed. 'Spinks believes our killer came tooled-up for this crime. It was planned. For whatever reason, someone wanted that student dead, and they chose this place. Doesn't that strike you as odd?'

'Anyone that wants to kill another person is odd in my book, Sarge.'

'Put yourself in the killer's shoes for a minute, Ollie. Picture someone you'd like to kill.'

His eyes darted to her and then away. 'Okay.'

'So, you spend weeks thinking about it, and then you decide you're going to do it. Maybe you investigate different methods. For whatever reason you decide you want to drive a spike through their head. You locate the appropriate tool, maybe you even test it on a watermelon so that you're certain it will work. You psych yourself up and then you head out to make your move. All that time, all that planning, and then you carry out the crime in a place like this. A public car park, where any number of people could disturb you. A car park where security cameras operate. In St. Mary's where you're likely to encounter multiple potential witnesses as you make your escape. It doesn't fit.'

Capshaw was nodding along. 'Like I said: all killers are odd.'

She shook her head. She was wasting her time. 'Right, get your notebook out. I want you to wake the manager of the nightclub. I want their camera footage from last night. There's a good chance the victim was in there, and maybe his killer was too. I also want the footage from these two car park cameras too. I want you to trace the owners of every car that enters and exits the car park from nine p.m. to midnight. I want the list of names on my desk before you go home tonight. Also, there is a church across the road. Find out if there was a service there last night or whether it was open late for confession. I'll get uniform to start knocking on doors. Someone must have seen what happened. If they didn't then we are dealing with one lucky son of a bitch.'

Two murders on her patch in as many days. It was going to take some juggling to manage the workload. Beth was scheduled off this weekend, and having worked nonstop for the past ten days, she wasn't going to be able to avoid the rest. She was going to need D.C.I. Payne to be more involved than originally planned.

11

Kelly parks on the kerb and kills the engine. She subconsciously puts a finger to her mouth and then catches herself. She's been biting her nails all day, and she must stop. They look in a terrible state. The thing is, she hasn't been able to stop thinking about what happened outside the club last night. She shouldn't have killed Josh. That was wrong. There was no reason for her to do it. No, scratch that. She shouldn't have allowed him to escort her outside. She knew what he was planning when he said they should go somewhere quiet to chat. What man has ever meant that immortal line?

She allowed herself to be misled, because she wanted to believe there was someone out there for her. She doesn't want to spend the rest of her life forcing men to have sex with her. Not that she's exclusive to men. She's messed about with girls before as well, and the thought of ending up with a girlfriend rather than a boyfriend doesn't frighten her. She is comfortable with who she is, and she refuses to allow society to dictate who she can or cannot see. She wishes that whoever she is destined to love turns up soon.

She saw her brother watching the local news earlier. Josh's death was the main story. They hadn't called it murder, for now it was just a suspicious death. The car park had been closed all day, and the woman who had chaired the press conference hadn't said for how long it would remain closed. The whole area is draped in blue and white tape, and Kelly can see a sole officer, wearing a high visibility vest, guarding the entrance. He looks bored. What wrong thing did he say to the wrong person to wind up with such a lousy assignment?

Two suspicious deaths on consecutive days in the city. She knows her brother will connect the dots soon enough, and then she will be in trouble. They have carefully built a new life together, and her reckless actions last night now threaten to spoil everything. She catches herself chewing her fingernail again.

She thought she had satisfied her blood lust. Before Todd on Wednesday night, she hadn't killed in more than a year. Why wasn't she able to maintain control? Was it simply because Todd had looked at her strangely? No, that wasn't it. She'd lowered her guard, and let Todd in, but he'd betrayed her. She'd killed him because she was angry at herself. But what about last night? What had driven her to kill Josh? She'd told herself it was for a higher purpose: that she had been saving future girls in his sights, but that was a lie.

It is time to admit the truth. She killed Josh because she wanted to feel that all-encompassing power. Holding someone's life in the balance is a massive adrenaline rush. It's better than any cigarette, alcohol, sex or even narcotic-induced euphoria. Live or die. It is the ultimate bet. When faced with such a decision, most will choose to save the individual. It takes a lot of courage to choose option two. It isn't the act of killing that's hard, it's dealing with the emotional impact that follows: the guilt, the empathy, the regret. She was riding that rollercoaster right now. She didn't regret that Josh wouldn't be able to force himself on other women. She regretted exposing herself, and more importantly, her brother.

That's why she has returned to the scene of the crime. She needs to know for certain whether there is anything that will lead the police to her door. The club and car park are twenty metres up the road, to her right. The club isn't open, so she has no way of checking whether their initial meeting at the bar was captured on camera. The church is to her left, but it looks closed. She is about to exit the car and approach the officer when she hears voices from behind. She glances in the rear-view mirror, and gasps when she recognises the detective from the press conference arguing with the man she saw urinating outside the church last night.

How can they have found her so quickly? What could she have left at the scene that means they knew she'd be here tonight? Had they seen her driving out of the car park? Was that it? Was that the mistake that would be her downfall? She continued to watch them, waiting for the inevitable sound of sirens, ready to haul her away. She thought about starting the engine and tearing away, but they'd catch her eventually. If they knew her car, they knew her identity. There was probably a search team at their house now. Her brother is going to find out everything. Her bladder feels like it might explode. She looks through her window, expecting to see the female detective staring back at her, but she is surprised to see the man and woman have continued to walk. They haven't stopped to question her. They are still arguing, but they are now directly outside the church. She cracks her window so she can hear what they are saying.

'What are we doing here?' the man asks. He is much better looking up close. There is an intensity in his eyes, and although he has a large frame, she can tell it is mainly muscle, rather than fat. His skin is as dark as the night that surrounds him.

'There's nothing like returning to the scene of the crime, is there?' the detective asks.

'Scene of…what the hell are you talking about, Beth?'

'A twenty year-old student called Josh Grabban was murdered in the car park across the street last night.'

'What's that got to do with me?'

'We obtained footage from all the security cameras in the area, including the one ten feet in the air above you.'

He looks up.

'I'd hoped it would be pointing in the direction of the car park and might help identify the person responsible, but unfortunately it only covers this side of the street. I spoke to the vicar here. He said he had the camera installed after a spate of vandalism last year. Apparently it took weeks to scrub the graffiti from the church doors last time. He didn't mind us taking a look at the footage anyway. Have you any idea how embarrassing it was when one of my team watched the footage and saw *my* ex-boyfriend pissing against the doors?'

'Ah…I see. I can ex –'

'Save it! I don't want to hear your excuses. What I need to know is whether you saw anything or anyone suspicious in that car park across the road.' She pointed for emphasis.

He scratches his head. 'Not that I can remember.'

'You didn't hear anyone screaming for help, or the sound of two men fighting?'

'No, as I said, I don't remember anything like that. Is that why you brought me here? For that?'

'Not just that. What were you doing here last night, apart from emptying your bladder of course?'

He looks away. 'I was…uh…chasing a lead for a case, that's all.'

'Is that right? This lead doesn't happen to wear a baseball cap, and go by the name of Tyrell does he?'

He shakes his head.

'Come on, Johnson, what do you take me for? I'm a police officer. You think I don't know what goes on in this area? Word on the street is someone had a serious beef with a local dealer. Apparently, this mystery man attacked Tyrell and his hired muscle. You wouldn't happen to know anything about that would you?'

He shakes his head again.

'Tyrell wasn't interested in naming names or pressing charges. When he was spoken to at the hospital, he seemed to have developed a bout of amnesia. Word is he's on the lookout for vengeance.'

'I told you: I don't know anyone called Tyrell. Why are you telling me all this?'

'That's what friends do isn't it? I'm worried about

you, Johnson. Melissa told me you missed Anita's funeral.'

He groans.

'She's worried about you too. We all are. Melissa thinks you're suppressing your grief when you should be letting it out. It's not healthy. Talking to a friend will bring you more relief than anything you can buy in a bottle or a syringe.'

He stares at her until she makes eye contact. 'Is that what we are now? Friends? It's not too late to be more.' He took her hands in his. 'I still love you, Beth, and the fact you invited me here today, tells me you still love me.'

She pulls her hands back, and turns to walk away. He grabs her shoulder and tries to kiss her. She fights his embrace and pulls away. 'No. I've told you I can't. It's too late for that -'

'It doesn't have to be. I know the miscarriage affected us, but I still love you, Beth. I need you.'

She slaps him hard across the face. 'How dare you! You think just because a few months have passed I've forgiven you for what you did?'

'I didn't do anything wrong.'

'You killed a man, Johnson!' She remembered where she was and lowered her tone. 'You killed the chief suspect in a murder investigation without a second thought. You made me an accessory for not reporting what I witnessed. Have you forgotten all that?'

He rubs his cheek gingerly. 'James Lennon drugged vulnerable young women, tortured, and raped them. When he was finished with them he disposed of them like rubbish. I didn't kill him. He fell over the edge of a building, and he simply slipped out of my hands.'

She waves her finger in his face. 'Bullshit! I saw the look in your eyes when you released your grip. You knew he'd fall to his death.'

'So what? There's one less scumbag in the world. You should be praising my actions, not chastising me.'

'You know for a fact he was guilty, do you? Okay, Sherlock, where's your proof?'

'You know he did it, as well as I do. He had videos of the girls he'd abducted.'

'The suspect had a hard drive of images he could have downloaded from the internet. It's hardly a smoking gun.'

'So why did he run when he saw us?'

'Some people are overly paranoid.'

'I found his latest victim in a locked bunker in the garden.'

'But she couldn't identify the man who had abducted her. In fact, not even survivor Freya Coleman could confirm his identity.'

'Why are you being like this, Beth? You don't think he was guilty?'

She throws her hands into the air. 'Of course I *think* he was guilty, but what I think doesn't matter. We don't *know* he was guilty.'

'He was guilty.'

'And therein lies the problem with us. You can't differentiate between the truth and supposition. Every bone in my body tells me Lennon was guilty, but we will never get the chance to prove that in court, because you decided he deserved to die.'

He tries to pull her close again, but she pushes him away. 'No, Johnson. I don't have time for your bullshit. I'm under a huge amount of pressure at work with White away and Tapper on training. Everyone in the office is looking to me for direction, and I've had my stripes the least amount of time. With two murders in as many days, and the press all over both, I can't be dealing with your problems as well. I invited you here because I thought you might have been able to help me, but I can see it was a waste of time. You need to sort yourself out.' She stormed away.

Kelly continues to watch the man she now knows as Johnson. She sees him in a new light: strong, handsome, rugged, and not afraid to get his hands dirty. She keeps low as he walks past her window and disappears into the night. The butterflies in her stomach are fluttering. Yes, she will have to find out a lot more about him.

SATURDAY

12

'Anger management. It's the perfect solution.' Melissa's eyes had twinkled as she'd spoken. 'After we met Wendy yesterday, I went to the building where the church meets. They host counselling sessions at the weekend and some evenings. At ten a.m. on Saturday, there's a session for those needing to deal with their anger management issues.' She'd raised her eyebrows. 'It's your way in.'

He hadn't been so sure. He still wasn't sure Wendy Barlow's unsubstantiated claims were anything more than the paranoid misgivings of a lonely woman. 'There's no guarantee he'll even been there,' he'd told Melissa last night before they'd left for the day.

'Even if he isn't, it'll get you in through the door. You can have a poke around. Come on, it's not like anyone would doubt you have issues with anger, is it?' She'd winked at him to show she meant no harm. 'Don't forget you're meeting Tom Dewis afterwards. If he is the son of the murdered factory owner, it could be an interesting case to take on.'

Carmichael found the former men's social club easily, and arrived two minutes before the meeting started. He was encouraged to write his name on a sticky label and attach it to his shirt. He decided to use his Seb Carter alias again. The main hall was larger than he'd expected. Chairs were laid out in a circle and half of them were occupied. He helped himself to a cup of coffee and took a seat. Only one of the men in the circle was named Paul, so it was safe to assume he was the preacher Mrs Barlow had spoken of.

With the meeting now finished, Paul approached him. He was younger than Carmichael had expected, maybe in his late thirties. He was wearing navy blue jeans and a black polo shirt.

'Welcome, Seb. I'm Paul. Was this your first time here? I don't recognise your face.'

'Yeah, my girlfriend wanted me to…what I mean is, she thought I should…'

Sanza nodded. 'I understand. There's no judgement here. None of us are perfect. It's good you came to find out what it's all about. What did you think of the session?'

'It was interesting to hear how others identify their triggers. I think that's something I can go away and think about.'

'That's as good a starting point as any. We all have emotional triggers, whether they cause positive emotion like happiness, or as in the case here, they cause anger and resentment. The key to coping with our anger is to recognise those triggers and take appropriate action when they occur.'

Carmichael nodded. 'Are you involved with the church here?'

'I am, yes. I'm the founder and chief preacher as it goes.' He smiled proudly. 'Are you a religious man, Seb?'

'I used to be. Tell me, how long have you been based here?'

'Our church moved to these premises about five years ago.'

'And where were you before that?'

'When the church first formed, it was based in a disused farmhouse in the middle of a field near Cadnam. The farmer who owned it was an old friend, and he allowed me to make moderations to make it suitable for a gathering.'

'How come you moved?'

'Praying in the middle of a field isn't always practical, particularly in winter. When I found this place, it seemed sensible to move the church to somewhere more accessible. Attendances have increased since the move. If you're interested, I have a couple of pamphlets about the church, what we do, that kind of thing. They're in the office. Come with me, and I'll show you.'

Sanza led him through the main hall, past the podium and altar, and into a small office at the rear of the building. He passed two glossy leaflets to him. 'Here you go. The first one tells you a little bit about who we are, what we stand for, and how we could help you. The second gives you the times of the various meetings we hold here. As well as anger management, we offer counselling for alcoholism, drug addiction, gambling, that kind of thing.'

'Thanks, I'll give them a look.'

'Do you think you'll attend next Saturday's meeting? There's no pressure. A lot of our regulars were sceptical the first time they attended, but were pleased they returned. I think it's one of those things where you need to judge the benefit after the second go.'

'How did you get involved with all this? I mean the church, and the counselling.'

Sanza smiled. 'I was in a dark place in my life seven or eight years ago, and when I thought I couldn't go on, I heard God calling to me.' He paused. 'I can see from your face you think I'm crazy, but I promise you that's what happened. It wasn't like a burning bush or anything, but He came to me in a dream.'

'What did He say?'

'It's hard to put it into words...I didn't have a conversation with Him, it was...I woke the next morning knowing what I needed to do. My attitude to life changed overnight. I'd been selfish, and suddenly my heart was filled with God's love. As I said, it's not easy to explain...tell me, do *you* believe in God?'

He forced a smile. 'Let's say I'm open-minded to the possibility, but also to the impossibility. The jury's still out as far as I'm concerned.'

'I'm not surprised. The biggest challenge I hear from those I meet is: how can God exist, when you see all the pain and suffering in the world. It's a fair argument, to be honest. You can't turn on the news without seeing a story about an unnecessary murder, or one nation threatening another with nuclear war. There's so much negativity in the world that it can be difficult to hear God's message.'

'But you can hear it?'

'Of course.'

'What makes you so special?'

'Nothing! Anyone can hear God's message if they choose to listen. So many people pray for help, and complain when they don't hear God speak back to them, like they expect him to speak English or something. Everything God wants to say to us, he already has.' Sanza tossed a large book at Carmichael, who just managed to catch it. 'His plan is all in there.'

'The Bible is hundreds of years old, how can you argue its message is still relevant?'

Sanza eyed him carefully. 'Do you want a theological discussion, or are you trying to goad me?'

He smiled again. 'Maybe a little of both.'

'I appreciate your honesty. Okay, let me put it this way: have you ever bought a piece of furniture from IKEA?'

'Sure.'

'Good. So, when it arrived it was flat pack, right? Bits of wood and metal, and a ton of screws and bolts in a transparent plastic bag.'

He nodded.

'Okay, so let's imagine you've bought, I don't know, let's say you've bought a chest of drawers. You've seen what it looks like in the store, and there's even a picture of it on the box, but how do you ensure you get all the right pieces in the right place?'

'Use the instruction booklet.'

Sanza clicked his fingers. 'Exactly! But what would happen if you didn't have the instructions? Do you think you'd manage to build the chest of drawers?'

'I suppose so, eventually.'

'Yes, but it would take several attempts until you worked out what went where. You might even accidentally damage some of the parts along the way. Now, there are some people who can look at the flat pack kit, and know how it will all fit together without the need of an instruction booklet. These people are rare. I'm not one of them. If I didn't have the instruction booklet, I think I'd grow impatient and throw the apparatus at the wall. I persevere because I have the instructions, and I know that if I follow them, I'll soon have a practical piece of furniture. Now, imagine the bits of wood and metal represent your friends and family, and key moments in your life. When you first open the box, you have no idea how they will all fit together. Now let's also imagine the bag of nuts and bolts represent the important decisions we each take in our lives. They link together our friends and family, and of course those key milestones. Most of us will eventually get it right, with the occasional accident along the way, but if we all had the instructions, we'd get there quicker.'

'What about those people who can't follow the instructions. I've known people that were rubbish at building flat pack.'

It was Sanza's turn to smile. 'Touché. You're right, you can lead a horse to water, but you can't make it drink. There are those people out there too, but they're in the minority.'

Carmichael turned the book over in his hands. 'So you're saying this is our instruction manual?'

'Exactly! Everything we need to know about how to lead our lives is already written for us. That's why people think God doesn't answer them. If they read his instructions they'd find their answer.'

'It's an interesting philosophy, but it must be the world's biggest instruction manual. If I bought a chest of drawers with this many instructions, I think I'd quit before I started.'

'There is a lot of detail in it, I grant you, but that is why He gave the gift of interpretation to church leaders. Every priest, monk, imam, rabbi, and pujari is there to interpret God's instructions and to help us on the path to righteousness.'

'So why you? There are already so many churches out there for people to choose from, what's so special about the Church of Eternal Light that they should ignore the others and come here?'

'Do you like stand-up comedy, Seb?'

'I guess.'

'Okay, well, let's say you go to watch your favourite stand-up comedian, and he keeps saying the same jokes every time you see him. Eventually you'd grow bored, maybe stop going to see him so often; maybe stop going altogether. The same ennui is gripping modern day Christian churches. Have you ever been to church?'

'My parents were Roman Catholic.'

'Okay, so when was the last time you went to Mass?'

'It's been years.'

'I bet if you went tomorrow, you'd find it matches the memory of your last visit. Nothing will have changed. Okay, there might be different hymns, and different readings, but the format and the prayers won't have changed. You'll still recite with the rest of the congregation, like drones. I don't believe that's what God wants us to do. He gave us the Bible as a user guide about how to live our lives, and we need to pay reverence to its divinity, but robotically repeating mantras isn't respectful.'

'So you think Christian churches are wrong?'

'I didn't say that. Don't put words into my mouth. I'm not saying there's anything wrong with Christian services. That works for some, but not for all. I'm hoping to find those that want God's comfort, but are put off by all the rules and doctrine. I want to help those that fall between the cracks. I believe we all have free will, and choose how we live our lives. I don't try to recruit people to join our little community, but I welcome all those who come by.' He paused. 'Now it's your turn. Why are you really here?'

'Excuse me?'

'I've been hosting counselling meetings for years. I always make an effort to introduce myself to first-timers when I see them, but most will say or do anything to get out of the door. You on the other hand have engaged me in debate and seem genuinely interested in what I have to say. Something doesn't sit right.'

Carmichael eyed him carefully. 'I was just interested that's all.'

'Don't kid a kidder. Who are you really? Is your name even Seb? You don't look like a Seb. In fact, it strikes me that wild horses would have to drag you to an anger management session unless there was an angle in it. I'm a good judge of character. Come on, tell me the truth. I won't be cross.'

'I am telling the truth. My wife told me I should -'

Sanza snapped his fingers. 'Ah, there you go. It was your girlfriend when we met. I knew it!'

Carmichael scrunched his eyes closed, angry at his own slip. 'Okay, okay, my name's not Seb. You got me.'

Sanza was grinning now. 'So what are you? A reporter?'

'Not exactly. I'm a private investigator. I was hired by the mother of one of your -'

'Let me guess: Wendy Barlow?'

'Yes, how did you -'

'She rings here all the time, throwing out accusations about what happened to her daughter. It was such a tragedy, but unfortunately she turned her back on God's message and fell into old habits.'

Carmichael passed him a business card. 'I'm sorry about the deceit. I wanted to get a sense of who you are without you being defensive.'

'There's no need to apologise. Hopefully, I've done enough to put your mind at ease. There's nothing sinister about what we do here, Johnson. I only want to help people. We have a service here tomorrow. You're free to stop by and see for yourself. You can come and speak to some of our members. You'll soon see that we mean no harm.' He eyed Carmichael carefully. 'Can I be honest with you?'

'Please.'

'I see a darkness behind *your* eyes, Johnson. There is something troubling you personally. I'd be happy to talk to you about it. Maybe I can help you find God's guidance in the great book.'

'I'm fine, believe me!'

'Are you sure? I'm able to hear confessions if there's anything you'd like to tell God.'

Carmichael stood quickly, suddenly keen to be out of there. 'I've taken up enough of your time. I should be getting on.'

Sanza watched him leave, certain it wouldn't be the last time their paths would cross.

13

'Shit, piss, fuck, bugger,' Beth yelped, as the steaming macaroni cheese dripped onto her hand. She dropped the plastic container on the plate, and rushed to the sink. The cool water brought light relief. 'That'll teach me to read while cooking,' she said to herself.

Her day off work had started reasonably well. She'd managed to sleep through the noise of the screaming baby next door, and hadn't crawled from bed until after nine, which was something of a record for her. She'd fixed herself a pot of tea and headed for the bath. It was so rare that she ever had time to mope about the flat, and she was determined not to do anything that came close to constituting work. With all the recent overtime available, she couldn't remember the last proper day off she'd enjoyed. D.C.I. Payne had insisted Beth take some downtime. The trouble with shift work was burning out.

By ten o'clock, however, she was bored. She was bathed and dressed, and looking for something to do. The television was a waste, as she wasn't into cookery programmes, detested all forms of sport, and was over the age of twelve.

'What do normal people do at the weekends?' she'd asked herself over and over again. When no obvious reply was forthcoming, she did what she knew best, and fished out her work satchel.

She'd used the living room floor to sort the evidence she'd amassed so far for the two murders. On the left side of the room, she'd started with Todd Francis' casefile. She had the photographs taken by the forensics team of the victim, and the few points of interest they'd captured. The handcuffs were made of leather and fastened with a buckle. Although they were black in colour, it was impossible to conclude whether they had belonged to the victim or his killer. Beth had found a dozen online sites where similar cuffs were available for purchase. Iron chains had then be used to restrain the cuffs to the bedframe beneath the headboard. The chain looked like the sort that could be readily purchased from a DIY store, so that too was a dead end. The blood found on the cuffs belonged to the victim only.

The most interesting aspect from the case was the stray strand of hair that had been found at the scene. Spinks had concluded that the hair was synthetic, rather than human, and that pointed to the killer wearing a wig. Did the victim know his killer was wearing a wig? Role play and costumes went hand-in-hand in the bondage and sadomasochistic culture. One of Chagrin's team had analysed the strand and although they couldn't offer a direct link to a suspect, it wasn't a total waste.

The report said that in some cases it was almost impossible to tell the difference between natural hair and the synthetic variety, owing to the denier and texture of the latter. The killer may have chosen the synthetic variety because of its easy maintenance. The wig wouldn't require styling, could be worn in all weathers, and was likely to be less expensive than a natural variety. That told Beth a thing or two about the killer. The report also noted synthetic wigs could not be restyled, which meant the killer would either need an alternative wig or their look would remain the same. Beth had already put a call out to local wig merchants to see if any similar purchases had been made in the last six months, which was the likely timespan of a synthetic wig. Nobody had returned her call yet.

The door-to-door enquiries had been fruitless. Only one other resident had been in on Wednesday night, and she hadn't heard any noise from the upstairs flat. The only real lead Beth had was an image captured from the security footage of the café where Todd had spent the evening with a tall blonde. It was too much of a coincidence that his date had long platinum blonde hair. Unfortunately at no point did Todd's date face the security camera, meaning they only had a shot of the back of her head. Capshaw had interviewed the barista who had been working that night, but he'd been unable to provide a description of the woman.

To the right of the living room was the paperwork related to the Josh Grabban murder. His student identification had been found in his wallet, and a call to the university had revealed he was a fresher, living in the Glen Eyre halls in Bassett. The university had put Beth in touch with two other students who said they were with Josh in the club on Thursday night. They confirmed they arrived shortly after opening at ten, and left shortly before two.

'Josh pulled and left before midnight,' one of his

friends stated. 'We didn't see him again, so we assumed he'd gone back to her place.'

They had been shocked to learn of Josh's true fate, but the security camera at the club's exit confirmed they didn't leave until closing, which ruled them out as suspects. Beth had studied the last known shot of Josh, leaving the club with a tall blonde in pursuit. Again, the image was of the back of her head only. Beth compared the image with the one from the café. It was impossible to confirm for certain if they belonged to the same woman, but Beth's gut was screaming that it had to be. But that raised the question of who she was and why she'd chosen to kill two unconnected strangers.

Beth had been through both victims' backgrounds with a fine toothcomb, and there was nothing to connect them. Todd was Southampton born and bred, in his early forties, and worked for a bank. Josh by contrast was twenty, and raised in Norfolk. He'd only lived in Southampton since joining university in September. They didn't share any tastes, and a cursory glance at their bank accounts confirmed they hadn't visited any of the same shops in the last year.

Beth turned the tap off and patted her hand with a towel. The cheese had left a red mark where it had burned her skin. She gently blew on it. Steam was still rising from the ready meal, as she picked up a fork and gave the contents a stir. It was lazy cooking, but that was all she ever seemed to do these days. If her meals weren't purchased from a fast-food establishment, they came out of the freezer. Her mother would turn in her grave if she could see Beth now. She'd believed that food should be grown, rather than bought, but then she'd been backward in a lot of her thinking. It still hadn't stopped the cancer taking her when Beth was eighteen.

She leaned against the kitchen work surface in the open plan flat, systematically blowing on her food and then taking a mouthful. She knew it wasn't good for the digestive system to eat while standing, but with all the paperwork spread out, there wasn't anywhere to sit. She took another mouthful, and then, out of the corner of her eye, something caught her attention.

She dropped the fork into the container and marched purposefully over to the image of Josh leaving the nightclub. How hadn't she seen it before? It seemed so obvious now. She reached for a magnifying glass and focused in on the speck of colour that had stood out from the kitchen. She excitedly snatched her mobile phone and dialled D.C.I. Payne's mobile. Payne was someone Beth admired greatly. A capable D.C.I. who was both competent, and popular amongst her peers, whilst managing to balance the demands of the job with a husband and family. She was living proof that the two worlds could coexist. Beth was almost giddy as the line connected.

'Ma'am, it's Beth Taylor. Are you free to speak? I think I've found something.'

'Now's not a great time, Beth. I'm about to take my daughter to her dance class. Is it work-related?'

'Oh, I'm sorry, Ma'am, I didn't realise it was your day off too.'

'That's okay, Beth. With White away, I told you to contact me if you needed anything. What is it?'

'It's about the Josh Grabban case, Ma'am. The

student who was killed in the car park in St Mary's?'

'Amber, put your bloody shoes on, and get in the car will you? Sorry, Beth, teenagers are a nightmare! Don't have kids. Stay a career woman. God knows I wish I had.'

Beth laughed nervously.

'Anyway, Beth, what were you saying about the Grabban case?'

'I think I know what the murder weapon was, Ma'am.'

'Have you spoken with the pathologist?'

'No, not yet, I thought I should update you first.'

'Jesus, Amber. *Not* the red ones. The *pink* ones. For God's sake! Sorry, Beth what were you saying?'

'The murder weapon, Ma'am? I think I know how she killed him.'

'I'm listening.'

'The image we took from the security camera shows Grabban leading her away from the club, we can't see her face, but we *can* see her shoes. Stilettos, Ma'am. They must be at least four inches high, if not more. I think that's how she did it. She must have pushed the heel into his ear until she killed him.'

'Is that even possible? Death by Jimmy Choo's?'

'It's the right thickness, and length, and explains the dark bruising around his temple. The woman in the café with Todd Francis is also wearing stilettos. Granted they're a different colour, but the same sort of height. Josh's friends said he left with a tall woman. Stilettos would make any woman look tall, wouldn't they?'

'Amber, if you don't get into the sodding car now, you won't be going anywhere. I don't care what your dad said. You can live by his rules on his time. When you're with me, it's my way or the highway. Do I make myself clear?' A pause. 'Sounds good, Beth, That's good work. Let me know what Spinks says, and then find those shoes and our killer. I'll see you on Monday.'

The line went dead. Beth returned to her lunch. She hadn't been sure what Payne would say, but she hadn't expected her to be so distracted. It was strange to hear her boss not in control. Beth dismissed the thought. Payne was just having a bad day. The pressures of the job and family were tough on everyone. She made a note to check the criminal records database for any recent parolees with a penchant for expensive heels. It was a break. Only time would tell how significant a break it might be.

14

Carmichael leaned against the doorway while his host busied himself making tea, 'So this is where your mum stabbed your dad to death?'

Tom Dewis shot him an angry look. 'Not exactly. There's more to it than that. That's why I called you.'

Carmichael couldn't understand how, let alone why, a twenty-three year-old would choose to live in the house where his father was brutally murdered sixteen years ago. It gave him the creeps just being in the house.

Tom led him through to the living room, and once they were both seated, he began. 'I don't know how much you remember about my mother's case. It was in all the newspapers, both local and national, at the time. It was sensationalised to sell more copies. Nobody was interested in the truth.'

'And what is that?'

'My mum didn't kill my dad.'

'That's not what a jury of her peers concluded.'

'They had little other choice. The police decided mum was guilty from the moment they arrived. She was their prime suspect from day one, and they overlooked other suspects.'

'That's a bold accusation to make. If you have proof of that, you should take it to the Independent

Police Complaints Commission. Maybe they could have the case reopened for you.'

'If I could prove my mum didn't do it, she wouldn't be behind bars now. She'd be here, in her home, where she belongs.'

'When you phoned my office on Thursday, you didn't mention exactly why you wanted to meet me.'

'I wanted to meet you before I decided whether I should hire you.'

'Hire me to do what?'

'Find the evidence that clears my mum's name.'

Carmichael sipped his tea. 'From what I've read, your mum was charged sixteen years ago, and sentenced nine months later. Don't you think it's a little late for that? Why now?'

'It's never too late to overturn a miscarriage of justice.'

'True, but it's one thing to believe someone else killed your father, but it's another to prove it.'

'That's why I want to hire you.'

'I think you've got the wrong idea about me, Tom. I'm used to spying on cheating spouses. That's my speciality. What you're looking for is someone who can dedicate weeks to digging through the past, trawling through evidence and interviewing witnesses who have probably forgotten the most pertinent details of what happened. Even if you found someone willing to spend the time on such an investigation, the chance of finding answers is too slim to consider.'

'I'm sure when you hear what I have to say, you'll change your mind. Give me until you finish your tea. Then, if you're still not interested, I'll pay you for your time this morning and you can be on your way.'

Carmichael checked his watch and nodded.

'My father, Ben, was born and raised in Southampton. He had the city in his veins. He went to The Dell every game to watch Saints, he was involved in community activities, and he loved that this was his home. Mum told me he'd tried his hand at almost every career, and was working in a telephone exchange when she first met him. She said it was love at first sight, and they married within a year of meeting. He promised her he would find a way to buy them a house, and that she would be able to raise a beautiful family there.' He stood and selected one of the frames from the wall, before handing it to Carmichael. About eighteen months after the wedding, he met George Murphy, a Dubliner who had settled in the area. The two of them were working as market traders and mum said they were as thick as thieves. They were always getting into scrapes, though mum assures me it was George who led my dad astray, rather than the other way around.' He pointed at the photograph. 'That's the two of them. George is the one on the right. The picture was taken the day they secured the bank loan to open their textile factory. It had been George's idea for them to go into business together, and dad's idea to focus on ladies hosiery. There were already a couple of similar businesses in the city, but the owner of the largest one died suddenly, and my dad and George were able to purchase the land and business from his grieving widow for a cheap price.'

Carmichael passed the photograph back and reached for his tea. 'That must have all been before I moved to the area.'

'Oh, I'm sure it was. They took over the factory in Eastleigh in the late seventies I think, and despite neither of them managing such a large team of employees before, they did a good job. The business grew, and they bought out one of their biggest rivals, until they were the first port of call for hosiery in the county. It was quite an operation by all accounts. Mum said they'd never been so well off. He bought this place without the need of a mortgage. Mum says he used to call his staff his "second family". I can remember going to the annual Christmas party he threw for the staff and their families. Everyone was always so complimentary about him.'

'It sounds like you were happy.'

'We were, but then…things turned sour. I still remember the day when my dad came home and broke the news to my mum. The look on his face, he was ashen, like all the blood had been drained from him. They'd taken on a huge contract to deliver lingerie for some major retailer in the US. It would have made my dad and George millionaires. They mortgaged the business to cover the cost of purchasing materials, and offered staff overtime to meet the demand. They'd completed half the order when the retailer went into administration. The factory was stuck with half the completed order, and supplies to complete the remainder. News got out that the business was struggling, and the sharks circled. They were unable to complete new contracts as they didn't have the funds to buy new materials. They tried offloading the completed work to other retailers without success. The business went into meltdown. With no income, my dad couldn't afford to keep the regular staff on, and most were laid off. He was devastated. He blamed himself for gambling the company's future. He became depressed, and when things couldn't seem to get any worse, they did. An anonymous call was placed to the Inland Revenue, as it was at the time, claiming my father had been embroiled in creative accounting. When the taxman decided to follow up on the allegation, they discovered the company pension fund had been embezzled. The pension account was empty, and there was no sign of who or how it had been taken. Of course, fingers were pointed at my dad. He declared his innocence, and offered his full cooperation to the investigation, but that didn't stop the press making unsubstantiated accusations. It seemed to be the only story in the papers for a fortnight. My dad was a broken man. He'd lost his business, his "second family", and was seriously facing the prospect of imprisonment.'

'What happened next?'

'On Saturday 25 March 2000, my mum found him bleeding to death in the kitchen. He'd been stabbed multiple times.'

15

Kelly hasn't heard from her brother all morning. Josh's death is still the lead story on the local news. Her brother hasn't mentioned the murder to her, so she's confident he doesn't suspect. He knows what she is capable of, but he believes he can keep her from those urges. For a long time he has. The police haven't announced that they've connected the two murders. If the police do come calling, she is confident her brother will protect her.

They've always been close. She is sure they're closer than most brothers and sisters, but she likes the fact she can turn to him when she needs support or a shoulder to cry on. He's always looked out for her, and likewise, she has done things for his benefit. They are a strong team.

That's why she has ventured out now. She wants to do something nice for him, to show him how much she appreciates what he does for her. He would never ask her to do what she is planning, but she can sense this is something he wants. It is lunchtime, and the roads are jammed with people making their way to the beach on what promises to be one of the hottest days of the year.

She is in the car park of KFC in Millbrook, two and a half miles from the city centre. She ordered her food at the drive thru, and has been eating it while she waits. Her fingers are greasy, and she uses a paper napkin to wipe them. She knows the meal will do nothing for her larger frame, but she hasn't eaten since breakfast, and needs to maintain her energy levels for what she has planned. She slurps her strawberry milkshake, watching people entering and exiting the McDonald's next door.

The girl she is waiting for is called Claire, and she used to go out with Kelly's brother. They had met at a friend's party, and had hit it off almost immediately. They had dated for several months, though Kelly warned him about her. She's always had a sixth sense when meeting new people, and she hadn't liked Claire one bit. For starters, Claire has no morals, practically sticking her tongue down his neck within four hours of knowing him. Kelly made it clear to him she didn't like Claire, but, for once, he ignored her guidance. He tried to see Claire behind her back, but she found out, and things turned sour between them for a brief time. She forgave him, of course, after all, he is her brother, but she has never forgiven Claire for encouraging him to be deceitful to his sister.

Kelly had sensed that Claire was trying to trap her brother. Claire kept throwing herself at him, always trying to get him into bed. He isn't that kind of guy: he has morals. He fell in love with Claire, but told her he wanted to save himself for their wedding night. Kelly didn't approve of their relationship, but she admired her brother's resolve.

One night Claire got him drunk and seduced him. Kelly found Claire wandering around the house, naked and beaming from ear to ear. Kelly stormed out, allowing her bother to deal with the repercussions of the whore's actions. He bottled it, and didn't end things as he should have, even though Claire betrayed his wishes.

They continued to see each other for several more weeks, until Claire dropped the bombshell: she was pregnant. She told him it was his, and that they'd now be able to get a council house together, so she could raise their child.

He was devastated. He'd showed Claire nothing but kindness, and suddenly he was facing an uncertain future he had no control over. Kelly wasn't sure how to help him, but eventually went to visit Claire, and told her a few home truths. Claire didn't react well and phoned Kelly's brother, giving him an ultimatum: it was her or Kelly. Claire didn't realise Kelly heard the whole thing. Kelly told her brother it was time to move on, and he reluctantly agreed to end the relationship.

Claire sent him a letter weeks later, telling him she'd had an abortion, as she couldn't live with bringing his child into the world. That was the last straw.

He shut himself away for weeks, refusing to see anyone. Kelly took care of him, and, after much persuading, he eventually put the whole sorry mess behind him. The memory of that time still haunts him to this day, not that he ever discusses it with Kelly, but she knows him too well. He's turned over a new chapter in his life now.

Kelly is less forgiving. She's never forgotten how Claire treated him. Kelly has decided today is the day the whore will get what's coming to her. She knows

Claire works at the burger restaurant, and that she is there right now. It is a matter of waiting for her.

Claire's shift ends and she emerges shortly after one. She still looks the same: shoulder-length brown hair, tied in a small ponytail. She is nearly twelve inches shorter than Kelly, at only five foot. Kelly knows how to use her height to dominate others. Claire walks back to her flat, along a shadowy footpath. She doesn't hear Kelly following slowly behind.

Kelly isn't surprised to discover Claire is still living in the same high-rise flat. When Claire is inside, Kelly knocks at the door. Claire opens the door a crack, and Kelly forces her way in. She puts the cloth over Claire's mouth, and drags her back into the flat. Claire is fighting to escape, kicking her heels into Kelly's shins, but her attempts are futile. She soon passes out on the floor. Kelly places the cloth back into her handbag, next to the small bottle of chloroform. It won't be long before Claire regains consciousness; there wasn't much of the chemical on the rag.

Kelly pulls a chair over and ties a silk scarf around the ceiling rose above it. She lifts Claire into a standing position on the chair, and ties the other end of the scarf tightly around her neck. Kelly lifts Claire, and kicks over the chair. She isn't sure whether the ceiling rose will hold Claire's weight, so she takes a deep breath as she lets go of the body.

The knot tightens around Claire's throat, and the sudden drop has woken her. Her legs wriggle as she tries to prise her fingers between the scarf and her neck. The more she struggles, the tighter the noose becomes. Her face is turning purple already. Kelly watches, unable to hide the grin from her face. She steps out from behind Claire, so she can watch as the life drains from the whore's eyes. Claire sees her, and her panic increases, but it is already too late. Claire is already feeling lightheaded, and it won't be long until she passes out again.

Kelly removes a piece of paper from her handbag, and holds it high so it is the last thing Claire will see. It is a typed suicide note. Kelly folds the piece of paper and leaves it on the floor beneath Claire's feet. She remains standing there until Claire's legs stop kicking. She pulls out her phone and takes a picture. She likes a keepsake, and this is a memory she will happily relive in the future. Pleased with her afternoon's work, she closes the front door and walks back towards her car. She finishes the strawberry milkshake, before driving home.

16

Tom made Carmichael a second cup of tea, before continuing his story. 'On the night he was killed, my mum had gone out to the cinema with her best friend. They'd been to watch 'The Insider' with Russell Crowe. Have you seen it?'

Carmichael shook his head.

'My mum is a huge Russell Crowe fan. She'd been itching to see the film since its release, but my dad wasn't particularly sociable at that time, what with everything that was going on. Mum decided to go with my Auntie Pat. She's not my actual aunt, but that's what we used to call her. Anyway, the film started at half past six, and was on for a little over three hours, including adverts and previews. Auntie Pat drove mum home, and dropped her shortly before ten o'clock. My mum went straight to bed, without seeing my dad, but something woke her shortly after. She cannot recall if it was a noise or a light that disturbed her, but something had. She crept downstairs, wondering if they were being burgled, and that's when she found him.'

Tom suddenly walked out of the room. Carmichael remained where he was until Tom called for him to come out to the kitchen.

'That's where she found him,' he said, pointing at

the radiator to the left of the doorway. The kitchen was about three metres square, with a backdoor leading to the garden near where he was pointing. 'It was weeks before they managed to clean the mess,' he added.

Carmichael watched him carefully. What kind of person could live in the house where his father had been murdered? He shivered.

'My mum checked for a pulse, but it was weak. She told me his shirt was soaked red through. She tried to talk to him, but he was unconscious. She didn't know what to do, and then remembered our next door neighbour was a vet. She rushed to their house and made them call for an ambulance. The vet returned to the house with my mum, and they waited together for the paramedics to arrive. My dad was rushed to hospital, but…he died of his injuries before they reached the hospital.'

'I'm sorry.'

'Owing to the blood on her clothes, the police made my mum their prime suspect. They described it as a crime of passion. They took her away and questioned her for days. My sister Annie and I went to stay with my Aunt Helen, my dad's younger sister. She didn't have children of her own, but my dad had bought her a small house when the business had been thriving, so she owed him. My mum was eventually released. From day one, she said she was innocent, and that she loved my dad. You can imagine the field day the newspapers had. My dad's death seemed to give them the confirmation he'd stolen the money. It didn't matter that he couldn't defend himself. They painted it as a massive scandal. They portrayed my mum as some jealous harlot who had killed him because he wouldn't tell her where the money was. It was all lies, and they eventually printed an apology when George threatened them with legal action, but it was too late by then. You can't make people unread something though, can you? The damage was already done. She was guilty in most people's eyes.'

'Were there any signs of a break in? Anything to suggest an intruder had been in the house?'

'None. They concluded that dad must have known his killer and let him in, or...well, the killer had a key to the house. It was easier for them to blame my mum than investigate who else might have had a motive to kill him.' Tom led him back to the living room. 'A week after she was released from questioning, one of her so-called friends went to the papers and told them my dad used to beat my mum, and this was a more likely motive for her violent retaliation. The police brought her back in for questioning, and, under pressure, she admitted she had been the victim of some minor domestic abuse. He'd first lashed out at her two months before his death. It was right after the Inland Revenue had begun their investigation. I'm not making excuses for him, but he was under so much pressure. The police found a note on her medical record that she'd been treated at The General for a sprained wrist. She'd told doctors she'd fallen down the stairs, when in truth, they'd argued, and he'd pushed her over. Even after intense interviews, she still maintained her innocence. The police now had motive, all they needed was the evidence to support their belief. The blood on my mum's clothes was circumstantial, but her fingerprints were also found on the kitchen knife that had been used to stab him. Her solicitor argued she'd been chopping vegetables before she'd gone to the cinema, but hers were the only prints they found on the handle.'

'That's not enough to get a conviction though.'

'No, but I think what nailed it was the account the vet and his wife gave. They told police they heard arguing at about half past ten. My Auntie Pat confirmed she'd dropped mum home shortly before ten, so she had opportunity as well as motive. The police kept asking what she was doing between ten and when she claimed to discover the body at eleven. My mum had originally told them she'd been dropped at home at eleven, and that she'd found the body on her return. When they questioned her about this discrepancy, she couldn't explain it. The case went to trial at the Old Bailey in London, as it had become high profile by this time. She tried to take out a mortgage on the house to cover her barrister and solicitor's fees, but the bank refused as they didn't believe she'd be found innocent. I think George paid in the end. Her barrister told her to plead guilty, as she'd get a lesser sentence. She refused, as she was innocent. Unfortunately the jury were unanimous in finding her guilty, and she was sentenced to life imprisonment with no chance of parole, as she'd shown no remorse for such a violent and callous act. That was sixteen years ago.'

'Did she appeal against the conviction?'

'Of course. At her first appeal, her defence team argued the conviction should be reduced to manslaughter on the grounds of provocation. They said she was the victim of abuse, so any intent to kill was in self-defence. She wasn't happy with this approach, but was desperate to get out for me and my sister. The appeal was refused on the grounds that the thirty seconds it took for her to locate the knife, did not constitute "a sudden and temporary loss of self-control". The murder was therefore considered to be pre-meditated, and provocation could not be accepted as a defence.'

'What happened about the Inland Revenue's investigation into the stolen pension fund?'

He snickered. 'Nothing. It ended the moment my father was declared dead. The lead investigator ruled the monies untraceable following my father's death, and the case was closed. The staff never got a penny of their money back.'

'Does your mum have any idea where it went?'

'I asked her once, and she told me if my dad had taken it, he did a great job of hiding his guilt. She is more certain than ever that he didn't take the money, and that whoever took it is still out there. It is my belief, Mr Carmichael, that whoever framed my father for stealing the money, also killed him to cover their tracks.'

'Can I ask you a personal question?'

'Sure.'

'How can you be so certain that your mum is telling you the truth? Is it not possible she is telling you she's innocent, so that you'll continue to visit her?'

Tom folded his arms. 'I've looked into her eyes. I know she didn't do it.'

'What happens if I find evidence that points to your mother's guilt? What would you do?'

'I spoke to my pastor about that. He believes in the power of forgiveness. *If* that happens, I will have to learn to forgive her. I believe she's innocent, so I don't think that will happen.'

'What does your sister think about all this? She's older than you, right?'

'My sister took off as soon as she turned sixteen. She was thirteen when it happened, and I don't think she ever forgave my mum. She went travelling with her boyfriend, and I haven't seen or heard from her in a couple of years. I think my aunt is still in touch with her.'

'Your sister thinks your mum did it?'

'Annie believed what she read in the papers. She was always closer to my dad than my mum. When he died, she shut herself away. She fell in with a bad crowd at school, and shut me and our aunt out of her life. I always assumed we reminded her of what had happened to him, and she couldn't deal with it.'

'If I agree to look into this, I'd want to speak to her as well.'

Tom beamed. 'So you'll take the case?'

'I didn't say that…but, I'll think about it.'

'You can have access to anything you need. I can arrange it. I've taken some time off work so that I can help you out.'

'That won't be necessary. I already have an investigative partner. I won't need you hanging around too. Can I ask you another personal question?'

Tom nodded.

'Why do you still live here? Just knowing that someone died here gives me the shivers.'

'My dad was attacked here, but he died in the

ambulance.'

'Even so, knowing he took his last breaths here, doesn't it...I don't know...doesn't it make you uneasy?'

'I understand what you're saying. My aunt Helen said something similar when I decided to move in. For me, this house holds a lot of happy childhood memories. I was seven when I left here, but I can still remember birthday and Christmas parties. I remember kicking a football in the back garden with my dad. All the photographs on the wall are reminders of happier times. I'm not ready to close that door yet. I want to remember my father for the good that he did, not by how his name was tarnished in that final year.'

'Which room do you sleep in incidentally?'

'The same bedroom I've always slept in. I kept my parents' and sister's rooms as they left them. You're welcome to take a look if you want. I believe this house holds the clue to what happened all those years ago.'

'I want to meet your mother. I appreciate you telling me you believe in her innocence, but I want to assess that for myself.'

Tom looked giddy, as he stood and thrust out his hand. 'I'll arrange it as soon as possible. Hopefully I can get you in this Tuesday. That's when I'm next due to visit her. I'll speak to the Governor and see if he can grant you special access, given that you'll be aiding her appeal.'

'Good. If I'm satisfied with what I hear, I'll see what I can find.' Carmichael shook his hand. 'You said the stolen pension money was never found. I think that's the best place to start. I've got a contact who might be able to provide some background on why the police weren't involved in the Inland Revenue's investigation.'

Tom led him to the front door. As it opened, a woman with straggly auburn hair was coming in. She was wearing a checked tabard, and carrying two large shopping bags. Carmichael put her in her mid to late forties. She took a step back when she saw his large frame staring back at her.

'Aunt Helen, this is the private investigator I was telling you about,' Tom declared. 'Johnson Carmichael, this is my Aunt Helen.'

She blinked several times, before nodding politely, and pushing past them into the kitchen, placing the carrier bags on the counter top.

'You'll have to forgive her,' Tom whispered. 'She's a bit set in her ways. She thinks I'm wasting my money in hiring you. She pops round to bring me food once a week. I think she still sees me as a child who needs her to do things for me. I know she means well. God knows where Annie and I would have gone if she hadn't agreed to take us in.'

Carmichael stepped outside, handing over a business card. 'This has got my mobile number on it, as well as the office number. Once you've sorted out Tuesday, give me a call. Meanwhile, I'll have Melissa draft a contract for you to sign, and I'll look into what happened to the pension monies.'

SUNDAY

17

Beth stepped into the elevator, and the rickety doors closed with a sigh. The metal walls were adorned with lewd comments drawn in permanent marker. There was the faint whiff of urine too. She felt unclean just standing there. She was relieved when the lift finished its journey and she was able to escape into fresh air again. A uniformed officer was standing at the door which led to the flats in the council-owned high rise. He held the door open as she waved her identification. She found D.C.I. Payne waiting for her outside flat fifty-eight.

Beth stifled a yawn. 'Morning, Ma'am, it's not often we see you so early on at the crime scene.'

'The rest of the team were called in overnight for an Operation Fortress raid. Big haul of cocaine from all accounts. The only reason I didn't send you was that I thought you deserved a weekend away from the office. Unfortunately, we got this shout, and I've had to bring you in anyway. I am sorry. You didn't have anything planned for today did you?'

'Nothing I couldn't move,' Beth lied. The truth was she'd been relieved to receive Payne's call. The thought of another day on her own filled her with dread. 'What have we got?'

Payne ushered her into the flat. 'Girl's name is

Claire Willis. She was supposed to be going to her mum's place for dinner last night, but when she didn't show and didn't respond to calls and messages, her mum became worried. She came round and found Claire hanging from the ceiling rose in the main room.'

Beth grimaced. 'Suicide.'

'Evidently so. The paramedics who arrived on scene discovered a suicide note on the floor beneath the body. It's not exactly poetry. It says she's sorry to have let everyone down and has had enough.'

'Sounds pretty straightforward. I can get one of the D.C.s to complete the paperwork if you like. There's no point in us both wasting our Sunday. I'm sure you'd rather be spending the day with your husband and children.'

'The victim's mother insists her daughter had no reason to take her own life and is claiming foul play was involved.'

'You're kidding!'

Payne shook her head. 'We'll have to give it the once over. You know, as well as I do, the victim's families in these cases never accept that their loved one just gave up.'

'Where's the mother now?'

'I had a Family Liaison Officer escort her home. She was making a right noise when I first got here, threatening to go to the press if we didn't treat this seriously. You know the kind of thing. Let's get down to brass tacks: it's an open-and-shut suicide. Show the family some empathy, ask a few awkward questions, kick over a couple of stones and then close it. Okay?'

Beth nodded. 'Sure. Can I see the suicide note? It's

an idea to read it before I meet the mother.'

Payne snapped her fingers and one of the white-suited forensics officers brought over the letter in a transparent wallet. Beth scanned the letter with her eyes. It was as brief as Payne had described.

Beth passed the letter back. 'Do we know if the neighbours heard or saw anything suspicious?'

'Uniform are doing door-to-door now, but I wouldn't pin any hope on that. You know what this estate is like: they don't talk to the police, until it benefits them. I'd be surprised if any of them even admitted to knowing the girl.'

'Did she live alone?'

'As far as we know.'

'And there were no signs of forced entry?'

'None. The door is fitted with a fairly sturdy lock, which can only be opened by a key. The victim's mother had a spare, which is how she got in.'

'Was the victim depressed, or on anything?'

'That's the mother's argument. She reckons her daughter was happy, and expressed no suicidal tendencies or signs of depression.'

'When was the last time anyone saw the victim?'

'She finished her shift at the burger joint at lunchtime. We spoke to her shift supervisor, and he said she didn't seem unhappy when she left. He said there was no reason to suspect what she would go on to do.' She looked off into the distance. 'I guess you never really know what goes on in someone's life once the doors are closed...' Her words trailed off, as she gazed out of the window.

'Ma'am? Is everything okay?'

'What? Yes, fine, everything's fine. Get this one

closed off as soon as you can, Beth; you've got enough on your plate with the two homicides.'

Payne left the room.

Beth smiled at one of the forensics officers she recognised. 'Are you guys nearly done in here? Do you mind if I have a snoop?'

The officer lowered his face mask and smiled back. 'We're done in this room, so feel free.'

He was clean-shaven, and his blue eyes sparkled. He was far too handsome to work beneath a mask. Beth realised she'd been staring for too long without speaking. 'It's Harris, isn't it?'

He smiled again. 'That's right. My friends call me Mark.'

Beth turned when she felt her cheeks redden. She moved to the chest of drawers at the side of the room, and waited for Harris to leave. She admonished herself for acting unprofessionally. The drawer unit was fixed to the wall, and consisted of three long drawers. The bottom drawer was filled with DVDs, the middle drawer with CDs, and the top drawer with odds and ends. She focused her attention on the top drawer, pushing papers and stationery out of the way. There were a couple of bank statements, final notice utility bills, and some family photographs.

She frowned, as a thought troubled her. She moved across to the table and picked up the suicide note. She brought it back to the unit. For all the scraps of paper in the drawer, there were none that matched the piece of paper she was holding. Puzzled, she called Harris back into the room.

'Have you guys removed any paper from this drawer?'

He frowned. 'We haven't taken anything. We only dusted for prints. We didn't find anything of significance in the unit.'

'What's missing from this picture?'

He glanced around the room, unsure what she was getting at.

She held up the letter. 'This was on the floor, right? It's a letter typed, rather than handwritten, on a piece of paper that matches none of the paper in the room. What's missing?'

He glanced around again, and then saw what she meant. 'There's no computer in here.'

'Exactly! How could she have written the suicide note?'

'Maybe she typed it somewhere else and brought it back with her.'

'Like where?'

'I don't know…maybe she wrote it at work, or at a friend's house.'

'She works in a fast-food restaurant. I doubt she'd have access to a computer and printer, besides, it would be a huge risk to write something like this there, where any number of colleagues could catch her. And who goes to a friend's house to compose their suicide note? Again, there's too much of a danger that you'd be caught and then your friend would try and talk you out of it. It makes no sense.'

'What are you saying?'

'I don't know yet. It's odd, that's all. Something doesn't add up here.'

18

Carmichael watched the men and women piling in to the former working man's club. They weren't dressed as Wendy Barlow had suggested. The men were wearing shirts and smart trousers, and there were no ankle-length dresses in sight. It looked like any congregation at any normal church. He checked his watch. The service was due to start in three minutes. He didn't like being awake so early on a Sunday. He crossed the road, and headed for the door.

The hall was filled with chairs spiralling around a small round stage in the middle of the room. There was a narrow walkway separating the chairs, along which they walked. There had to be more than a hundred people already seated, and chatting. He found a vacant chair.

Looking around the room, the congregation still looked normal. He hadn't been sure what to expect, but he had assumed there would be something different.

The woman next to him offered a warm smile. 'Is this your first time here?'

He smiled back and nodded. 'Are you a regular attendee?'

'Oh yeah. It's the highlight of my week. Genuinely,

I always feel better after Paul's services. He just…I don't know…he has a way of connecting me with God's words. Do you know what I mean?'

'He does seem to have a way with words.'

'Have you met Paul yet?'

'I have. He's the reason I'm here today.'

Someone tapped Carmichael on the shoulder. 'Is this seat taken?'

He looked up and was surprised to see Tom Dewis staring back at him. 'What are you doing here?'

Tom sat. 'This is my church. I didn't realise you were a member too.'

'I'm not. I just…I don't know why I'm here really.'

'I was the same the first time I came here. A friend of mine dragged me along, and it moved me so much that I had to come back. With everything that happened with mum and dad, it's been good to be able to communicate with God.'

'I never took you for the religious type.'

'I told you yesterday that my pastor preaches the power of forgiveness. Have you met Paul yet? He's quite an engaging man.'

'So I've heard.'

'I have to be honest: h's made such a difference to my life. He's so easy to talk to. When I'm feeling down about mum, he's always there for me.'

'Not everybody shares your optimism. Paul's been accused of trying to brainwash his followers.'

'Ha! People fear new things. You wait and see: there's nothing sinister about the service. People question what they don't understand. I've never felt so close to God. Oh look, Paul's coming. Relax and enjoy it. Let God speak to you.'

Carmichael craned his neck and saw Paul Sanza moving along the walkway. As Paul walked, he shook the hands of those seated on the ends. He stepped onto the stage, closed his eyes and lowered his head. Those seated lowered their heads too.

'Dearest father, your flock come before you today to seek forgiveness and to ask you to guide them on their way. We are at your mercy, and we willingly give ourselves for your divine mission. Heavenly father, hear our prayers.'

The congregation declared 'Amen,' in unison.

Sanza opened his eyes and slowly looked at the sea of faces before him. 'Welcome one and all. I see a lot of familiar faces here today, and for that I thank God. I see love and happiness before me.' He looked directly at Carmichael. 'I also see a couple of new faces amongst us, and I would like to extend a warm welcome to those individuals. We do things a little differently here. Please don't be worried or alarmed by what you see or hear. We are all here for the same purpose. We believe. Let me hear you friends: do we believe?'

'We believe,' the group responded.

'God was born as man and died to save our souls. Praise be to God.'

'Praise be to God.'

Carmichael kept his head bent low, but watched the crowd eagerly replying to every line Sanza offered.

Sanza lifted his arms out wide. 'Let us pray. Heavenly father, we hear you calling to us and we answer you with Amen.'

'Amen.'

'We hear your truth from the words you gave us in

the Gospel.'

'We hear you.'

'The outside world chooses to ridicule us, but we will not hear them.'

'We will not hear them.'

'They will laugh at us and call us names, but we will rise above it.'

'We rise above it.'

'They challenge your name and your word, but we will ignore their jibes.'

'Ignore them.'

'We will turn our back on those who besmirch your name.'

'We turn our back.'

'We will not give in to the temptation of alcohol.'

'We say no to temptation.'

'We will not give in to the temptation of drugs.'

'We say no to temptation.'

'We will not give in to the temptation of nicotine.'

'We say no to temptation.'

'The devil will call to us, but we will say no.

'We say no.'

'Heavenly father we give ourselves for your mission only. Hear our prayers. Amen.'

'Amen.' The group broke into applause.

Sanza quietened them by gently waving his hands. 'I sense God is here in the room with us today. Let's test His words. Who's got something troubling them in their personal life? Don't be shy. God is ready to answer your prayer.' He lifted a copy of the Bible above his head. 'The answer to every question can be found in here. Who will be first? God wants to help you.'

A nervous hand lifted into the air across the room. All eyes turned to face the owner.

Sanza encouraged the middle-aged woman to stand. 'It's Jennifer, isn't it? Tell me, Jennifer, what troubles you? What do you need God's help with?'

The woman glanced nervously at the eyes upon her. 'It's my neighbour…she…I believe she poisoned my cat…little Whiskers was so innocent.'

The crowd let out an empathetic groan.

Sanza shook his head in dismay. 'That is so sad, Jennifer. I see why you're troubled. God hears you calling to him. Why do you believe your neighbour caused the cat's death?'

'I found poison on my lawn, by the fence that separates our properties. I didn't put it there. It could only have come from one place. She always hated my cat. She is such a wicked woman.'

Sanza indicated for her to sit, before addressing the rest of the group. 'This world is full of wicked people. I'm sure each and every one of you can think of at least one person who is as wicked as Jennifer's neighbour. Probably most of us can think of more than one. The Bible tells us the whole world is lying in the power of the wicked one. The Book of Revelation says that Satan is misleading the entire inhabited earth. Many imitate him, and that is why there are so many cruel people out there. What does God teach us? Matthew's and Luke's gospels tell us when injury is dealt upon us, we must turn the other cheek. We must not take an eye for an eye. It is the devil who tells us revenge is sweet. It is the devil we see at work each day. How many of us have watched the news and thought 'Can things get any worse?'

There is tragedy and cruelty wherever we look, and there is one reason for that. It is not because God is cruel. It is because Satan is among us now, and he wants us to rule with greed and selfishness, because these are the qualities he admires most. The devil wants to cause havoc upon the earth because God threw him out of His kingdom. When the devil enters our lives we have one choice to make: allow him in or keep our hearts pure for God. You must forgive your neighbour, Jennifer. You must grieve for your cat, and then allow forgiveness to enter your heart. That is the only way to keep Satan at bay.'

The crowd erupted into a unanimous, 'Amen.'

'God hears us best when we sing our love to him. Let us all stand and sing the Lord's Prayer. Let's show God we want Him in our hearts.' He looked directly at Carmichael again.

Carmichael glanced at Tom as he stood. He was beaming from ear to ear. Tom glanced over to him and smiled, and Carmichael couldn't help but smile back. He opened his mouth and began to sing.

19

The door-to-door enquiries conducted earlier in the day at the Millbrook estate had yielded no witnesses. As anticipated, there hadn't been a queue of neighbours volunteering to offer insight into what had happened in Claire Willis' flat. The uniforms who conducted the search had left Beth a list of properties where the occupants had actually opened their doors to speak. The list of flats where no answer was received was much longer.

Beth locked the car. 'Payne wants us to get this one closed ASAP. You start at the top and work down. I want to take another look inside her flat, and then I'll work down from there. Okay?'

Capshaw nodded.

The thought of spending any more time in the rickety old lift that stank of piss made her stomach turn. She could hold her breath for five floors, so long as it didn't stop on the way up. Poor Capshaw would have to put up with it for the full ten floors.

The lift pinged as it arrived on floor five. Beth stepped out, and once the doors were closed and Capshaw was on his way up, she exhaled. She would use the stairs to descend each floor. Flat fifty-eight still had a layer of blue and white tape across the doorway. She ducked beneath it and unlocked the door using the spare set of keys Claire's mum had loaned them. The door stuck slightly as she pushed it open. She stepped inside, and left the door resting on the sticky frame.

Remnants of black dust on surface tops was the only sign that the SOCOs had spent the best part of the day milling about inside. She put herself in Claire's shoes.

She walked slowly forward, speaking aloud to herself. 'I've just finished my shift at the fast-food restaurant. It was a five hour shift. Am I tired? Maybe. Do I know at this point that I want to kill myself? Am I depressed? Have I already decided that I'm going to hang myself?' She stepped into the main room, and looked up at the ceiling rose. 'Why do I choose to hang myself? Why don't I just swallow a handful of pills?' The silk scarf that had been used as a makeshift noose had been taken down and was being tested at the lab for DNA evidence. 'Why do I use a silk scarf? If I've planned my suicide, why don't I buy a proper rope? How do I know that the ceiling rose will support my weight?' Claire was only five foot tall, and wasn't overweight, so it was reasonable to assume that the light fitting would support her.

Beth walked over to the large window at the rear of the flat and looked out at the Millbrook bypass below her. It wasn't an inspiring view. 'Why do I leave my suicide note on the floor? Why don't I leave it on the table?'

She frowned and walked to the bedroom. The duvet was still curled up in a pile in the middle of the mattress. There was more black dust on surface edges. The curtains were closed in this room, but there was still a lot of light in the room. A thought struck her. She moved to the chest of drawers and pulled open the top one. She found underpants, tights and socks. In the second drawer she found vest tops and t-shirts. In the third drawer she found long-sleeved tops and cardigans. In the final drawer she found jumpers. She checked the top drawer again: no scarves of any kind, least of all silk ones.

'Did she buy the scarf to hang herself with? Why? She could have used a pair of tights to equal effect. Why would she buy a scarf to kill herself with when she could have bought a rope?'

There were too many unanswered questions. D.C.I. Payne had told her to conclude the case as quickly as possible and focus on the murders of the banker and the student, but the little voice in her head was telling her Claire didn't commit suicide.

She stepped back into the hallway when she spotted a pair of eyes staring back at her from the front door. The breath caught in her throat. The man realised he'd been spotted and quickly disappeared from view. Beth rushed to the front door and pulled it open, almost walking into the cordon. She ducked just in time and saw the shadowy figure disappearing into a flat three down from Claire's.

Beth ran to the flat and banged on the door. 'This is the police. I know you're in there. I just want to ask you if you saw anything at flat fifty-eight yesterday.'

There was no answer.

Beth banged the door again. 'I saw you go in. Please, I only want to ask you some questions.'

She could hear movement beyond the door, but it was going away from the door, rather than moving towards it. Beth stooped and pushed open the letter box hatch with her fingers.

She peered through the gap. It was difficult to see anything in the darkness of the hallway. 'Hello? My name is D.S. Beth Taylor. I just want to ask you some questions.' She spotted movement at the far end of the dark hallway. 'I know you, don't I? Your name's Victor, isn't it?'

The dark figure stopped moving, and looked towards her.

She could just make out the white of his eyes. 'Do you remember me, Victor? My name's Beth. We met last year. Do you remember? I was giving a talk at the community centre. You came over and told me I smelt nice.'

The figure took a step closer.

She remembered Victor approaching her after the talk at the community centre. He'd seemed shy, but after speaking with him, she'd realised he wasn't all there mentally.

Beth pushed her business card through the door. 'Here you go, Victor. You can see it's me. I don't mean you any harm. Can you just let me in for a bit?'

The figure stepped into the patch of light coming through the hatch. 'I know you,' he said, his West Indies accent unmistakeable. 'You're the pretty police woman.'

'That's right, Victor. You know me.'

He opened the door a fraction, and glanced through.

His skin was as black as his hair, and his wide-eyed stare looked almost comical. She smiled back at him to show she wasn't a threat. 'Can I come inside, Victor?'

'What d'you want?'

'I just want to ask you some questions about Claire Willis. She lived at flat fifty-eight. Did you know Claire?'

He grinned at mention of her name. 'She gonna be Victor's wife. She a good girl. She buy Victor bread some time.'

'You liked Claire, did you, Victor?'

'She a pretty little t'ing.'

'Can I come in, Victor?'

He considered her for a moment before opening the door, and allowing her to enter. The stench hit her immediately, and it was all she could do to stop herself from retching.

'Toilet blocked,' he said when he saw her eyes watering.

She pinched her nose and followed him along the hallway to the main room. Empty food packets littered the floor. He closed the door to the living room once they were inside. She instinctively opened the window, and pushed her head out breathing deeply until the nausea passed. She left the window open.

She looked around the room. There were more empty food containers on the floor and sofa. The only object free of food was the leather armchair in the middle of the room that Victor was sitting in. She spotted a small pile of crystals on a crumpled piece of foil on the table. There was a lighter next to the foil, along with a small pipe, and a discarded syringe. Was he high now?

'How long has your toilet been blocked, Victor?'

'Long time now.'

'How do you…I mean, when you need to…what do you do?'

'Victor go when luck present.'

She remembered he'd been difficult to understand when they'd met last year. She tried to interpret. 'Is that what you were doing at Claire's flat this morning? You were looking to use her toilet?'

He grinned back at her. His teeth looked like they were coated in golden syrup.

She tried to hide her distaste. 'Did you see Claire yesterday?'

'Mischief come by da poun' and go by da ounce.'

'Mischief?'

'Dat girl alway' bring da rain.'

'Wait? Are you saying Claire was in trouble?'

'Trouble nu set like rain.'

'Who was she in trouble with Victor? Did someone come to her flat yesterday?'

His eyes widened with fear. 'Bad joo joo.'

'Bad joo joo? Bad magic? Are you saying Claire was bad?'

'I warned her, victory nu come fram lie dung inna bead. She no hear. Bad joo joo come fa' her.'

'When was this, Victor? When did the bad men come for her?'

He tutted. 'Yu shake man han, yu nu shake him heart.'

'You met the man?'

He tutted again. 'Be no man of dis plain. She come and move with dem high shoes. Bad joo joo come.'

'It was a woman? You saw a woman at Claire's flat?'

He nodded. 'Alligator lay egg, but him nu fowl.'

'What did this woman look like, Victor? Can you describe her for me?'

'Mountain move.'

'She was tall? What colour hair did she have?'

'Golden like corn in da sunshine.'

Beth wrote tall and blonde in her notebook. 'Is there anything else you can tell me? Was she fat, was she thin?'

'Man no like da bones of da goat.'

'She was fat?'

'Nah, dem curves be there, but not too many.'

Beth reached in to her pocket and pulled out the security camera image from the coffee shop in Totton. 'Was this her?'

Victor didn't answer, but his face was the picture of fear. He leapt to his feet and grabbed the small pipe from the table before returning to his seat. 'You go now. Me no want bad joo joo coming for Victor.'

'It's okay, Victor. You don't need to worry. I can protect you. Was this the woman you saw at Claire's flat yesterday?'

He lit the end of the pipe and inhaled deeply, closing his eyes.

'Victor, was this who you saw?'

He wasn't listening, he slowly exhaled, and his shoulders relaxed. She could have arrested him for possession of a Class-A substance, but she didn't need the hassle. She tried to talk to him again, but his mind was elsewhere. She left her business card on the table with a twenty pound note, before holding her breath and heading for the front door. She closed it behind her and checked the next flat number on her list. *If* Victor was right, and the mystery blonde had called at Claire's flat, that linked her with three deaths in a week. It had to be more than mere coincidence. She knocked on the next flat with the security camera image tightly grasped in her hand. Victor wasn't a reliable witness, but she hoped one of the other residents might have seen the woman too. Who was this woman? And why was she suddenly killing in the city? Beth was sure there had to be a connection, but try as she might, she just couldn't see it.

20

Carmichael fastened the zip on his anorak. Although it had been a warm summer's day, a cool breeze was now blowing as he walked beneath the stars. The occasional car drove past, but otherwise the street was empty.

He saw the sign for Aldi, and crossed the road. He glanced around as he made his way around the back and into the car park. He saw the large black Range Rover with tinted windows parked in the far corner beside a builder's skip. He walked straight towards the vehicle. The window was down by the time he arrived.

'I was told I could score some gear from you,' Carmichael began.

'Oh yeah, and where did you hear that?' the pimply kid said from inside.

Carmichael removed a roll of notes from his pocket. 'I don't want any trouble, okay? I've got the cash, I just need to score some uppers.'

The kid nudged the large black guy behind the wheel, and laughed. He turned back to Carmichael. 'I don't know who you are or why you think I can help, but you've come to the wrong place. Now, fuck off!'

Carmichael squeezed the bridge of his nose in frustration. 'I'm not police, and I'm not wearing any kind of listening device, alright? Look.' He lifted his shirt and twirled around. 'I asked you outright, so if I was trying to trick you, I'd be guilty of entrapping you. Come on, you know the law better than me. Have you got what I need or not?'

The pimply kid considered him for a moment. 'I told you, pal, you've come to the wrong place. Now, don't quote me, but you see that kid standing by the moped over there?' He pointed over Carmichael's shoulder. 'I've heard a rumour that if you're looking to score, he knows people. If you're looking to purchase drugs, he'd be a good person to try.'

The tinted window rose, and Carmichael was left staring at his own reflection. He turned away. What was it with these paranoid pushers? Why had such a simple transaction become so complicated? He crossed the car park and approached the lad sitting on a small petrol scooter. He was busy tapping something into his phone, and didn't even bother to look up as Carmichael stopped in front of him.

'Your mate over there said you are the person I need to speak to, to score.'

The lad didn't raise his eyes. 'What you after?'

'Twenty hits of Dexampex, if you have it?'

'You're a Dextroamphetamine user are you? Are you looking to lose weight, or improve alertness? Do you suffer with ADHD, or what?'

'I don't think that's any of your business. Have you got any or not?'

'I don't have Dexampex, but I can you do you twenty of Dexedrine. It'll work in the same way.'

'Great. How much?'

'Two hundred and forty.'

'It usually costs two hundred.'

'Not from me it doesn't. You want the pills? That's the cost.'

Carmichael counted the notes out. 'Your competitor is cheaper than this.'

'Oh yeah? Who's that then?'

'Tyrell, down the road.'

'Word is Tyrell is temporarily out of business. By all means, take your money to him instead.'

He passed over the money. 'Here you go. Where's the gear?'

The lad pointed back at the Range Rover. 'You can collect your items from over there. I only take the money.'

'What the fuck is this? Argos? What happens when I get over there and they say I haven't paid?'

'Chill, man. I've messaged him to say what you want and what you've paid. He's waiting for you.'

He wanted to push the kid off the scooter and teach him some manners, but he resisted the urge. He sighed as he walked back across the car park. The window wasn't lowered until he was standing outside the car.

The pimply kid was holding a small transparent bag of pills. 'My mate says you usually deal with Tyrell. Is that right?'

He ground his teeth to control his frustration. 'What does it matter? I used to deal with Tyrell, and now I deal with you. Can I have my gear, please?'

The kid held the bag out, and Carmichael snatched it before it was yanked back in. The kid watched him. 'Tyrell is a good friend of mine. He told me one of his regulars got heavy-handed last week and broke his wrist. He wasn't happy, I can tell you. Funny actually, the bloke he described looks just like you. What a coincidence.'

He pocketed the bag and backed away. The two rear doors of the vehicle opened and two large men climbed out.

The kid opened his door. 'Tyrell put word out that if any of us should come across the wanker who broke his arm, we should let him know. What would he say if I sent him your picture?'

'Listen, I don't want any trouble. We've done our business and I'm happy to leave it at that. I'm sure you've got more important things to be getting on with.'

The posse advanced towards him, spreading around. The pimply kid remained directly in front. 'The ironic thing is I should probably thank you for incapacitating one of my rivals. Business has been booming the last five days. The thing is: he's a mate, and I don't like the look of you.' He nodded his head and the two goons charged at Carmichael. He managed to connect a fist with one of them, before the second tackled him to the ground. The two goons each grabbed an arm and hoisted him back to his feet.

The pimply kid squashed his fingers into a knuckle duster. 'I imagine this is going to hurt *you* a lot more than me.' He drove his fist into Carmichael's face, and followed it up with a blow to the stomach. The two goons kept him upright as the kid delivered blow after blow. His head burned in pain. Satisfied, the kid turned and walked back to the Range Rover telling the goons to finish him off. They released his arms, and he crumpled to the floor.

He rolled himself into a ball as they kicked him in

the back and legs. He closed his eyes and prayed for it to stop. Still the beating continued, and as he thought he would pass out from the intense pain, the sound of a siren in the distance caused the goons to stop and race back to the Range Rover, which tore out of the car park with the smell of burnt rubber in its wake. He was in too much pain to move.

The siren grew closer. He managed to open one of his eyes, and willed himself to get up. If he was found in this state in possession of amphetamines, he could kiss his investigator's licence goodbye. He rolled onto his knees, and growled as he pushed himself to his feet. The siren was closer now, and the faint flash of blue lights were beginning to reflect off the windows of the supermarket.

He was in no condition to run.

He had to hide.

He spotted the builder's skip, and stumbled towards it, tumbling over the edge as an ambulance flew past. He lay there staring at the stars. What the hell was he doing: risking the job he loved for a hit? Risking imprisonment for a temporary fix. What would his daughter think about what had become of him? He continued to stare at the stars as the tears cascaded. For the first time in ages, his prayers had been answered.

MONDAY

21

Melissa appeared in front of him as he reached the top step.

'Good morning,' she chimed eagerly.

He hadn't slept well, and although his face didn't show any signs of the beating he'd taken last night, his whole body ached. He'd flushed the pills down the toilet as soon as he'd arrived home, determined to turn over a new leaf. He'd regretted the decision from the moment they disappeared around the U-bend.

'Hi,' he said, trying to sidestep her.

'Have you got a minute? There's something I need to speak to you about.'

'I've got a ton of stuff to do today. I'm meeting Sue Dewis first thing tomorrow, and I still don't know enough about her background yet.'

She looked disappointed.

'Okay,' he relented. 'Come to my office.'

She followed him into his office, glancing nervously back at the couple sitting at her own desk.

'What is it?' he asked, hanging his jacket on the back of his chair, and booting up his computer.

Melissa sat across from him, and let out a deep breath. 'Well, I was moved by Mrs Barlow's story, the other day, so I did some checking into that church she mentioned. What's it called, the Church of Eternal…?'

'Light,' he finished for her. 'What about it?'

'The thing is, I figured if Mrs Barlow is right, and I'm not saying she is, but *if* she is, there must be other examples, other cases of a similar nature. Right?' She continued when he nodded. 'So, I did some digging, and guess what? I found someone else who lost a child to the church.'

He rolled up his sleeves. 'I don't see what any of this has to do with me.'

'Hear me out. Okay? I know you think Mrs Barlow is an old kook, but what if you're mistaken? I think you need to hear what this other family have to say. I think they might change your mind.'

He sat and offered a sympathetic smile. 'I'm sorry Melissa, but I don't have the time to -'

'They're here now,' she interrupted, smiling passively back at him. 'They're in my office right now.'

He stretched his neck so he could see into her office.

'Please, Johnson? I'm only asking that you listen to their story. It's ten to twenty minutes at most. Please?'

He checked the time on his monitor and snarled. 'Fine.'

She clapped her hands together excitedly, leapt to her feet, and returned a moment later with the couple and two spare chairs. 'Mr and Mrs Bush, this is my colleague Johnson Carmichael.' The three shook hands. 'Now, I want you to tell Johnson everything you told me. Don't leave anything out.'

Mrs Bush spoke first. She was in her late sixties, with silver hair. Her face was heavily made up, but did little to cover the signs of age. She looked at Melissa. 'I'm not sure where to begin.'

Melissa placed a reassuring hand on hers. 'Tell him about Greg.'

Mrs Bush smiled back at her, before turning back to face Carmichael. 'Our son Greg was born in 1978, his real mother died during childbirth, his father was unknown, and so he was taken into care immediately. He spent several years in care homes and foster homes, before we found him in 1988. We fell in love with him immediately, and although we were warned about his antisocial behaviour, we were assured that all he needed was to be loved. I made it my mission in life to provide him with the love and support he needed to develop. He had spent years building walls around his emotions, and it took me as long to break through his defences, but I got there. My proudest moment was seeing him achieve three A-Level passes at college. We couldn't afford to send him to university, but that wasn't something he wanted to do anyway. He got a job working in the local supermarket in Lordshill, and I think that was when he was at his happiest. He had a number of friends in the store, and always seemed to have a smile on his face. He was there for six years, but was sacked when he got into a fight with the store manager, John Duggan.'

Carmichael flinched at the sound of the name, but tried to hide his look of recognition.

'Can you believe it? Greg told me he'd overheard the manager making lewd comments about one of Greg's friends, and so he challenged Duggan. They got into an argument, and, unfortunately, Greg threw a punch. Despite his previous exemplary record, he was dismissed. The irony is that Duggan is in prison now for killing his own wife. Hardly a shining example of good behaviour is he? Anyway, Greg drifted in and out of other jobs for a couple of years, but he couldn't settle on anything he enjoyed as much. He became introverted, and lost a lot of weight. He no longer smiled. I worried for him. Eventually, he moved back home, and I was relieved I could make sure he was eating properly.'

'You said you'd been warned about his behaviour at the time of adoption. What were you told?'

She took a deep breath. 'There were rumours of abuse at his last foster home, and he'd attacked the man accused of the abuse; broke his nose.'

Carmichael scribbled a note on some paper. 'So there was already a history of violence.'

'My son is a good boy, Mr Carmichael. He isn't a troublemaker.'

'Tell him about Sanza, Mrs Bush,' Melissa encouraged.

'Oh yes. In 2009, Greg signed on for Jobseeker's Allowance. He was desperate to find a job he didn't hate, and that's when he met Paul Sanza. I'm not exactly sure how they met, but -'

'Sanza was handing out leaflets outside the Job Centre,' Mr Bush confirmed. He looked a similar age, but his hair was brilliant white, and his face was supplemented by a bright white bushy moustache.

'Oh that's right,' Mrs Bush continued. 'Greg returned home telling us about this man he'd met in town. He had a leaflet from the Church of Eternal Light. He said he and Sanza had hit it off straight away, and they'd gone for a coffee, which Sanza had paid for. It was the first time I could remember him smiling since he'd lost his job. He said he was going to go along to the service that Sunday and he asked us to give him a lift. We obliged and I went into the service with him. Don't get me wrong, Mr Carmichael, we're not a religious family, but even I found the service uplifting. Greg stayed behind at the end, and one of the other attendees gave him a lift home.'

Mr Bush wiped a tear from his eye. 'That should have been a warning sign to us.'

Mrs Bush patted his leg. 'I was relieved to see him happy again. He bought a bike, so he could cycle to and from the church whenever he wanted. He spent most of his time there or handing out leaflets in town. He stopped looking for jobs altogether, as he was so passionate about the church's activities. The only way I can describe it is that it was like he had been called for a higher purpose. He played a vital role in helping the church move to its new premises in Millbrook a year later, and it was shortly after when the trouble started.'

'What trouble?' Carmichael asked.

Mrs Bush sighed. 'I remember it was bonfire night in 2010. It was a Friday. Greg burst through the door before nine, and went to his room. I went to check on him, and heard him sobbing. I tried to go in, but he locked his door. I asked him what was wrong, but he didn't answer. I left him a plate of food outside his door, but when I rose the next day, he was gone, but the food was still there. He didn't return on Sunday night, and so I telephoned the police. They said they would look for him, but I wasn't convinced they were taking me seriously. We still hadn't heard from him by Tuesday night, so I decided to pay Sanza a visit at the church. That's where I found Greg. He was inside the church, cleaning the floor. I asked him where he'd been and why he hadn't called, but he stared at me vacantly, like he was in a trance or something. He spoke to me, but it was like someone else's words coming out of his mouth. He told me I was worrying for nothing and he was fine as he was with his new family. He told me to leave and not to come back. It broke my heart to hear him speak that way. I didn't know what to do, so I did as he instructed, and returned home.'

'I was away on business that week,' Mr Bush picked up. 'I returned the following weekend and she told me what had happened. I went to the church myself, and dragged Greg outside. I demanded to know what was going on, and warned him to treat us with more respect. He laughed in my face and told me to leave him alone. I have to be honest, my first thought was that he was on drugs.'

Mrs Bush blew her nose with a tissue, which she tucked into her sleeve. 'At the start of December, we were woken, in the middle of the night, by the sound of breaking glass. I panicked that we were being burgled, but it was Greg. He came into our room in tears. He apologised over and over again. He said he didn't know what had come over him, and that he didn't ever want to go back to the church. He said they drugged him, and made him do bad things. He slept in our bed for a straight twelve hours. When he woke up, he was like a different person. He jumped at every strange noise. He kept saying they were after him, but wouldn't say who 'they' were. He said they were watching *us*, and he begged us not to go to work. He said they would come and get him if we left him alone. When he wasn't panicking, he would cry or sleep. There was clearly something wrong with him. I tried to take him to see a doctor, but he refused because he thought they would get him while we were out. He eventually agreed to let me call the doctor to our house, but when our family GP arrived, Greg refused to speak to her, saying she was one of their spies. Our GP told us he might be suffering with some kind of paranoid schizophrenia, or dissociative identity disorder. She told us we needed to take Greg to a specialist clinic for a proper diagnosis. I told her Greg wouldn't leave the house, so she prescribed a mild sedative, which I mixed in with his food. When he fell asleep, we drove him to the clinic, where they recommended we leave him for observation. It was the hardest thing I've ever done. He begged and pleaded for us not to leave him there; that *they* ran the clinic, but we took the doctor's advice, and returned home. That was the last time we ever saw our boy.' She burst into tears.

Mr Bush wrapped his arm around her shoulders. 'Greg used a bed sheet to hang himself in the clinic, Mr Carmichael. The doctors told us they hadn't realised he was suicidal when they had put him to bed. We spoke to the police about what had happened, and asked them to investigate what Sanza was up to, but they said there was nothing they could do. We were beginning to think Greg had imagined it all, or that he was mentally ill. When Melissa phoned and said you had evidence the church is brainwashing people, we - '

'Whoa! Hold on,' Carmichael interrupted. 'Melissa told you what?' He glared at her.

She shrugged sheepishly. 'Well, not evidence exactly, but someone else has approached us making similar claims about the church.'

'I'm terribly sorry, Mr and Mrs Bush,' Carmichael said, still glaring at Melissa. 'I appreciate how difficult it is to lose a child, believe me, nobody in this room understands your loss better than me. I can see how raw the pain still is for you, however, my partner has misled you. It's true we were approached by someone who made certain claims against Sanza's church, but I have personally investigated those claims and found them to be false. I wish to thank you for coming here today, and sharing what is clearly a difficult history. I need to be clear with you: we are not investigating the Church of Eternal Light for claims of brainwashing, or inappropriate behaviour.'

Melissa opened her mouth to speak, but Carmichael raised his hand, and she closed it again. He watched her show them out, angry that she'd gone behind his back.

22

Beth pressed the 'Add Sugar' button three times. The hot drinks dispenser beeped as it reached the maximum number of sugar shots. The plastic cup dropped into the dispenser and the machine whirred to life. She hated the filth the machine dispensed in the name of tea, but she could just about stomach the coffee, if it was sweet enough. The whirring stopped, and Beth removed the cup of tar-like substance. She sipped it and grimaced. It would have to do.

She spotted Harris, the SOCO with the intense blue eyes, standing by her desk.

Has he come to see me?

She felt unusually warm, as she pulled out her chair and sat. 'It's Harris, isn't it?'

What am I doing? I know it's Harris. And he knows I know it's Harris.

He nodded, and she caught herself staring at those eyes again.

She looked away. 'Are you after me?'

'I was looking for Olly, sorry, I mean D.C. Capshaw. Is he around?'

Beth glanced at her watch. 'Six o'clock? He's probably grabbing dinner. That one can eat for England. Is there anything I can help with?'

'Maybe.' He lifted a small box onto her desk. 'Are

you working on the Todd Francis' investigation?'

'The murdered banker? I'm leading it.'

'Perfect! We recovered a laptop at the scene, and the tech team have finished examining it. It can be logged into evidence now. I said I'd bring it across.'

Beth lifted the lid off the box, and removed the laptop. 'Did the tech guys find anything interesting?'

'There's a printed copy of their report is in the box too.'

Beth reached back into the box and removed the report. She began to flick through it.

Harris cleared his throat. 'Can you let Olly know I stopped by, and tell him I'll see him tomorrow night?'

Beth was too engrossed in the report to hear him. She skim read the report, and then re-read the final part in detail. 'Have you seen this?' When she looked up, Harris was already gone.

She opened the laptop and turned it on. A low battery indicator flashed up on the screen. She reached back into the box, and located the power cable. She plugged it in using the power socket beneath her desk. The machine slowly booted up. The laptop was running an outdated operating system, and took an age to open Internet Explorer. When examining the machine's internet history, the tech guys had found the usual slew of pornographic sites; nothing underage. They also found the URL of an internet dating site. According to the report, the victim's profile was on the site.

Beth opened the dating site from the computer's list of favourites. The victim had left himself logged in, and his profile picture filled the screen. It wasn't a particularly flattering picture, but it had clearly been taken several years earlier, as the man in the picture looked much younger and slimmer than the man she'd seen bound to the bed.

According to the profile, Todd was in his early forties, and looking for 'friendship and maybe something more.' He described himself as 'fun-loving, with a great sense of humour.'

How many other members use that line?

Beth had never felt the need to seek a partner online. The demands of the service meant relationships were strained at best. In hindsight, it was amazing that her relationship with Carmichael had lasted as long as it had. When she'd discovered she was pregnant at Christmas, she'd been ready to move in with him and cement their relationship. But then the Coleman case changed everything. Beneath his dark brooding, and constant crusade for justice, she was sure there was a good man.

The victim's profile had been viewed a dozen times. It didn't seem a lot. He'd been a member of the site for six months, and only twelve people had considered him suitable dating material. It made her pity him more.

She referred back to the report. According to the internet history, the victim had been messaging one of the site's other members. She found the name and typed it into the site. Her mouth dropped when she saw the broad shoulders and golden hair. She pulled out the security camera image from her jacket pocket, and compared it to the profile picture on the screen.

It's her! I've found you!

The blonde on the screen went by the name Kelly Knowles. She claimed to be thirty-four, single, and 'looking for love.' Beth stared at the face again, committing every line and blemish to memory. It had to be the same woman from the café. The report included a transcript of the exchanged messages between Todd and Kelly. Evidently, they were due to meet at the café at half past eight on Thursday night. That tied in with the receipt they'd found in his flat.

It didn't mean this was the woman who'd killed Todd. All she could prove so far was that Kelly was probably the last person to see Todd alive. Even if she didn't kill him, she might be able to provide insight into what happened to Todd after the café. The security footage showed the two of them leaving together, but the footage from the nearby traffic camera showed him alone leaving the area in his car.

Beth held up the security camera image from the nightclub. Was the blonde seen leaving with Josh Grabban the same woman? It was possible, but circumstantial. She would need to find a way of tying Kelly Knowles to Josh. Frustratingly, a search of the site didn't pull up profiles for Josh or Claire.

Beth returned to Kelly's profile. It listed her date of birth, but there was no address, or useful information. She could request a warrant to demand the owners of the website turn over Kelly's personal information, but that would take time; time she didn't have. She had a better idea.

She pulled out her mobile and dialled the number. It was answered on the fourth ring.

'Carmichael Associates,' Melissa greeted.

'Hi Melissa, it's Beth. Is he around?'

'Hi Beth, he's not I'm afraid. He left about half an hour ago. Have you tried him on his mobile?'

'No, but it was you I wanted to speak to.'

'Me? Okay.'

'I was wondering if you could do me a favour. I'm trying to locate a woman in the area, but all I've got is a name and date of birth. I've run a trace this end and she isn't known to us. If I give you her name, do you think you could see what you can dig up for me?'

Melissa was quiet for a moment. 'I don't see why not…can I check why you aren't asking Johnson for help?'

'To be honest, we're not on the best of terms at the moment. He made a pass at me on Friday night, and I pushed him away.'

'Are things no better between you two then?'

Beth sighed. 'I'm not sure they ever will be.'

'It's such a shame. You were good for him. He was certainly a much kinder boss when he was seeing you. He's been such a grouch recently.'

'Has he spoken to anyone about his grief yet?'

It was Melissa's turn to sigh. 'He won't even talk to me about it. I wish he would talk to someone – anyone – about his pain.'

'Where is he now?'

'God knows! He stormed out of here with a face like thunder. He's probably out trying to score more pills…wait, I shouldn't have said that -'

'Don't worry about it: I'm aware that he's been popping pills. I'm sure he'll open up when he's ready. It doesn't matter how much we bang our heads against the wall, we won't get through to him until *he's* ready. You know what he's like.'

'You're probably right. Who do you want me to look for?'

'She goes by the name Kelly Knowles. I'll email you a link to her online dating profile so you'll have her picture and date of birth.'

'Great. How quickly do you need the information?'

'As soon as you can. Oh, and Melissa, be careful, okay? She's a person of interest in a murder investigation. Just be careful who you ask about her. Okay?'

'Sure thing. I'll tread lightly.'

Beth thanked her and hung up the call. She printed off Kelly's profile picture and pinned it to her soundboard. As soon as Capshaw returned, she'd send him to Josh's friends to see if they could identify her as the blonde from the club.

23

Carmichael swirled the glass in his hand, watching the ice cubes crash into each other. He placed the glass to his dry lips and waited for the final drop of bourbon to fall onto his tongue. He pushed the small round table across the carpet, so he could stand. The table wobbled as it came to a rest. As he stumbled to the bar, he glanced back over his shoulder to make sure his jacket was still on his chair; he didn't want to lose his table. The pub had been getting busier for the past hour, and space was becoming scarce.

It was two days since he took the last of the Dexampex he'd scored from Tyrell, and he was suffering from withdrawal. He'd naively thought that going cold turkey would work. He hadn't slept properly in two days either. Every time he closed his eyes he saw Anita. Tonight's plan was to get so paralytic that sleep would take him instead. He'd been in the pub since five, when he'd had enough of Melissa's nagging.

His eyelids were heavy, as he looked to see where the barman had gone to. He covered his mouth to hide his yawn. He stared at the crisp packets hanging from the back wall. He couldn't remember the last time he'd eaten.

'Salt an' vin'gar,' he declared.

'Be with you in a minute, pal,' the barman called from further down the bar.

Carmichael blinked several times. He was sure someone had asked for his order. He shook his head in an effort to clear the fogginess. Reaching into his pocket he pulled out his wallet. Only a five pound note remained in the fold. He checked the wallet again. He was sure there'd been sixty pounds in there earlier. He looked at the woman next to him. Could she have taken the money without him realising? She smiled warmly back at him.

'You're pretty,' he smiled. 'I'll get y'a drink.' He snapped his fingers at the barman who still hadn't appeared.

'That's kind,' the woman replied, 'but I'm fine.'

He furrowed his brow. 'My money no good to ya? It's cos I'm black in'it?'

The woman glanced nervously around, desperate for the ground to swallow her. 'No, it's not…it's just _'

He waved his arm. 'It's your loss.'

The woman stepped away from the bar, and returned to her table.

'Fuckin' racist,' he called after her, and then shouted for the barman's attention.

'Calm down, pal, or I'm going to have to throw you out of here.'

'You shouldn't threaten me. You should serve m'a drink, 'kay?'

The barman shook his head and poured a fresh glass, adding fresh ice. He held his hand out for the fiver Carmichael was clutching.

'Where's my crisps?'

'You didn't ask for any crisps.'

'I did. I chose salt and…the green ones, yeah.'

The barman grabbed a bag of crisps and dropped them on the bar, snatching the money and returning twenty pence change. Carmichael tried to pick it up, but his vision was blurring again, and his fingers kept missing. He finally waved his hand dismissively and returned to his table. He raised his glass and toasted the photograph of Anita that was staring back at him from the table.

'I'm so sorry,' he slurred. 'I should have been there for you, Anita. I wish your mother hadn't hidden you from me. I wish you were here now. I should have done more. Were you happy? Well, of course you were; you were a shining light.' He sipped the whiskey, and yawned again. 'I should have been a match.'

A shadow fell across the photograph. Carmichael looked up and saw a familiar face smiling at him. 'Do you mind if I sit for a moment?' Paul Sanza asked.

Carmichael's lips moved but no words came out. Sanza sat on the chair next to him, pushing the jacket along to make space.

'Are you here for the quiz?' Sanza asked.

'Nah, just a quiet drink.'

'Well you're welcome to join us, if you fancy?'

He shook his head. 'I'm not in the mood.'

'I know how you feel. I'm not a big fan of quizzes myself. Some of the girls from the church suggested we come and participate. My general knowledge isn't up to much.'

Carmichael opened the packet of crisps, and offered the bag to Sanza, who politely declined.

'Who's Anita?'

Carmichael frowned at him.

'I overheard you,' Sanza clarified. 'Is she a girlfriend of yours?'

Carmichael shook his head. The table wobbled.

'A friend then?'

'She was my daughter.'

Sanza picked up the photograph. 'Is this her? She's pretty.'

Carmichael snatched the photograph back, and placed it in the pocket of his jacket for safekeeping. 'She died.'

'Oh gosh, no. I'm so sorry, Johnson. Was it recent?'

He nodded.

'Oh, I'm so sorry to hear that. She looks so young as well.'

'She was. She was only nineteen.'

'That explains your sombre mood. If you'd like, I can pray for her soul at mass on Sunday.'

'How can you pray to a God that can be so...so...so merciless?' He slammed his hand on the table. 'She was nineteen! I'd only just met her, but He took her from me!'

Carmichael didn't notice the people at other tables glancing over at them. Sanza took it all in his stride. 'We don't always know what God's plan is for us. Sometimes it can seem to not make sense, but I assure you, there *is* a plan. As much as you might hurt right now, it's for a reason.'

'It's punishment! It's karma. If I'd been better...'

'You can't think like that. God will judge us all on the last day. He doesn't inflict punishments in this life.

We are all accountable for what we do on Earth. You mustn't blame yourself. It isn't your fault that Anita - '

'You know nothing!' he interrupted. 'How can you believe in something that isn't there?'

'That's the gift of faith, Johnson. In our darkest times, we must search even harder for the light. Take your friend Tom Dewis, for example. He lost both his parents when he was only seven years-old. A father murdered, and a mother imprisoned. Does he seem bitter to you?'

'What's your point?'

'My point is, Tom hasn't given up on God. He hasn't turned his back on the world. Instead, he's embraced God's message and he is living his life to the maximum. You could learn a thing or two from him.'

Carmichael finished his drink and slammed the glass on the table. There were more glances. The barman looked over.

Sanza placed his hand on Carmichael's, and gently whispered. 'I understand the pain you are going through, Johnson. I have experienced loss, and I have counselled others through the grieving process. It is okay to be angry, in fact, it is part of mankind's natural response to shock. You need to be angry, but you also need to let your anger go. Whilst you see Anita's loss as a punishment, I see it as a blessing.'

Carmichael glared at him.

'Hear me out. You resent the fact you barely knew your daughter, but you are failing to see how much richer your life was because she was in it. It's tragic that your time together was short, but imagine how much worse it would have been if you'd never met her at all? If you'd found out about her after she'd died, wouldn't you have given anything to spend an hour with her? Wouldn't you have done anything for the chance to spend a few months getting to know her? I know it doesn't make it any easier for you right now, but, in time, hopefully you will see the plan and be thankful for it.' He paused. 'My door is always open to you.'

'Ha! You think I need saving?'

'No, but I'm not offering you redemption, Johnson. The Church of Eternal Light is about more than religion. You've seen the counselling service we offer. I sense a real darkness in you, and I'm not referring to your grief. I see something in you, something I have seen in myself in the past. You've done bad things in your life, but that doesn't mean your future has to remain in the shadows. Let me help you find your path again.'

'Wendy Barlow thinks you brainwash people.'

'What do you think?'

'I don't know what to think.'

'Is that what you think I'm doing now? Do you think I am trying to manipulate you?'

Carmichael shrugged and placed the empty glass to his lips.

'Have you spoken to anyone about your loss?'

'I don't need a shrink!'

'It doesn't have to be a trained specialist. Accepting and talking about loss is part of the grieving process. I know people who've found solace in talking to the deceased. I know it sounds crazy, but visiting the grave and talking openly is a great way to start the healing process. It can allow you to say all the things that you weren't able to before she passed.' He paused. 'Allow me to do one thing for you now. Let me phone for a taxi for you. You're in a pretty bad state.'

'I'll walk.'

'No. Wait here, and I'll call the taxi for you.'

Sanza stepped away from the table and moved to a quieter corner, placing the phone to his ear. Carmichael grabbed his coat and headed for the door.

24

Kelly spots Carmichael leaning against a lamppost, as soon as she emerges from the pub. He can barely keep himself upright. She noticed him drinking there earlier, and couldn't deny the attraction. She's been daydreaming about him taking her in those strong arms, and dominating her. It is unusual for her to allow others to take control, but there is something in those dark eyes that she yearns for. She feels a connection with him that is more than lust.

She thought about approaching his table and introducing herself, but she was worried he might reject her advances. She could tell he wouldn't fancy her like this; she didn't expect to see him, and isn't dressed for glamour.

He pushes himself away from the lamppost, and stumbles forward, awkwardly shifting his bulk from one leg to the next. He looks like a toddler learning to walk. He is stretching his arms out ahead of him for balance. He looks like he might fall over at any minute. He veers to the right, and loses a foot over the kerb-edge, nearly falling, but just about remaining upright. He looks back and curses the kerb, before continuing across the road. A passing car blasts its horn.

She continues to watch him. Should she step

forward and offer him support? Something is holding her back.

As he makes it to the other side of the street, he seems unable to decide which direction to walk in. He faces one way, looking for something familiar, before turning and repeating the exercise. He eventually settles on a direction, and stumbles forward.

Three youths exit the pub to her right. They spot Carmichael across the road, and she overhears one of them saying they should jump him, and steal his watch and phone. She steps back into the shadows. One of the lads is wearing a white polyester tracksuit, and has greasy curls. He seems to be the leader of the group, flanked by a fat kid with a crew cut, and a shorter kid with glasses. They can't be much older than eighteen. They reek of Lynx and cheap cigarettes. They are all wearing shiny white trainers.

The kid in the tracksuit spits on the floor, before leading the other two across the road. Kelly remains where she is, watching. Carmichael is leaning against a lamppost again. He is peeing against a line of bushes that border the pavement. Beyond the bushes is a small wooded area with a path to the flats beyond it. The group hangs back until Carmichael is moving again. They call after him, as he nears the break in the bushes. He turns unsteadily to face them.

They are mouthing off at him, but Kelly can't make out what they are saying. The kid in the tracksuit pushes Carmichael, causing him to fall against the bushes. Carmichael waves a finger of warning in his direction, and struggles to regain his composure. They are laughing at him now. He stumbles into the path, and the youth in the tracksuit urges them to follow.

Kelly steps out of the shadows and quickly crosses the road. There is a second break in the bushes to her right and she sneaks through, all the while watching the group taunting Carmichael.

He is shouting at them now; telling them to back off. He warns them that he is an expert in hand-to-hand combat, but they laugh at his bluff. He clenches his fists and charges at the one with glasses, knocking the youth to the ground. The other two erupt into laughter, but stop when they see him punching their friend in the face. They grab Carmichael's arms and pull him backwards, before kicking him in the midriff. He curls himself into a ball, and grabs the standing leg of the youth in the tracksuit, causing him to fall. Glasses is back on his feet and is kicking Carmichael too.

A twig snaps, as Kelly emerges from the darkness, but nobody notices the sound. She launches a kick at Fatty's back, sending him sprawling with a yelp. She is glad she isn't wearing heels tonight. Glasses has noticed her and signals to Tracksuit, who turns and smiles at her. 'Welcome to the party,' he sneers, pulling out a flick-knife.

Kelly smiles back. She hasn't brought a weapon with her tonight, but is ready to take his. She backs away, allowing them to move towards her. Fatty is back on his feet, and the three circle her. Carmichael isn't moving on the floor.

'You want to stick me with that?' she shouts at Tracksuit.

He glances nervously at his friends, and nods.

'Come on,' she challenges, lifting her shirt and revealing her abdomen. 'I'll give you one chance.' She smiles at him, as he glances nervously at his friends again. He takes a step forward. 'Make sure you stick it in nice and deep,' she warns.

His hand is shaking as he points the blade forward. She knows he has to accept her challenge, otherwise Glasses and Fatty won't respect him. She assumes he is sweating, though it is difficult to see, with only the faint glow from a nearby street light. She is watching him out of the corner of her eye. He lunges and in one quick motion she grabs his wrist, pulls him towards her, spinning him into her grasp. She forces his hand to his throat, and presses the blade against his skin. She is stronger than he had anticipated, and now he is panicking. She presses her knee into the back of his, and he drops to the floor, the blade in his hand still pressed against his own throat. Glasses and Fatty back away.

'Should I kill him?' she asks them. 'I tell you what: I'll give you a choice: one of you can take his place and make the ultimate sacrifice, or I can run this blade against his throat, and you can watch him die helplessly. You decide.'

Fatty glances at Glasses and then back to Tracksuit, whose eyes are wide with panic. Nobody speaks.

'Times up,' she declares and pulls the knife across his throat. She releases her grip on his hand, and, as he crashes to the muddy ground, his hands desperately try to stem the flow of blood. Fatty and Glasses step backwards, both wanting to run, but too scared to move.

She grabs the knife. 'Who's next?'

Before they can answer, she charges at Fatty, and

pushes the flick-knife into his left eye, before swinging an arm around and catching Glasses in the throat with her wrist. Fatty screams in agony, whilst Glasses falls to his knees, clutching his own throat. She steps behind him, wrapping her arm around his neck, and gripping his chin in her left hand. She places her right hand behind his head, and pulls up and twists in one motion. His neck snaps and he crumples to the floor.

Fatty is squealing like a pig, and is sure to attract attention. He is bent forward, clutching his face.

'If you want to live, you need to let me remove that blade,' she says, circling him like a tiger stalking its prey.

'Leave me alone!' he shouts, uncertain where she is.

'If you don't get help, you'll bleed out like your friend in the tracksuit. I can help you, but this is a onetime offer.'

He stops screaming. She can tell he is thinking. He is considering his options. He doesn't want to die, but he doesn't think he can trust the person who just killed his two best friends. Survival is the basest of human emotions.

'Okay,' he finally says.

She stops in front of him. 'Good. Stay still. I'm going to move closer. You need to keep still so I can pull it out. If you move, it could do more damage. Do you understand?'

'Yes,' he spits.

She steps towards him, hoping he doesn't do anything stupid. She tentatively reaches for the knife.

He shudders as she coils her fingers around the

handle.

'Are you ready for this?'

She pulls the knife out, and, before he has chance to straighten, she drives her knee into his face. He stumbles to the floor, still clutching his face. She kicks him onto his back, and drives the knife into his chest, piercing his heart. The blade gets stuck in a rib. He is screaming again. She slams her foot onto the handle, and it continues through. She places a gloved hand over his mouth and nose, until he stops moving.

She removes her phone and shines the light over Tracksuit. Although his hand is still by his throat, his eyes are lifeless. Satisfied with her work, she walks across to Carmichael, and helps him to his feet. He is slurring his words, but seems to have no recollection of what has happened. She places his arm around her shoulders and walks him back through the break in the bushes, and back to the pub's car park. She helps him into the back of her car. He lies down, and is snoring within seconds. She fastens the belt around his large frame, before fishing in his pocket for his wallet. She opens it and removes his driving licence. She recognises his address, and climbs into the front of the car.

'You owe me one,' she says into the rear-view mirror, before pulling out of the car park.

TUESDAY

25

Carmichael knew he was going to be sick as soon as his eyes opened. Saliva was pooling beneath his tongue, and his stomach was churning. His forehead glistened with sweat. He pushed the duvet cover back and raced for the box-like bathroom, crashing to his knees and lifting the toilet seat in one swift motion.

His throat was hot, and dry when he finished. He placed his head beneath the sink tap and filled his mouth with cool water. It did little to satisfy the dehydration. He stared at his reflection in the round mirror hanging from the wall opposite the shower. His face looked tired and ropy, like a dark and worn chamois leather. Small bags hung beneath his eyes. It had been over a week since he'd last used a razor, and the stubble on his chin was a mixture of black and grey. He noticed a small bump to the right of his temple. He leaned in for closer inspection, and nearly fell forwards. He pressed his hand against the wall for balance and studied the bump. It looked fresh, but he didn't remember being in a fight last night. As his right hand gently pressed the bump, he spotted grazes on his knuckles. He pulled back and examined the backs of his hands. His left hand was slightly swollen.

He tried to recall where he'd been last night, but the aching in his head wouldn't allow it. He opened the medicine cabinet and looked for anything to dull the pain. There was nothing. He'd already made the most of the painkillers he kept for such occasions. He slammed the cabinet closed, but regretted the petulance as his head throbbed again.

He showered as quickly as he could, and dressed in his favourite dark grey suit, and grey shirt. His tie was still knotted and discarded on the bedroom floor. He placed it over his head and did his best to resurrect the knot. He turned on the television as he made a cup of coffee.

As he returned to the room, a story on the news caught his attention. The screen cut to a familiar looking pub, and panned round to a wooded area across the road. There was a police cordon surrounding the break between the bushes.

'The three bodies were discovered shortly before two this morning. Police have yet to confirm cause of death, but it is believed the incident may be gang-related. Witnesses have confirmed the three young men had been drinking in The Hatchett pub on Twyford Road in Eastleigh, prior to closing, and police are canvassing for witnesses who may have seen what happened in the woods beyond me. The Hampshire Major Investigation Team are expected to make a formal statement later on today.'

Carmichael turned the television off and looked back at his knuckles. He remembered being at The Hatchett, but he still couldn't remember when he'd left, or even how he'd made it home.

He rushed to the kitchen sink. The smell of fresh coffee didn't help his nausea. Last night's clothes were heaped on the floor, near the washing machine. He dived at them, lifting his trousers, and shirt, examining them for any sign that he'd been in a fight. There was a thin trail of blood on the white shirt, but it was impossible to tell whether it was his own or somebody else's. He sniffed the shirt, and noticed faint traces of perfume, but he didn't recognise the scent.

He slumped to the floor, and took several breaths. He was being paranoid: just because he happened to be in the same pub as three recently deceased men, didn't mean he'd done anything wrong last night. The grazes on his knuckles could have come from anywhere. There was no logical reason to assume he'd been in any way involved in their deaths. He'd remember...wouldn't he?

He closed his eyes, and took a deep breath, letting it out slowly. He had no memory of a fight, but for safe measure, he grabbed his shirt and stuffed it into a polythene bag. There was no harm in getting rid of the blood-stained shirt. Even if the blood had nothing to do with the dead men, the chances of getting the stain out were slim, so he'd replace it instead.

He stuffed the polythene bag under the front passenger seat of his car, and started the engine. He was due to collect Tom on their way to see Sue at Bronzefield Prison.

26

Beth looked up at the sound of her name. D.C.I. Payne was sheltering beneath some branches, waving her over. Beth acknowledged her with a nod.

'Thanks for coming, Beth. I'm sorry to do this to you, with everything else you've got on your plate, but I need someone to coordinate efforts here, until Tapper returns from her training course. She's due back tomorrow, but in the meantime, I need someone level-headed as S.I.O.'

'Don't mention it, Ma'am. It's part of the job.'

'I'd happily do it myself, but I'm being pulled from pillar-to-post with this joint-op with the Operation Fortress team. Did I tell you about it? It's all very hush-hush, but they suspect cocaine is being smuggled in via Venezuela and Norway in boxed fresh fish. More than half the unit are tied up with surveillance. It's a killer.'

'I had wondered why the office has been so quiet recently.'

'I'd have pulled Tapper off the training, but she wants to push for D.C.I. this year, and I don't want to hold her back, if you catch my drift. Forget I said that.'

Beth winked. 'Said what, Ma'am?'

Payne offered a grateful smile. 'I'll let the M.E. fill you in on the victims -'

'Victims? Plural?'

'That's right. Three of them. What we know so far, is that they were drinking in the pub across the road, but we don't know when they left. Estimated time of death is between nine and ten, according to Spinks. We got hold of the pub landlord this morning, and he identified the three youths. Unfortunately, the pub's CCTV is out of action, so we will have to make an appeal for witnesses. Are you happy speaking to the press at the right time?'

She nodded, but inside she was screaming, 'No!'

'Good. You don't know what a relief it is knowing that you're on scene.'

'What do you want me to do about the rest of my workload?'

'Capshaw is competent. Make more use of him.'

Competent wasn't the word Beth would have chosen to describe him. 'Is there anything else you can tell me, Ma'am?'

'The landlord is trying to put together a list of regulars who were in The Hatchett last night. We'll need to get in touch with them ASAP, as they're going to be our best hope of finding out exactly what happened to the three.'

'I heard mention of gangs on the radio news on the way over.'

'One of the youths has a tattoo on his wrist, which is consistent with the Thompson crew in the city. When you see what happened to them, you'll understand.'

'Why? What happened?'

Payne grimaced. 'I'll let Spinks fill you in. I hope you didn't eat too much for breakfast this morning.'

'Did the other two have tattoos?'

'No, but the one who did looks barely eighteen, so he can't be that high in the crew yet. He's probably only a bit-part player, which is why I'm not totally convinced by the gang-related theory, but I'll leave you to draw your own conclusions.' Payne lit a cigarette. 'I take it you've got everything you need?'

Beth nodded. 'I thought you quit.'

'I did. Sometimes home life can be just as stressful as the job.' She didn't say anything else, before crossing the road and heading to the pub's car park.

Beth inhaled deeply. She just had to treat the case as the distraction she probably needed. Unless one of the pub regulars confirmed the sighting of a mysterious blonde, at least this would give her conscious mind something different to chew on. She made her way through the break in the bushes and headed for the crime scene entrance. Four murders in a week; White had picked a great time to go on holiday.

27

Bronzefield Prison opened in 2004, and is a facility built to house female inmates and young offenders. It has been the home to some of the UK's most notorious women, including Rosemary West. Located in Ashford in Middlesex, it is a ninety minute journey from Southampton in fair traffic. Unfortunately for Carmichael and Tom, heavy traffic around Farnborough slowed the journey. The prison visitors' centre opened at one, and they were expected to arrive half an hour before their visit, for a variety of security checks.

Carmichael smiled at the uniformed woman behind the counter as she examined his photo card driving licence. She didn't smile back. Instead she asked him to remove any valuables and to place them in one of the designated lockers. He did as instructed, swiftly realising there was no place for a sense of humour today.

'You're allowed ten quid in change,' Tom whispered to him, 'but that's all. No phones, no cigarettes, no jewellery. It's in case you try and pass it to one of the inmates.'

He understood the protocol. The two men returned to the counter where he was directed to a white wall so his photograph could be taken. Finally his fingerprints were scanned.

'What happens to my data?' he asked.

'We hold it on record here for the next time you visit,' she advised. 'Don't worry. It's not shared with any third parties.'

There was a small canteen where two pensioners were busy nattering as they boiled kettles.

'You can't take drinks or food in with you,' Tom warned, when he spotted Carmichael watching them. 'There are facilities inside in case you get thirsty or hungry. I would advise you go to the toilet out here though, as there isn't one in the main building.'

'You're kidding! What happens if you need to go?'

'One of the guards will escort you back here, and wait while you go, before escorting you back. If one of the occupants needs to go, they're taken back into holding.'

Carmichael waited until two, before heading to the gents, and fifteen minutes later found himself sitting at a small table, waiting to meet Sue Dewis. He wasn't sure what to expect. He'd seen her picture in the various newspaper reports he'd read, but those images were all from sixteen years ago. She'd been in her early forties when she'd been convicted, but the woman who approached their table was a shadow of her once more glamorous self. Here was a woman with tired eyes, a permanent scowl on her face, and hair in desperate need of a wash and blow dry. She hadn't looked like a killer in the photographs he'd seen, but she resembled one now.

He'd expected her to be pleased to see him, but she barely registered his presence, instead offering a thin smile in Tom's direction. Incarcerated for sixteen years for a crime she hadn't committed: he had thought she would have welcomed any glimmer of light at the end of the tunnel, but if anything, she looked angry.

'Mum, this is the guy I was telling you about. Johnson Carmichael, I'd like to introduce my mother, Sue.'

'It's a pleasure to meet you,' he offered.

Sue made eye contact, but didn't respond.

Tom suddenly stood. 'I'll fetch us some tea and cake. Why don't you two get to know each other?'

'Tom's a good lad,' he said, when they were alone. 'You must be proud.'

She stared coldly. 'Why? Because he's the son of a killer?'

'No, I meant…I just meant any mother would be proud to have such a well-intentioned boy. He was telling me on the journey here that he visits you three times a month. I imagine his visits are a highlight.'

'Listen, Mr Carmichael, if there's one thing I've learned in here, it's how to spot a bullshitter. Hiring you was not my idea. In fact, I think it's a bloody ludicrous idea. Now, I don't know what rock Tom found you under, but I do wish you'd scurry back under it.'

'He's convinced you're innocent; that you were wrongly convicted of his father's murder. Is he right?'

She considered him for a moment. 'What's your angle here? Hmm? What's in it for you?'

'I don't understand.'

'Oh, please, don't give me that. Nobody in their right mind would willingly take on a sixteen year old investigation like this. You must be after something.

If you're hoping to write about my case, and sell the movie rights, you can forget about it! I don't want to be the subject of a one-sided online documentary series either.'

'I'm not a charlatan, Mrs Dewis. I'm a legitimate private detective, and I'm good at what I do. I'm not here to cheat you or Tom. He wants me to find the truth about what happened in 2000.'

'You shouldn't waste your time. The police proved my guilt beyond a reasonable doubt. What makes you think they're wrong?'

'Aren't they? Tom seems pretty convinced. If he's wrong, you should tell him, so he can stop wasting his time holding onto the possibility that his mother isn't a killer.'

'I've exhausted all my appeals. There's nothing you can do to get me out of here.'

'I disagree. If you didn't kill your husband that means the real killer is still out there. If I can find him, the courts would have to look at your case again.'

She spoke calmly, a woman who had accepted her fate. 'Even if you did manage to find him, what would be the point? I'm an old woman now. I'll be sixty next year. I've missed watching my children grow. The little money I ever had in savings has now been used up on solicitor and barrister fees. The world's a different place. I'm better off in here.'

'What I don't understand is why you've never made a deal after all this time. You were sentenced to serve a minimum of twenty-three years, but had you said you were guilty and shown some remorse, you'd already be out of here.'

'I'd be out, but I'd be labelled a killer.'

'You've already got that label, so what difference would it make?'

'You wouldn't understand -'

'No? Try me.'

She looked over to Tom, who was still queueing for drinks. She turned back. 'Do you know what I see when I look in the mirror? I don't see myself. I see a woman who is being held against her will for a crime she didn't commit. She's a fighter. She refuses to give in despite the persistent knocks she suffers. When she's kicked, she clambers to her feet and she goes on. She refuses to allow her spirit to be crushed. She's an inspiration to me. I watch her make it through each day, a second at a time. She's the picture of adversity. If I were to lie and accept responsibility for something I didn't do, I'd be turning my back on her. Suddenly, I wouldn't be looking at someone else. I'd see myself through the eyes of a killer, and that's not something I can do. I didn't kill Ben, Mr Carmichael, and no amount of cajoling or promise of freedom will make me say otherwise.'

28

Carmichael took Sue's dry and wrinkled hand in his own. 'So let me help you. Where's the harm? Worst case scenario, I'm unable to find the man who killed Ben. Your life will continue as it is now. Best case, I clear your name and you walk out of here with your head held high.'

She looked back towards Tom. 'I don't think he can take it. His faith in me has never wavered. I worry what dragging up the past will do to him. He was seven when his father died. I'm sure he has repressed feelings and memories about that time, and I don't want to see him reliving that nightmare.'

'Surely that's his choice to make though. He wants to do it.'

'Are you a father, Mr Carmichael?'

He wasn't sure how to answer. 'No.'

'Well, sometimes parents know their children better than they know themselves and make decisions to protect them. I don't think it's in Tom's best interests to go through all this again, which is why I want you to decline his offer.'

'I don't understand why you would turn your back on the chance to clear your name.'

'Maybe one day when you have children you'll understand.'

'He's a grown man who knows his own mind. You've got another seven years to serve of your sentence. Don't you want to spend that time with your son and your daughter for that matter? What aren't you telling me?'

She dabbed her eye with a tissue. 'I want you to walk away from this, okay?'

Carmichael fixed her with a stare. 'Tell me why first.'

She leaned in so he could hear her whisper. 'I won't serve my whole sentence in here…the doctors have given me three years until…' She broke off as Tom placed a tray of tea and fruit cake on the table.

He smiled at them both. 'Well, what are you two talking about?'

'Your mum was about to tell me about the night your dad died.'

Sue shot him a look of anger, and smiled at her son. 'Are you sure you want to hear this, Tom? Perhaps it would be best if Mr Carmichael and I discussed these matters on our own.'

'It's okay, mum. I've read the newspaper reports a hundred times or more, trying to find something – anything – the police might have missed. I know the gruesome details inside and out. You don't have to protect me.'

She sipped her tea. 'Very well. The first thing you should know, Mr Carmichael, is that Ben wasn't nearly as bad as the papers made out. They accused him of being a cheat and a bully, but that wasn't the man I fell in love with and married. I don't know where they got their gossip from, but it was painted in such a way that it was his behaviour that had caused me to lash out.'

Carmichael took a bite of cake. 'One of your friends told the papers that Ben used to beat you.'

'Ben was under an increasing amount of stress that year…with the Revenue's investigation hanging over his head, he was struggling to relax. Don't forget, he was being accused of stealing his workers' pension fund. That was their savings; their future. He loved every one of his employees like they were his family. He could never have done what he was accused of. It was killing him. He was drinking heavily every night, and working ridiculous hours searching for whoever took the money. That much pressure…something's bound to give eventually. He lashed out at me, but I preferred that, to him taking it out on Tom and Annie. I'm not excusing what he did, but I know he didn't mean to do it.'

'How many times did he hit you, Sue?'

She waved away the question. 'It happened a couple of times, that's all. The prosecution made it into something bigger. They produced medical reports confirming I'd had stitches for a cut over my eye, and suggested his violence was the reason for my alleged actions. Can you believe my barrister suggested I claim mitigation? I had to keep reminding *them* I wasn't guilty.'

'The papers also claimed he'd been seeing another woman behind your back.'

She sighed. 'I read that one. I wanted to seek damages as it was untrue. Ben was married before he met me, but the first marriage fizzled out. He had a son from that relationship that he'd never met. About a week before his death, the son turned up at our door asking for money. Ben felt guilty and offered him a place to stay, but the lad was only interested in cash. With everything else that was going on, we didn't have any money to spare. They argued at our house, and then the kid left. We never heard from him again. Ben went to see his ex a few days later and they must have been spotted talking by one of her neighbours and the story was published as him having an affair with his former wife. It was a ridiculous story, but once these things are printed, the mud sticks. So, suddenly my beloved Ben was painted as a rat. Juries are supposed to ignore such speculation, but there's no way to ensure they do.'

'The missing money is the part of the story that I find the most interesting, to be honest. It was alleged that the pension fund was worth a million pounds, and that it disappeared. I don't understand why the Revenue's investigation stopped with Ben's death. There seems to be little mention of the money once your trial began.'

'Well, if Ben did take that money, I never saw a penny of it! If I knew where it was, I would have hired a better defence team to represent me in court!'

'Do you have any idea who might have taken it?'

She shrugged. 'If I had to guess, I'd suspect George Murphy.'

'You mean Ben's business partner?'

'That's right. I never trusted George, but he and Ben had been friends for years, and Ben wouldn't hear a word against him.'

'Why wasn't Murphy under investigation as well?'

'The thing is: Ben was the one responsible for the money side of the business. George handled the contracts and new orders, and Ben handled the books and the accounts. They were a good pair.'

'So what makes you suspect George?'

'I don't know…a gut feeling I suppose. Don't get me wrong, George was charming, and we used to go out for dinner with him and his wife, but I never trusted him. He was always looking for ways to expand the business. He wanted money fast, and wasn't afraid to cut corners to get it. Ben was more sensible, and believed in growing steadily.'

'The embezzlement scandal was so high profile, so I don't believe the Inland Revenue would have written the money off as untraceable without good reason.'

'Well, you'd have to ask them about that.'

'Do you think the person who stole the money could have killed Ben?'

'Do you know how many times I've asked myself that question in the last sixteen years, Mr Carmichael? The police described it as a crime of passion. They said the nature of the attack was so frenzied that it had to have been carried out by someone close to him. I was found covered in his blood, so I was their prime suspect from day one. It didn't seem to matter that I wasn't capable of such violence.'

'That's not what your sister-in-law claimed though, is it? She appeared as a witness at your trial and said you'd once threatened her with the knife used in the attack.'

Sue raised her eyebrows. 'That was the thing that shocked me most in court. I'd always been kind to Helen, but I knew she depended on Ben, and I think she wanted to see his killer punished. She had always looked up to him, and I don't think she liked it when he married me. She'd longed for a child of her own for a number of years, but she was barren. She'd been ill as a child and due to complications it made her unable to conceive. I don't blame her for what she said, but the truth is I never threatened her. I suppose if I'd been in her shoes I might have made up something as well. I think she is easily led. I mean, Tom will tell you, it doesn't take much to persuade her to your way of thinking.'

Tom sat forward. 'It's true. When I was growing up, if I wanted something, I knew what to say to get it. Annie was worse though. She could get anything she wanted: new makeup, alcohol for a party, anything. Aunt Helen has always been a soft touch. But to her credit, she took good care of us. Even now, she still pops round once a week to make sure I'm eating properly.'

'She lied about the threat?' Carmichael pressed.

Sue nodded. 'It was complete fiction.'

'Didn't your barrister challenge her testimony?'

'He did, but it was her word against mine. She was a star witness. The victim's endearing sister who had taken custody of the children. What jury wouldn't believe her version of events over that of the accused?'

'You don't sound bitter though.'

'As I said, if I knew a little lie would help convict Ben's murderer I'd have done the same. Helen believed everything she read about me in the newspapers, and thought she was helping justice be done. I don't bare a grudge. Ultimately, her lie was only one piece of the circumstantial evidence against me.'

Tom glanced at his watch. 'Our time's nearly up. So, Mr Carmichael, will you take our case on?'

'Please Tom,' she said. 'Don't waste your inheritance on this frivolity. I'm begging you.'

Tom took her hand in his. 'Trust me, mum. If it helps free you, it's worth it. You don't deserve to be in here. Let Mr Carmichael do his job.' He turned to Carmichael. 'Well, you've heard what she had to say, will you take it on?'

Carmichael looked back at her. Her eyes were begging him to decline the offer, but his gut was telling him there was something she was hiding. 'I'll do it.'

Tom pulled him into an embrace. 'Thank you so much. If there's anything you need, names, addresses, let me know. Thank you so much for agreeing to work on it. I prayed for this. When I saw you at the church on Sunday, I just knew you were sent from God. He's going to do it, mum: he's going to get you released.'

A bell sounded overhead, and all the prisoners stood and were escorted back through holding. Sue didn't look back at them as she was escorted away.

WEDNESDAY

29

Carmichael pushed the pay-and-display parking ticket against the windscreen, before closing the door, and locking the car. He'd arranged to visit the Hartley Library on University Road that morning. As part of the university, the library stored court transcripts where precedent had been set. It was his best shot at understanding how the judge had determined Sue's sentence sixteen years ago.

He was certain she was telling the truth when she denied killing her husband; her body language had indicated as much. Yet, when pressed about other details of that night, she had crossed her arms, and gazed into the distance. The question was: what was she hiding? What was she so desperate for him not to find that she'd be prepared to remain behind bars until her dying day?

He'd already developed a broken picture of the events following the discovery of Ben's body on Saturday 25 March 2000, from newspaper articles, but there was so much detail missing.

It had been years since he'd visited the library. He tried to ignore the occasional stares as he sat at one of the many terminals and typed in the details of Sue's case. He located the case reference number, and managed to collar a pretty young student to help him locate the large book it was buried in. The library smelled musty, and this was heightened as he opened the book on the table. He pulled out a pad and pen and scribbled the timeline of events cited in the transcript.

The first date recorded in the transcript was from the end of January. A prosecution witness, and former colleague, had claimed Sue told her Ben had been violent towards her. The day after Valentine's Day that year, Sue was reported as missing two days of work. A medical report from the General Hospital confirmed she'd been treated for injuries following a fall down the stairs. The inference was she lied to the doctor treating her, and that Ben was the cause.

On the night in question, Sue visited the cinema with her best friend Pat. They attended the evening screening of The Insider, at the Odeon in Southampton. They left the cinema around ten, and headed back to Highfield, a ten to fifteen minute journey by car. Pat claimed she had waited until Sue entered the property, before driving off. That put Sue in the property at half past ten when the next door neighbours reported hearing arguing and banging at the property. The neighbours couldn't make out what was being said, only that they heard raised voices and what sounded like something heavy being banged against the wall. Fearing for Sue's safety, they telephoned the police to report what they heard.

Sue appeared on their doorstep moments later, covered in blood, begging them to save his life. The neighbour, a vet, had done what he could to stem the flow of blood. Shortly before eleven, Sue telephoned for an ambulance. A recording of the call was played to the jury in which Sue claimed she had only just returned to find her husband in such a state. This cast doubt upon Sue's version of events. She was home for at least forty-five minutes, which remained unaccounted for. The prosecution argued that lying on the 999 call showed Sue's calculating nature, as she tried to cover her tracks.

The ambulance arrived at 23:10, and although they treated Ben, he died from significant blood loss before they reached the hospital. Sue did not travel with him in the ambulance.

The police arrived on scene and a preliminary statement of events was taken from a clearly shaken Sue. He noted that the First Officer Attending was Naomi Payne, Beth's current D.C.I., who was a P.C. at the time. It would be good to hear if she remembered anything significant about that night. He made a note to give her a call later.

The murder weapon, a long-blade chef's knife was found covered in blood beside the puddle where the body had been slouched. At 00:30, Sue is still covered in Ben's blood and is asked to hand over the clothes and change so she can accompany them to the station. The neighbours next door agree to watch the children.

Sue was questioned on and off by the police for the best part of three days. A week after the murder, Helen Dewis, Ben's sister, makes a statement at the police station where she tells them about the threat Sue made to her life. Helen claimed, during an argument in the kitchen, Sue grabbed the same chef's knife and waved it at her. She also claimed Sue threatened to stab Ben if he was ever violent towards her again.

In early April, Sue was arrested and formally charged with Ben's murder. Due to the violent nature of the crime and the possible threat to the lives of her children, Sue was held on remand until her trial seven months later. The prosecution argued her motive for the killing was revenge for the domestic abuse, and to steal the missing pension funds. On 23 November 2000, she was convicted and sentenced to a minimum of twenty-three years in prison without parole, until she showed remorse for her crime.

Carmichael re-read his notes, and turned to a fresh page to raise the questions that troubled him. Sue never appeared in the witness stand, so the transcript did not record her version of what happened between her arriving home, and when she appeared on the neighbour's doorstep. This left nearly forty-five minutes unaccounted for. He made a note to ask her for an explanation on his next visit. He also wanted to speak to Tom and his sister Annie. Both were in the house at the time, but neither reported hearing the violent argument in the kitchen below them. Tom would have been seven and Annie would have been fourteen at the time. He made a note to ask Tom how he could contact Annie.

He also noted Ben had probably known and let his killer into the property. Sue fitted into that category, but who else? Sue mentioned Ben's former business partner George Murphy as the most likely suspect, so Carmichael put him at the top of the list of alternative suspects. Sue also mentioned Ben's estranged son from his first marriage, so he was added to the list too. The final question Carmichael scribbled was: what happened to the money? Somebody, somewhere, knew where the million pounds had gone, and it was now vital to learn who that was. That had to be the key to what happened to Ben.

30

Beth lifted the photograph into the light and compared it to the image on the computer screen. If only the blonde had glanced at the camera in the club, she'd know for sure, but there was too much room for doubt. She had spent the afternoon reviewing the details of Josh Grabban's murder in the HOLMES-2 system. It was used to log each piece of evidence, as well as witness testimony and potential suspects, and then to look at it in a logical manner. She'd already linked it to the Todd Francis murder. Melissa's search for Kelly had been as fruitless as her own. Beth was now comparing Kelly's online dating profile picture to a recently-paroled offender.

The woman on screen, Roxanne, was overweight, and her hair was a darker blonde than the suspect, but given they knew she was wearing a wig, Roxanne's natural hair colour was irrelevant. She was in the right height bracket, and had been out of prison for two months. Roxanne's history included convictions for aggravated assault, shoplifting and prostitution. She was recorded as living at an address in the Shirley area of the city.

Beth compared the images again. Was it Roxanne? Had Roxanne met Todd with a plan to rob him and things had turned nasty? If so, why did she kill Josh?

She kept coming back to that question. She could devise a list of reasons Todd might have been killed, but Josh's murder made no sense. It couldn't have been pre-meditated as it was carried out in such an open place. In fact, the only thing linking the two cases was Beth herself. It was her refusal to accept that the blonde at the café wasn't the blonde seen being led from the club by Josh. She had spent hours comparing the still from the café to the still from the exit at the club. Other than the hair and build, there were no distinguishing features to tie the women, but she was certain in her gut it was Kelly.

Payne wasn't convinced, but she saw the fire burning in Beth and allowed her to pursue the theory, for now.

'Are you coming to the pub tonight, Sarge?' Capshaw asked, turning off his computer. 'They're doing two-for-one cocktails until eight.'

She glanced up at him, annoyed by the disturbance. 'No, I've still got loads to do.'

Capshaw failed to hide his relief. 'Okay, then. Well, I'll see you in the morning.' He tucked his chair under the desk.

'Are you ready?' Beth heard a familiar voice ask him. She looked up and saw Capshaw was now shaking hands with SOCO Harris.

Harris looked over when he noticed her watching them. 'Are you not coming for a drink, D.S. Taylor?'

He looked even cuter in a shirt and tie. Her cheeks reddened. 'Um, I can't…there's no rest for the wicked.'

He nodded. 'I understand, but everyone needs a break. You could come for one, and then head back here to finish off.'

She was tempted. God knew she wanted to say yes, but Roxanne's bitter eyes stared back at her. 'Thanks anyway.'

Harris and Capshaw said goodnight and joined the rest of the group who had amassed at the door. A moment later, the office was empty. Beth massaged the muscles in her neck. She was exhausted, but she wasn't ready to rest; not until she'd figured out who Kelly really was. She was certain the key was there, she just had to figure out how to find it. She walked to the small kitchen and boiled the kettle. Maybe a break from the screen would bring the enlightenment she sought.

On her way back to her desk she noticed the light was on in Payne's office. She was surprised to see the D.C.I. hadn't clocked off yet. She'd been in since six. Beth was the only one who knew when Payne had arrived, as she'd been in the office herself. She decided to offer to make a Payne a drink, and approached the door. She stopped herself from knocking when she saw Carmichael sat across the desk from Payne.

What the hell was he doing here? There was no way Payne would have contacted him. They'd met during the Freya Coleman investigation at Christmas, but Payne wasn't the sort to use a consultant on an active investigation.

Was he talking about Beth? Had he come to make trouble for her? Things had been bad between them since the miscarriage and their subsequent split, but this was a new low. She'd been within her rights to have a go at him on Friday night. Was that what he was complaining about? She had to find out. She knocked on the door and opened it.

'Ma'am, I've put the kettle on, do you want a tea?' She deliberately avoided eye contact with Carmichael, pretending she hadn't noticed him there.

Payne smiled. 'Thanks, Beth, but I'm heading home in a minute.'

Carmichael stood. 'I should get going myself. Thanks for your time, Naomi. I appreciate you meeting with me.'

'You're welcome, Johnson. It was nice taking a trip down memory lane. I'm only sorry I couldn't give you anything particularly useful. It was the first murder scene I ever saw, and I'll never forget the amount of blood on the floor. Let me know how you get on. If we did lock up the wrong person, there will have to be a full investigation.'

He thanked her again and pushed past Beth.

'I'll show him down,' Beth said, before closing Payne's door and chasing after him. 'What the hell was all that about?'

'Oh, it's nothing, just a new case I've taken on. It's alright, I know my way down.'

Beth waited until they were in the stairway before grabbing his shoulder. 'What the hell did you say to her?'

'What are you doing? I don't know what you're talking about.'

'Oh please! You only came here today to antagonise me. I thought I made myself perfectly clear the other night. There is no future for us.'

He shook his head. 'Is that what you think I was doing here? You've got quite the ego on you, do you know that?'

'So I'm expected to believe your new case happens to involve my current boss?'

'Yes. She was the first officer on scene. This is none of your business, Beth. I need to go.' He stopped, and turned back. 'I don't know what's going on with you these days. You say you don't love me anymore, but I can see it in your eyes. You either need to accept how you feel or move on. I won't wait for you forever, Beth. Mark my words. If you want to try again, you need to act before it's too late.'

She opened her mouth, but no words would come out. He fastened his jacket and continued down the stairs. Beth returned to the office in a huff.

Payne was closing her office door. 'Right, I'm off. Have you got much more to do?'

'I'm no closer to finding the suspect, so…'

'Can I offer you a piece of advice, Beth? Don't take this the wrong way, but you need to get out and have some fun. Believe me, if you spend every waking hour thinking about this job, one day you'll look back and regret not making more of your social life.'

'Surely, *you* don't have any regrets. The perfect family and your rank: I don't know how you manage it.'

Payne rolled her eyes. 'If you only knew. Oh, that reminds me, are you able to collect me on your way in tomorrow? My car's being serviced first thing. Do you mind?'

Beth smiled. 'That's fine, Ma'am.'

'Good. Oh, and Beth, it's alright to switch off, you know. You're young enough to get through the day on minimal sleep. Go and have a good time. That's an order.'

Payne smiled again, and then she was gone. Beth looked back at her screen. It wasn't like Roxanne was going anywhere tonight. She glanced at her watch. An hour of cocktails wouldn't do her any harm. She logged out of her workstation and grabbed her bag.

31

The sun was low in the sky, as it continued its descent. A single light through a downstairs window confirmed somebody was home. Carmichael rang the doorbell of the small detached house.

Sanza opened the door. 'Johnson, good evening. Have I forgotten we were supposed to meet?'

'No, there's something I need to talk to you about. You did say I could call on you at any time. I hope I'm not disturbing you.'

Sanza led him through to a small lounge-diner, barely large enough for the dining table and two armchairs it contained. A large crucifix hung from the wall.

'Please, take a seat,' Sanza offered. 'Can I get you something to drink? I don't have any bourbon, I'm afraid, though there might be an old bottle of Cointreau knocking about.'

He sat at the table. 'I'm fine.'

Sanza joined him. 'So to what do I owe this pleasure?'

'Sorry to call unannounced. You weren't in the middle of something were you?'

'I was washing-up as it happens, so your interruption is a welcome break.' Sanza smiled warmly. 'What's on your mind, Johnson?'

'I'm not even sure where to begin. I've not been sleeping well. I keep having nightmares, flashbacks of things I've done…I don't know how -'

'Is that why you were drinking so heavily last night?'

'What do you know about last night?'

'Don't you remember? I saw you at The Hatchett.' He paused. 'Actually, I'm not surprised you can't remember, you were pretty wasted. I was there for a quiz. You looked unhappy, so I came over to see if I could help. You weren't in a talkative mood if truth be told.'

'I don't remember any of that. The thing is, there's a lot about last night I can't remember.'

'For instance?'

'I don't remember how I got home. I assume I ordered a taxi or walked.'

'I think you must have walked. I tried to order you a taxi, but you took off before I had the chance. I looked for you, but couldn't find you.'

He raised his knuckles. 'I woke with these grazes on my fists, and a bump above my eye. I think I…I may have been involved in a fight last night.'

'Who with?'

'That's just it: I can't remember. I have a blackspot from arriving at the pub to waking this morning. The thing is, I saw on the news this morning that three youths were found beaten and dead in the wooded area across the road from the pub. What if…what if that was me?'

'Yes, I heard about that. Such a tragedy. The police said they suspected it was gang-related though. You're not part of a gang I presume?'

He frowned at him. 'Do I look like I belong in a gang? Of course I'm not.'

'That's okay then. It's probably nothing more than a coincidence. I'm sure you'd remember it if you'd attacked three youths. Did you know the boys?'

'Not that I'm aware of. The police haven't released their names yet, but I don't think I know anyone in that age bracket.'

'There you go then, I'm sure you're panicking for no reason. The state you were in when I last saw you, you could barely walk, let alone defend yourself in a fight. Is that it? Is that all that's troubling you? I've told you before, I'm happy to listen. I won't judge.'

Carmichael eyed him cautiously. 'I don't know if I can trust you. Wendy Barlow says you're no good.'

Sanza feigned a hurt expression. 'Men and women fear what they don't understand. You've seen the congregation. Do they look like they're being brainwashed?'

'I was approached by another set of troubled parents. They claimed their son, Greg Bush, was part of your church and changed after he met you.'

'Greg Bush was a troubled young man from birth. He had a history of antisocial behaviour issues. I opened the church's doors to him. God teaches that no person should be turned away. I thought I could help him keep on the straight and narrow. He became an active member of the church. I thought he'd made a real breakthrough, but he stopped taking his medication. Did they tell you that? He was bipolar. His medication kept him balanced, but as soon as he stopped taking them, he became unstable. I was devastated when I learned he'd taken his own life in hospital. I felt guilty for not doing more. Were there warning signs I missed? Should I have insisted he return home when I learned he was off his meds? That's the curse of hindsight, isn't it? What you've got to ask yourself is: what I would have to gain from manipulating the minds of those who attend the church? It's not like any of the congregation are in positions of extreme wealth or power. My flock are ordinary people crying out to hear God's infinite wisdom.'

'What makes you so special? Why does He talk through you?'

Sanza patted his hand. 'God didn't send His son to save the righteous. He sent Him to save sinners. I'm a sinner. I did bad things before I heard Him calling me. I'll be honest with you, to show you can trust me. I was in prison when I heard Him calling.'

'What for?'

'Theft. I had a challenging upbringing. I'm not making excuses, I knew what I was doing, but I was easily led. It's all in the past now. In fact, it's public record. But that all changed from the moment He called to me. I knew I had to change who I was, and realise my potential. God put me on this planet for a reason, as I'm sure He did you.'

'I wish I shared your belief.'

'Can I tell you something else, Johnson? I think I know why you're here.'

'Why?'

'I'll come to that in a moment. Before I do, I want to know what's troubling you. Tell me, what's it like in the dark of night when the demons come? Who do you see?'

He took a deep breath. 'I see the faces of the men I killed. They haunt me.'

'What do they do?'

'They take my daughter from me.'

'Anita? You mentioned her last night. You said she died recently.'

'She was terminally ill. She needed a stem cell transplant.' A single tear rolled down his face. 'I was tested, but…I couldn't save her.' He wiped the tear away. 'She died because I killed them. That's what my dreams tell me. I am being punished.'

'God doesn't punish us on earth. Since Eden, He leaves us to our own devices with His words as guidance. We will all face reckoning on the day of judgement. When bad things happen to us in this life, it is easy to blame it on an unmerciful God, but that's simply not the case. You were at the service on Sunday. It is the devil who runs amok on earth. He causes trouble and pain because he wants us to turn our backs on God. Anita's passing was not the will of God, but the churlish action of Satan himself. You are not to blame for Anita's death, Johnson. You must not hold yourself accountable.'

'That's easy for you to say.'

'I believe the reason you are here is to help me with God's work. When I first met you I sensed that there was a darkness within your soul. I instinctively knew you had taken human life before, but that God had sanctioned you to do it. He sees everything, and He wants us to battle back for Him. There are too many people who have let the devil into their souls and they need to be saved. That's why you're here, Johnson. Your initials are the same as the Messiah. God has called you. Can't you hear it?'

'I don't hear anything.'

'That's because you don't know how to interpret His message. You were brought to me through the tragic death of one of my followers. Without her, we wouldn't have met. That speaks volumes to me. God is rewarding you for following the path He has chosen for you. Allow me to be the vessel you use to communicate with God. He wants me to hear your confession.'

'You're not a priest though, are you? I mean, I know you lead your church, but you're not ordained like an Anglican vicar or a Catholic priest, are you? That means the rules governing confessionals do not apply to you, do they?'

'You're right that priests and vicars risk excommunication if they break the seal of confession, but did you also know any person privy to that confession is also held accountable under the seal? What is said in the confessional, remains there. Am I bound in the same way? Not by canon law, no. However, I made a promise to God in front of my followers that I would adhere to the seal of confessional. You have my word that anything you tell me now, will remain unheard by anyone else.'

'I don't know if I can trust you.'

'How else can I convince you? It was you who sought me out tonight. God told you to come here so you could offer those sacrifices to Him.'

He glanced around nervously. 'You're not recording this are you?'

Sanza shook his head. 'We are the only ones here. Who were these men you killed? How did they die?'

'Janus Stratovsky was a hustler and pimp in East London. He was part of the Russian mafia, and his uncle was the head of the crime syndicate. I was a detective in the Met police back then, and we had Janus under surveillance. I ended up in the backroom of one of his clubs and he offered me a bribe. I refused and we were fighting when his gun went off. The room was soundproofed so nobody heard the shot. Out of fear, I took his body and torched it in the back of an old banger. I may not have pulled the trigger, but if I hadn't been there he wouldn't have died -'

'Where do you imagine this man is now? I'm pretty sure he won't have made it past St. Peter. If he was as bad as you say, he's bound to be burning in hell. Is that a reasonable assumption?'

'For all the people he hurt or killed, hell would be too good for him.'

'What about this other man?'

'His name was James Lennon.'

'Who was he?'

'I'm surprised you haven't heard of him already. He was in all the papers at the turn of the year.'

'Wait, you mean the monster who abducted and killed all those girls?'

Carmichael nodded. 'I was there when he was found. I chased him through the darkness, and he tried to push me off a building, but he slipped. I held on to him as he dangled over the edge of the building. He admitted what he had done, and I…'

'What did he say to you before you let him go?'

'What? I don't know, I can't remember.'

'Yes you can, Johnson. Remember back to that

night. It was dark. You were holding onto him. You looked in his eyes and he said something that made you decide to release him. What was it?'

'I'm not sure…I don't…'

'Yes you do. God wants you to remember, Johnson. What did that monster say?'

'He…he was boasting…he was proud of what he'd done, and…then -'

'Yes?'

'Then he asked if I had a son or daughter. I thought about Anita in his clutches and I…' Carmichael buried his head in his trembling hands.

Sanza moved across and put his arm around him. 'Do you think it was an accident that God put you on a path with those two monsters? Or a coincidence? No, I believe God chose you to deliver His justice to those monsters. Don't you see what I'm saying, Johnson? It wasn't your fault they died: it was God's will! He chose you, and you more than proved you are up to the job.'

'I'm not so sure.'

Sanza was beaming. 'I have to admit, I'm excited. Very excited indeed. You've made a real breakthrough today. It's late. We both need rest. Go home now, and I will make a bet with you. I bet you will sleep better than you ever have tonight. If I'm right, it is because you have heard God's call and you are on the right path.' He showed Carmichael to the door. 'I will call you tomorrow, and we will see which of us is right.'

32

Kelly peaks out from behind the blind in the downstairs bathroom. The light is off so he shouldn't notice her as he leaves. She catches her breath as she sees him stop and look back over his shoulder. Can he sense her watching him? He only pauses for a moment, before continuing on to his car. He looks strong and powerful tonight. It's all she can do to contain her excitement.

It was a surprise to hear him talking to her brother. She cannot recall him mentioning that Carmichael would be calling by this evening. She was tempted to come out of her hiding place and introduce herself, but she is in no fit state to do so. Had she known he would be at their house this evening, she would have been ready for him, but her wig looks a mess, and she doesn't want to even think about what her face must look like without makeup on. No, appearing before him tonight would have been wrong. Still, he looks handsome in his shirt and jeans. He strides across the road like a man on a mission. It's intoxicating.

She watches as he climbs into his car, but he doesn't pull away as she expects. Instead, he sits there, with the car's internal light on. What is he doing? What is he waiting for? He is parked too far away for her to see if he is on the phone or if he is talking to someone else in the car. She coils the blind's cord between her fingers.

What if…

She dismisses the idea. It's ridiculous. She moves away from the blind and leaves the bathroom, but as she enters her room, she can't help but sneak another glance out of the window. He is still sitting there. The car hasn't moved.

She heard everything he told her brother. She knew for certain now that they were destined to be together. She didn't realise how similar they are. He has killed too. He's the only one who will understand the journey she's been on. Is it fate's way of bringing them together?

She laughs out loud at her own delusion. If he discovers what they've done in the past, what she'd done, there's no way he will be interested. That said, they do say lost souls are attracted to one another. Perhaps this is why she can't stop thinking about him.

She looks at her reflection in the mirror. Has she got time to get ready? He still hasn't moved. Maybe he's waiting to see if she'll come out to him. Did he know she was listening in on them? What if tonight is the night? Does Cupid want them to meet?

She tingles with excitement. She opens the wardrobe and pulls out the first dress her hand lands on. It is dark green, but it is made of thin cotton, so she won't get too hot. She curses as she realises she hasn't shaved her legs in days. She grabs a pair of sheer tights, and throws them in the large bag on the bed, along with the dress. Finally, she drops her makeup bag in, along with her green stilettos, and zips the bag. She checks he hasn't moved, and is relieved to see him still there. She creeps downstairs on tiptoes. The last thing she wants is to disturb her brother. He won't be happy if he knows she is going out, especially if he learns of her infatuation with Carmichael. She manages to open and close the front door, with barely a sound, and then she tiptoes down the drive to their car. She climbs in, as Carmichael starts his engine, and pulls out. She starts her car, and slips out behind him.

The butterflies in her stomach are distracting. She tries not to think about how good this evening could be. She turns on the radio and sings along to the music that plays. He is driving over the speed limit. He must be in a hurry to get wherever he needs to be. She hopes he is going home. She'd like him to invite her into his flat this time. Should she tell him about their encounter last night? Would it make a good ice breaker?

'Uh, you don't remember me, but I'm the bitch who stopped you getting mugged and possibly killed by three chavs. That's right, I kicked their arses!'

She blushes. That's not the way she's going to win him over. He's the kind of guy who likes to take command. She can tell that by looking at those big dark eyes. She's not the submissive type, but she thinks she could be for him.

He brakes suddenly. She is far enough back that he won't notice her car slowing. She sees his car turn into a road to the left. She is confused. This is neither the way to his office or home. In fact, she knows the area well, and it is residential. There isn't a pub or restaurant within two miles.

Does he know he's being followed? Is he trying to shake her off?

She drives past the road slowly, looking along it as she does. He has pulled his car onto the kerb, and he is getting out. She performs a U-turn and drives along the road. She needs to see which house he is at. She drives past his stationary vehicle as he reaches the front door of a semi-detached property. He hasn't noticed the sound of her car, so she continues to the end of the cul-de-sac before turning around and pulling in on the opposite side of the road, about twenty yards up from him. She turns off the engine and swivels around in her seat so she can watch him through the back window. A light is on at the property. The door is opening.

'No!'

She wants to scream out, but she doesn't want to draw unnecessary attention. The woman at the door is younger than him. She is a brunette, like that detective. Doesn't he like blondes? He talks to the young woman for a minute, before she invites him in.

Kelly slams her forehead against the edge of the steering wheel. She savours the warmth of the pain. She pictures him lifting the woman into his arms and carrying her to the bedroom. The woman tears at his shirt and fumbles with the zip on his jeans. Kelly feels sick and angry. She looks at the bag of clothes next to her. She pulls out the dress, and thinks about ripping it to bits: to stick up two fingers at fate.

She starts the engine and is about to pull out onto the main road again when she sees a cat crossing the road in her rear-view mirror. Shifting the car into reverse, she jams her foot on the accelerator and yelps with glee as the rear tyres bump over the unsuspecting animal. Feeling less than satisfied, she continues her journey home. He will be hers one day, but she will have to remain patient. For now.

THURSDAY

33

It is my belief that whoever framed my father for stealing the money, also killed him to cover their tracks.

Carmichael replayed Tom's words over in his head. It had helped to talk through his findings with Melissa last night. He'd left just before midnight, which was when Melissa had discovered that her cat had been run over.

Ben's murder had to be more than coincidence. From what he'd read, the investigators were camped out in the factory offices, pouring over every receipt, every invoice, desperately searching for evidence of Ben's alleged creative accounting. It made no sense why the investigation would suddenly cease. He needed answers, and as HMRC had replaced the Inland Revenue, they were his first port of call. He'd spent yesterday afternoon desperately trying to get through on the phone, and still hadn't managed to speak to a human being. There was only one number for HMRC and that went through to an automated voice that asked him to state what he was calling about. It didn't accept his first answer of 'embezzlement'. In fact, it hadn't accepted his first half dozen responses. He'd eventually slammed down the phone in anger. Half an hour later he had tried again, but there was no way past the automated voice.

He had eventually said his query related to self-assessment, and as the call had been transferred, he was relieved. Unfortunately, that had been short-lived as a new message had told him all the lines were engaged and he should phone back later, before the line had promptly disconnected.

Out of frustration he'd sent them an email, complaining about the lack of staff able to answer his query. He had ended the complaint with a lie, advising he had new information about what happened to the missing pension money and wished to discuss the matter with a member of the team who had been part of the original investigation. He'd hoped it would pique somebody's interest, but as he opened his email this morning, he saw a blanket response advising him that HMRC does not deal with work-based pensions and that he should contact The Pensions Regulator.

He was still swearing at the computer screen when there was a knock at the door. He looked at the pair of eyes staring back at him. He reluctantly opened the door, and saw Melissa wasn't in her office.

'Can I help you with something?'

The man was at least six inches shorter than Carmichael, and was wearing a tweed jacket, despite the heat. He wore small, round spectacles and had what resembled a small hairy slug above his upper lip. What remained of the man's hair was dark brown, but it only served to highlight the shiny top of his head.

'Are you, Mr Carmichael?' he asked with a strong Welsh accent.

Carmichael kept the stern look on his face. 'I am. Who are you?'

'My name is Owen Templeton, Mr Carmichael. I

wonder if we could step into your office for a moment. There's an urgent matter I wish to discuss with you.'

'Listen, pal, you need to make an appointment. I'm up to my eyes with work at the moment, and we're not actively taking on new cases. Perhaps you could leave a message on the answerphone, and I will arrange for my assistant to book some time in for you.'

The man removed his spectacles and wiped them with a handkerchief. 'You don't understand, Mr Carmichael. I came here in response to your email.'

'What email?'

He put the glasses back on and smiled to show he meant no harm. 'It was you who emailed HMRC about Ben Dewis, wasn't it?'

'Well, yeah, it was, but -'

'I read your email, Mr Carmichael and knew instinctively that I had to meet with you. I jumped on the first train from Reading this morning.'

'I don't understand. I received a response fobbing me off.'

'Oh, I know. I was the one who sent it. If you let me come in, I'll explain why.'

Carmichael stepped back and allowed him to enter the office.

'Would you mind closing the door behind you?' Owen asked. 'I appreciate it's warm in here, but what I have to say is strictly confidential. Loose lips sink ships, and all that.'

Carmichael closed the door and returned to his side of the desk. 'I'm listening, Mr -'

'Oh, please, call me Owen, that's what everyone

calls me. There's no place for formality in the valleys.'

'Very well, Owen. Perhaps you can start by explaining why you've come here today. Your email suggested you had no interest in the missing funds.'

'Actually, you're more right than you know, Johnson. You don't mind if I call you Johnson, do you?'

Carmichael waved his hand dismissively.

'Great. Well, Johnson, technically, we at Revenue and Customs don't have any interest in the running of company pension funds. It is The Pensions Regulator who you would need to follow up with. Back in 2000, they called themselves the Occupational Pensions Regulatory Authority, as we ourselves were the Inland Revenue, but I don't suppose you want a history lesson on the governing bodies.' He paused to smile, but quickly continued when Carmichael didn't smile back. 'Anyway, why did I come here? As I said, I was part of the original team sent to Southampton to undertake a review of the textile factory's accounts. I'd never been to Southampton before, and I have to say I found it a charming city, I did. You know when sometimes you get a good feeling about a place? They put us in a lovely little hotel in the city, only a stone's throw away from the shopping precinct, and about half a mile from the factory. I remember telling my wife all about it. I always said I'd bring her one day, but we've still not made it here.' He paused as he lost his trail of thought. 'Oh, where to was I going?'

'You were part of the original team called in to review accounts.'

'Oh, yes, that's right. We were a team of four. There was me, Alan, Dai, and of course Huw

Llewellyn, who was the lead auditor. He was a stern man, I can tell you. If ever there was a man in need of a sense of humour transplant, he was one.' He chuckled. 'I'm not one to bad mouth a colleague, but he truly was wicked. I remember when me and Dai decided to -'

Carmichael gritted his teeth. 'What instigated the audit in the first place?'

'Oh…uh…it was an anonymous tip-off I believe.'

'A tip-off?'

'Oh yes, it's more common than you might expect. Often we find it's a rival business trying to cause trouble for a competitor. You'd be surprised at how many tip-offs we get when big contracts are looming. I remember we once received a series of tip-offs about a chain of cash and carries in Coventry. We were contacted every month for a year, even after we'd been in and confirmed everything was above board. There are some cheeky scallywags -'

'Owen, did you ever trace the source of the tip-off?'

'Oh no, we never bother. More often than not, the alert is genuine and we find what we're looking for.'

'What about with this case? I read you were here for weeks.'

'Well, that's not strictly true. After what happened, the newspapers exaggerated their reports. It wouldn't surprise me if the anonymous tipster was also the source of those reports. The investigation started in late December and finished in March, but we weren't here for every day of that period. Due to other audits, we would sometimes be here for only a day. I remember we spent eight consecutive days in

Wolverhampton in February that year, so the audit wasn't as intense as it might have first appeared. Please do stop me if I ramble, Johnson. My wife says I can get carried away when I -'

'Owen, what did you find at the factory?'

'Oh right, yes, the truth is: we didn't find a thing.'

Carmichael frowned. 'I don't understand.'

'The books were clean. Okay, there was one receipt for some stationery that had been claimed for when it shouldn't have been, but that was all.'

'What about the missing million pounds?'

'Oh that, well, that wasn't part of our investigation. We were only here to look at V.A.T. and income tax.'

'I'm confused. The newspaper report said you'd discovered missing money from the company pension.'

'Oh no, we would never be involved in that side of the business. No, as far as we were concerned, Ben ran a tight ship. He was a nice man as well. Nothing ever seemed too much trouble for him. He kept us fed with tea and biscuits and was able to produce every receipt and invoice we asked for. Such a shame what happened to him, it was.'

'Why was he accused of embezzlement then?'

'That's the strange thing, I'm not sure. One night in January, Alan and I were in the hotel bar when Llewellyn approached us and said he'd been told of some irregular activities in the pension pot. He said we were to keep it under our hats, but he planned to look into it.'

'But I thought you said you didn't get involved in that kind of thing?'

'We don't, Johnson. That's just it! We had no

jurisdiction, but he went off piste and did it anyway.'

'Didn't you raise your concerns with your superiors?'

'Llewellyn was my superior, you see. I was in no position to challenge what he was doing.'

'So it was another tip-off?'

'I assumed it was.'

'And do you know who told him of these irregularities?'

Owen pushed the glasses back up his nose. 'I don't, but I have my suspicions, I do. I once saw Llewellyn skulking in a corner with a chap called Paddy Grantham. He was the head of the Staff Union. He was a weasel of a man himself, and always had a beady eye on what we were doing at the factory. He was suspicious of everyone.'

Carmichael jotted the name. 'And you think this Grantham told your boss about the missing money?'

Owen nodded.

'But how would he know anything about it?'

'Your guess is as good as mine, Johnson. As I said, he was suspicious of everyone, so maybe he stumbled onto something he shouldn't have seen. I don't know.'

'Did your supervisor report his suspicions to The Pensions Regulator?'

'You mean the Occupational Pensions Regulatory Authority? He did eventually, but it wasn't until a few weeks later. It was right before the story was reported by the local press. It was hugely embarrassing for all of us involved, to be honest. We were all warned not to discuss any of our activities with reporters.'

'Did you suspect Grantham of leaking the story?'

'Yes, him or Llewellyn. It wasn't Dai, Alan or me, because we didn't know much about it.'

'So you don't know what happened to the money?'

'No idea, that's why I came here today. Your email said you'd found something?'

Carmichael wrinkled his nose. 'I may have been a bit liberal with the truth. I've been hired to find out who killed Ben, and I thought it may have been tied to the missing money.'

'Oh I see. You thought I might know what happened to the money?'

Carmichael shrugged.

'Well, I am sorry, Johnson, but I can't help you, I'm afraid.'

Carmichael sat up in his chair. 'Hold on a minute. If Revenue and Customs have nothing to do with pensions, why on earth did you drop everything to come here today?'

Owen glanced around to check the door was closed. 'What I'm about to tell you is in the strictest confidence. It isn't based on any fact, and if I'm ever challenged, I will deny we had this conversation. Am I making myself clear?'

Carmichael leaned forward. 'What is it, Owen?'

He mopped his brow with the handkerchief he'd used earlier on his glasses. 'I never felt right about the way things ended here. Ben was clearly proud of the way he kept his books in order. He was meticulous with the detail. He never struck me as the kind of man who would steal the pension money. When the accusation was made by OPRA, he was a broken man. It was as if someone had torn out his soul. I'm certain he had nothing to do with the money being taken. I said as much to Llewellyn and the OPRA investigator, but neither would listen to me. It left a sour taste in my mouth.'

'If Ben didn't take it, who do you think did?'

'That business partner of his would be a good candidate, or that Kevin Lyons who was always milling about the place.'

'I'm aware of George Murphy, but I don't know that other name. Lyons, you said?'

'That's right. Lyons with a 'y' He was in his mid-twenties I suppose; not long out of college. He'd been employed to help take the company into the digital age or something. Full of ideas about how they could be working smarter and saving money. I got the impression Ben wasn't a fan.'

'Did you ever tell anyone about your suspicions?'

'I told Llewellyn, but he told me it was none of my business and sent me back to the office.'

'Does he still work for Revenue and Customs? I think I ought to pay him a visit.'

'Oh, that's impossible that is, I'm afraid. Llewellyn died a couple of months after the investigation ended.'

'He's dead? Was foul play suspected?'

'Oh no, I don't believe so. He had a heart attack I think. Died in his sleep, he did. I didn't go to his funeral. I thought it would be hypocritical. His wife bought a house in the south of France and has been there ever since. It was rumoured she received quite the windfall when he passed; life assurance or something.'

Carmichael thanked Owen for the visit and promised he would be in touch if he managed to find who stole the million pounds. Owen was the second person to name George Murphy as the most likely candidate to have stolen the money. An internet search revealed Murphy was now the co-founder of a local internet dating company in the city. As luck would have it, the company were hosting a speed dating night at a hotel in Southampton that night. Carmichael decided he would go along and see if he couldn't catch Murphy off-guard.

34

Beth placed two pieces of gum in her mouth and chewed. Her satnav told her she was five minutes from her destination, but traffic was at a standstill, so she would probably remain five minutes away for the foreseeable future. She belched and her stomach turned at the taste in her mouth. Last night was a mistake. Two-for-one cocktails were always a mistake, particularly for a lightweight like Beth.

She'd caught up with her colleagues at Turtle Bay in the heart of the city. They were celebrating the news that Capshaw's wife was expecting their second child. She could tell he was drunk from the moment she arrived, as he came racing over and grabbed her in a bear hug.

'Look who's here,' he cheered. Nobody else shared his enthusiasm.

Beth offered to get a round in, but from all accounts someone had beaten her to it, so she found herself alone at the bar, desperately trying to get the barman's attention. The place was heaving. A space opened up next to her and she was angry when someone else jumped into it. He put his hand in the air and the barman took his order. She was about to give him a piece of her mind when she recognised the handsome features of Harris.

'Oh shit,' he said. 'Were you next? I'm so sorry. I didn't realise who you were.'

He caught her off-guard. 'Oh that's okay,' she smiled. 'It's not your fault.' She hated herself for not giving him a piece of her mind.

'The least you can do is let me get you a drink. What would you like?'

'Oh, you don't need to do that. I can get my own.'

'Nonsense, it's the least I can do. I see you're looking at the cocktail menu. Are you a cosmopolitan kind of girl or do you prefer sex on the beach?'

She choked on her own saliva, and coughed profusely. 'Uh, I…uh…what do you recommend?'

'I like the sharpness of a mojito, but for you, I think I'd recommend a caipirinha.'

'Thank God,' she laughed. 'If you'd have suggested a slow comfortable screw against the wall, I think I'd have slapped you.'

He smiled that gorgeous smile again, and she went weak at the knees. He ordered the drinks and when they arrived, he led her back through the crowd to the area where the rest of the team were sitting.

'I'm surprised to see you here,' he whispered when they were seated. 'I didn't think this was your kind of thing.'

'Oh no? What makes you say that?'

'Okay, don't take this the wrong way, but I saw you as the all-work-and-no-play kind of girl. I've never seen you out with this lot before.'

'You've obviously been looking in the wrong places.'

'It's good you came. Everyone needs to unwind from time to time.'

Was he flirting with her? It had been awhile since any man had. Carmichael wasn't much of a flirt; he tended to say whatever was on his mind. She liked Harris' playfulness. She finished her drink and returned to the bar, bringing him a bottle of lager. They'd continued making small talk, while she waited for him to make a move. Her bladder got the better of her and excused herself. In the bathroom mirror, she psyched herself up to make a move on him. He was back at the bar when she came out, so she went over to him.

'What are you drinking this time?' she asked.

'We said we'd do some shots here and then move further into town. I'm in the mood for dancing. Do you fancy dancing?'

She wasn't much of a dancer, but if he was leading, she'd gladly follow. He passed her a shot of something colourless and she knocked it back. She hadn't touched tequila since getting paralytic on it when she was eighteen. The memories came flooding back.

'You're a dynamo!' he declared. 'I'd better order two more or the others will think they're missing out.'

She smiled through the nausea.

He smiled back, and she knew then the moment was right. She grabbed his face in both hands and pulled him in for a kiss. Their lips parted as soon as they touched.

He pulled a face. 'I am so sorry if you got the wrong idea about me, Beth. I thought you knew. I'm gay.'

She wanted the ground to swallow her up. Her cheeks flushed. 'Of course I knew. I was just being friendly. I kiss all my gay friends.'

He looked relieved. 'You had me worried then. My boyfriend is always saying I lead women on. I don't mean to.'

He lifted the tray of shots and headed back to the table. 'Who wants some tequila?'

There were whoops of joy from all. He passed Beth a shot, and as desperate as she was to tip it on the floor, she took a deep breath and knocked it back in one.

She made her excuses when the rest of them decided to move on. She claimed she had to make a phone call and would catch them up, but as soon as they were out of sight, she hollered a taxi and headed home. She hadn't been sick, but her stomach hadn't stopped turning since the early hours of the morning. She'd been tempted to phone in sick, but then everyone would know what a lightweight she was.

She parked outside the D.C.I.'s house. She envied Payne. Although ten years older than Beth, she looked good for her age, had a senior rank within the force, and was destined to climb further. Her husband ran his own landscape gardening business, and rumour was that their luxury four bedroom house was mortgage-free. They had two daughters at public school and a family beagle. Beth wished her life was so well organised.

She put her sunglasses on as she walked up the driveway and rang the doorbell. There was no answer, so she tried again. She checked her watch. Payne had said to collect her at nine, so it was odd she wasn't ready. Beth followed the path that ran through to the back garden and conservatory. She heard Payne before she saw her.

'How fucking dare you use that against me?' Payne shouted.

'It was *you* who decided to go and fuck your colleague. Why is it so difficult for you to understand why I want a divorce?'

'We will talk about this when I return later. Don't think I'm going to give up all this without a fucking fight.'

Beth turned the corner and saw Payne and her husband at the far end of the large lawn. Payne was smoking and waving her arms hysterically. Beth tried to turn back, but it was too late: she was spotted. Payne stomped the cigarette under foot. Beth followed her back to the front of the house in silence. They got into the car without a word, and it was five minutes later when Payne finally broke the silence.

'I'm sorry you had to see that. I didn't mean to have a domestic this morning. He can be…sorry, you don't need to hear me talking about my marital problems. Let's put it behind us, and pretend it never happened.'

'It's none of my business, Ma'am.'

'Even so, it's not professional of me to allow my personal life to impact the job. What they don't teach you when you join is that you'll have a choice to make: the job or a family. You can't have both. I thought I could defy the odds, and now look at me.'

'With respect, Ma'am, I'm sure things aren't as bad as you think. Once you've both cooled off, I'm sure you'll sort it out.'

Payne snapped. 'What do you know about it?'

'Nothing, Ma'am, sorry, I was just trying to be

supportive.'

'I don't need you to be supportive, Beth, I need you to drive.'

'Yes, Ma'am.'

'I've got high hopes for you, Beth. White won't be around forever, and I could do with a bright officer like you running the office. I've been impressed with the dedication you've shown this last week. I can tell you've chosen the job over family, and I admire you for that. I wish I'd been so level-headed at your age.'

Beth nodded, but she wasn't so certain she had made that decision yet. With last night's embarrassment weighing heavily on her mind, she thought about what Carmichael had said. Maybe he was right: maybe she did still have feelings for him.

35

George Murphy was leaning against the bar in the Novotel hotel. He proudly watched as the evening's speed dating activities commenced. Carmichael could see him from the leather recliner in the reception area. A pretty woman in her late thirties leaned in and pecked Murphy on the cheek. He must have cracked a joke, as the woman giggled, before moving to a table and taking her seat. Carmichael saw Murphy leering at her bottom as she went.

Murphy was in his early fifties, moderately overweight, wearing a shirt, jeans and suit jacket. His faded blonde hair was slicked back over his head and bounced off his shoulders. His sixty-a day habit had added gravel to his Irish accent.

Carmichael approached the bar. 'What's all this?'

Murphy turned to see who had addressed him. 'Speed dating, mate.' He nodded towards the large poster hanging above the bar. 'It's for members of our site.'

The barman asked Carmichael what he wanted to drink.

He stared at the Jack Daniels, and licked his lips. 'I'll have an orange juice,' he said through gritted teeth. He turned back to Murphy, who was now reading something on his phone. 'Excuse me, so you run this internet dating site, do you?'

Murphy looked up. 'I founded it, mate.'

'Is business good?'

Murphy grinned. 'We do alright.'

'It must be competitive though, right? I mean, you can't turn on the television without seeing an advert for one dating site or another.'

'True, but it's easier when you have a U.S.P.'

He played dumb. 'What's a U.S.P.?'

Murphy put down his phone. 'Unique selling point, mate. It's what makes us stand out from our competitors.'

'I see. What makes you stand out?'

'A lot of the other sites are national. They can match you with someone that lives in your area, but there's no guarantees. We are a local company. We are exclusive to Hampshire. If you join our site, we guarantee to match you with someone from within the county. Means we have a smaller database, so we can focus on the key qualities our clients are looking for.' He smiled broadly, and Carmichael spotted something green between his teeth. 'Plus, we don't just pair our clients: we organise the whole date for them.'

'How's that?'

'Let's say you joined our site – incidentally are you single?'

'I am.'

'Okay, so let's say you sign up, and we find a woman who matches what you're looking for, and she likes the look of you too. Other sites would pass on your details to each other and leave you to it. What if you decide to take her out to dinner, but choose a bad restaurant? That could be it as far as that relationship goes. She might not give you a second chance.' He paused for effect. 'What we do is organise the whole night for you. We take the stress out of dating.' He grinned like a used car salesman. 'We book you a table from a select list of venues, collect you both at a pre-arranged time, so you get to meet and get to know each other before dinner. At the end of the night, we drop you both home. We don't just cater for restaurant dates. We have good connections within the local sailing community as well, so, if you fancy a date on a yacht, we can do that too.'

'Sound like you've got all the bases covered.'

He grinned again. 'We like to think so.' He thrust a hand out. 'George Murphy. And you are?'

Carmichael shook his hand. 'Johnson Carmichael.'

'Nice to meet you Johnson. Are you local to Southampton or visiting?'

'I live in Eastleigh.'

'That is local! And you said you were single at the moment?'

He nodded.

'Tell me, Johnson, are you looking for love? Have you ever used an internet dating site before?'

'I haven't, no.'

'It's not the taboo it once was, you know. In fact, one in five relationships in the UK starts online apparently. And they reckon half of all couples will meet online in twenty years or so.'

'That's good news for your business.'

'Certainly is. I tell you what, Johnson, tonight's event is supposed to be for members only, but if you're not up to much, why don't you come and take part.'

He politely shook his head. 'Thanks, but I don't think -'

'I won't take no for an answer. There are some lovely ladies here tonight. You don't know who you might meet. All I need is to take a few details from you so I can add your profile to the site. Come on, what d'you say? There's complimentary champagne and nibbles for members.'

He'd played hard to get for long enough. 'Oh why not; what have I got to lose, right?'

Murphy slapped his arm jovially. 'Great stuff. Let me get a pen and one of our forms. I'll be back in a minute.' He returned a moment later with a clipboard and biro. 'I'll add your name. What's your date of birth, Johnson?'

'Would you believe 29 February 1972?'

'You're kidding! You were born in a leap year? How on earth do you celebrate your birthday?'

'I usually open any cards on March first. I managed to celebrate properly this year though.'

'Well, I think that should be your opening line when you meet your first lady tonight. It's a cracking ice breaker...now, I need a few more details from you. What's your occupation?'

'I'm a private investigator.'

Murphy dropped the biro. 'Forget what I said. *That* should be your ice breaker! I never would have guessed that's what you do. You're not how I imagine a P.I. would look.'

'I get that a lot.'

'I've never met a P.I. before, but I always imagined you'd carry binoculars and a camera. I guess you must be off duty, tonight, right?'

'Something like that. Is this going to take much longer?'

'You can complete the rest online. If you give me your email address, I can email you a link straight to your profile and you can fill in the rest tomorrow.'

Carmichael handed over his business card.

'Great, oh, there's one more question. How did you hear about us? If existing members encourage a friend to sign up, they get entered into a prize draw to win a magnum of champagne. I'll tell you what, if any of our ladies takes your fancy tonight, we can put down her name as the person who introduced you and she might win the bubbly. How does that sound?'

'Actually, I was given your name by a mutual friend of ours.'

'Oh, who's that then?'

'Sue Dewis.'

Murphy froze, the blood slowly draining from his face. 'Who, sorry?' He coughed.

'Sue Dewis. I believe you knew her husband Ben.'

Murphy looked away. 'I don't know anybody by that name.' He glanced at his watch. 'Goodness me, is that the time, I should be off.'

'The thing is, George, Sue hired me to find the person who stole the million pounds from Ben's company's pension pot. She suggested I should speak to you about it.'

Murphy leaned closer. 'I don't know what you're talking about,' he growled.

'Oh, I think you do, George. Now we can either go somewhere quiet to discuss this like gentlemen, or…' He coughed and raised his voice. 'Or I can tell everyone here all about it.'

'Okay, okay, keep your voice down, will ya? We'll go outside. My car's in the car park. I need a cigarette anyway.'

Carmichael followed him out into the warm night air. It was gone nine, and the last rays from the setting sun were disappearing on the horizon. Murphy leaned against the bonnet of his Volvo and lit a cigarette.

'This your car?' Carmichael asked.

'Yeah, what of it?'

'Nothing, I expected you to be driving something…fancier?'

'It's a decent run around. I can get all the promotional bits for the business in the boot.'

'Let me guess, your other car's a Rolls?'

'What gives you that idea?'

'Sue reckons you're the most likely person to have stolen the pension money.'

'Well she's wrong. I didn't take that money. Do you think I'd be wasting my time on an internet dating business if I had a million quid sitting offshore somewhere?'

'Yeah, but the shit car and lame business could simply be a cover.'

'Well it's not! There was one person who knew what happened to that money, and he's dead!'

'Sue is adamant Ben didn't take it.'

'How is she by the way? I've not seen her since…well, since the sentencing. I did think about visiting her, but I didn't think she'd want to see me.'

'You're right. She thinks the person who stole the money is the same person who killed Ben.'

'Oh great! Now she thinks I killed Ben too? He

was my best friend for Christ's sake!'

'I think it's only right to tell you I'm looking into everything that happened in 2000, and I will find out what did happen. I'm good at what I do, George, so why don't you save us both a lot of time, and tell me what I want to know.'

'I've told you already: I didn't take the money, and the person who killed Ben is already in prison. Her prints were on the murder weapon for feck's sake!'

'What happened to the money, George?'

'How the feck should I know? Ben was the one who looked after the accounts, not me. Do you know how difficult it would have been for me to forge the necessary paperwork to get my hands on those assets? Paperwork has never been my forte. The audit people cleared me of any involvement. It was Ben who took the money, though God knows what he did with it, and it was Sue who killed him.' He squashed the cigarette beneath his shoe. 'You're wasting your time.'

'Where can I find Kevin Lyons?'

'I wouldn't know. Why do you want to speak to Kevin?'

'I heard he and Ben didn't see eye to eye. I want to find out whether Lyons knew anything about the embezzlement.'

'Good luck finding him!'

'What's that supposed to mean?'

Murphy opened the car door and climbed in. 'It means I haven't seen him in over fifteen years. After the factory went under, he took off, and I never heard from him again. Not even a reference request.'

Carmichael remained in the car park, as Murphy pulled away into the darkness. He was certain Murphy was hiding something, but he wasn't certain what. Something told him Kevin Lyons might be the key to the whole thing. He needed to find out more about Lyons, and one person who was bound to shed light on him was the woman who Sue was with the night of the murder: her best friend, and the woman Tom referred to as 'Auntie Pat'.

36

Kelly pours the rest of the wine into her glass. The bottle rocks as she returns it to the table. If her brother knew how much she was drinking, he wouldn't approve. She has been in the restaurant for an hour, and all she has eaten is a single bread roll. The waiter eyes her suspiciously, like he is expecting her to cause some kind of scene. Part of her wants to confront him, but she is clinging to the last of her inhibitions. For now anyway.

The waiter approaches the table. He looks at his watch, before plucking up the courage to repeat the question. 'Is your date on his way?'

She doesn't answer him. She picks up the wine glass and drinks until it is empty. She wipes her mouth with the back of her hand. 'Just give me the fucking bill,' she slurs.

The waiter can't hide the wry smile from his face as he turns and heads to the bar.

There isn't a spare seat in the small Italian restaurant. There is a couple standing near the main door, waiting for a table to become vacant. They have been trying to glance casually at Kelly for the last ten minutes. She has noticed their glances, and it is this that has encouraged her to stay as long as she has.

The waiter returns and places a small silver plate

on the table. She snatches the paper and stares at the numbers. She drops a twenty pound note on the plate, before adding, 'I want my change too.'

He shuffles back to the bar, and returns a moment later with a handful of coins on the plate. She pockets them and grips the edge of the table as she attempts to stand. She is wishing she'd chosen flats for tonight's adventure.

The Italian restaurant is near Carmichael's flat. She has been waiting to see him walk past the window. In her imagination, she offers him a seat at her table, and he accepts. They talk and discover how much they have in common. There is a spark of electricity between them, and he invites her back to his place for a drink, and they passionately embrace. She is silly for allowing herself to believe it could happen. She has never had these kinds of feelings before, and she is uncertain how to handle them.

It is nearly ten o'clock, and she isn't ready to go home yet. Her brother didn't react well to the news that Claire had hung herself in her flat. It was the second story on this evening's local news, even though it is several days since she left Claire hanging there. She was surprised to see the story upset her brother so much. She wanted to tell him she'd done it for him; that it was what the bitch deserved, but she knows he won't hear her words. Despite everything Claire put him through, Kelly can now see how much she still means to him. She doesn't regret her actions. She knows her intentions were best and that the world is a better place because that money-grabbing whore is gone.

That's one of her brother's biggest flaws. He's

always looking for the good in others, even when they trample on him. Thankfully, she is made of stronger stuff. That said, she does not want to go home to his misery. The night is young, and the world is alive with sound in tonight's warm climate. She walks unsteadily towards the exit. The waiter is talking to the waiting couple, and then the three of them glance in her direction. She can tell they are talking about her, and she snaps.

She decides to give them a mouthful, when there is a sudden eruption of noise behind her. She turns, knocking into a nearby table. Half a dozen men emerge from the kitchen area, some dressed as waiters, others in white aprons and hats. They are singing in loud, deep voices, and approaching a table where a young couple are sitting. Kelly strains her neck to see what is going on. The staff finish their song, and the young man pushes his chair back, and falls on one knee. The young woman in a silver-sequined dress puts her hands to her mouth in utter shock. Kelly cannot hear what he is saying, but it ends with the woman throwing her arms around his shoulders. There is a flurry of tears and giddy excitement. Each of the singers shakes the young man's hand, and pat him on the back. The crowd disperses, leaving the couple holding hands and whispering sweet nothings to each other. The young woman is now admiring the shiny rock on her finger. Kelly watches them kiss, and in that moment she knows she would give anything to be in that woman's shoes. The couple look over when they feel her staring, and she quickly beats a retreat. As she reaches the exit, she cannot see the couple who had been waiting for her table. She knows what she wants to shout at them, but, as she turns, she sees they are already seated at her table. She is tempted to go back to the table, but her feet are sore, so she continues with her exit.

Once outside, she stumbles to her car in the public car park across the road from the restaurant. She is struggling to remember where she parked it. She eventually lifts her key remote into the air, and presses the unlock button. Two sets of orange lights flash over to her left. She smiles and walks over to the car. She climbs into the driver's side, but she knows she is not safe to drive. She isn't prepared to risk being stopped by the police. She opens the car door and is about to phone for a taxi when she sees the newly engaged couple leaving the restaurant. The man's arms are wrapped tightly around his new prize, and she is squeezing him equally as tight. They cross the road and walk towards Kelly. What do they want? She realises they are walking towards the car parked next to hers.

They are giggling, as he unlocks the car and opens the passenger door for his fiancée. Kelly wobbles towards them, before congratulating them. The young woman looks nervous at first, but is soon showing off the ring on her left hand. Kelly tells them she was in the restaurant during the proposal and says they make a lovely couple. The man walks back around to the driver's side of the vehicle. The young woman is about to get into her seat, when Kelly pulls out the flick knife she took from the youth in the tracksuit last night. She pulls the fiancée towards her and places her arm around the woman's neck. The woman screams, but stops when Kelly lifts the knife and the blade glistens under the street light. Kelly places the blade under the woman's chin and tells the man to stay calm. She tells him to get into the car and start the engine.

Kelly opens the back door and slides in, returning the knife to the woman's throat once she is seated.

They ask her what she wants and she tells them they need to do as they're told if they want to live. She tells him to start the car and to drive back to their place. They are only in the car for five minutes before he pulls onto a driveway in Valley Park. Kelly keeps the blade pressed firmly against the woman's neck as the three of them enter the mid-terrace property. Kelly tells them to go to the bedroom. The man obeys, but Kelly can see he is assessing the situation. She can tell he is trying to work out a way to overpower her. She needs to take decisive action to keep him in check. She tells them to undress slowly. Kelly unzips the woman's silver dress, and helps lift it over her head. The man continues glancing over at them, as he unbuttons his shirt. Kelly tells the woman to kneel by the bed and to place one cheek against the mattress. She obeys with no resistance. Kelly pinches the ear closest to her and quickly runs the blade against the lobe. The woman screams in pain and her hand rushes to what remains of her bloody ear.

Kelly holds up the small piece of ear so the man can see it. 'If you don't want me to dissect her bit by bit, you'll do as I say,' she threatens.

A small puddle of blood is already spreading across the bed sheet. Kelly grabs a nearby towel and presses it against the woman's ear. She yelps again, but takes the towel and presses it hard against the wound.

'Don't worry, it'll clot soon enough. You won't bleed to death.'

The young woman is sobbing. Kelly cuts through the woman's bra straps and tells her to lie on her back on the bed. The woman reluctantly does as instructed. Kelly tells the man to remove his underpants and to lie next to the woman. He is sweating. Kelly removes her mobile phone and switches on the video camera. She tells the couple exactly what she wants them to do. The man protests at first, but a wave of the knife is enough to deflate his resistance.

An hour later Kelly lets herself out of the house, a smile of satisfaction etched across her face. She puts the phone and knife away in her handbag and walks to the end of the road. When a man rapes a woman, particularly when they are in a loving relationship, the dynamic between them changes forever. Kelly knows the young woman will never look at her fiancé in the same way again. He has defiled her, and she will never be able to forgive him for not putting up more of a fight to protect her. Kelly whistles as she reaches the end of the road. She is beginning to sober up now, but decides to call her brother to get him to collect the car for her.

FRIDAY

37

Carmichael declined the call, and switched off his phone. Sanza had phoned him five times already this morning, but he was in no mood to talk to him. He put the phone back in his pocket. Patricia Rankin placed the tray in front of him, before sitting nearby. Tom's 'Auntie Pat' poured him a cup of tea and encouraged him to take a biscuit. He looked at the selection of digestives on the plate before politely declining.

'I understand you were a bridesmaid at their wedding?' he began.

'Oh yes, and Sue was my maid of honour when I married eighteen months later. We've known each other since school, and were as thick as thieves as teenagers. We used to spend every day of the summer holidays at the pool on The Common. Of course, none of the places we used to hang out at are there any more, but I suppose things have to change. I used to call her 'The Mad Cat Lady', because she used to take her cat for a walk using a piece of string for the lead.'

'What can you tell me about Ben and Sue? Were they a happy couple?'

'They were. Sue was always so immaculately dressed, a real perfectionist. She wouldn't even go out in the morning unless her underwear matched, in case she was involved in an accident. As for Ben, I liked him the moment we met. Sue and I both got jobs at the telephone exchange in the city, two years after college.' She smiled. 'They were some good times. We'd get paid on a Friday, and hit the pubs and discos straight after work. We'd dance until dawn, and then spend the weekend shopping. We had no cares, and no responsibilities. Ben was working at the exchange as an engineer. He wasn't there all the time, but he'd usually stop by a couple of times a week to fix one problem or another. Sue and I both fancied him. He was a couple of years older than us, but he had a way about him. He was charming, and funny, and chivalrous. At the time I was seeing a guy on and off, so Sue and I agreed she could go out with Ben. From the moment she agreed to go on a date with him, he only had eyes for her.'

'What happened about the guy you were seeing?'

'We broke up a week or so later. His mother was an interfering old battle-axe, but he refused to see it. If we'd have finished sooner, I might have put up more of a fight for Ben. Still, they made a lovely couple, and I went on to meet my husband at their wedding, so it all worked out for the best.'

'Ben and Sue were married within a year?'

'That's right. What you have to understand is things were different back then. Weddings weren't such lavish affairs. They were married in the church at midday, we ate at the pub straight after, and they were off on honeymoon by three o'clock. There should be some photos of the wedding in one of those albums I left out for you.'

'When did you last see Sue?'

Pat sipped her tea. 'I've only seen her once since she was sentenced. She insisted I should move on with my life and forget I ever knew her. She said it was the only way she could cope with being inside. She didn't want reminders of what she was missing out on. I obliged. To be honest, I hadn't thought about her in years prior to Tom's phone call last week. So do you think you can find something to get her out?'

'It's early days yet, but that's the objective. You believe she didn't do it?'

Pat looked away. 'Her Tom is such a good boy. She should be proud of the man he is becoming. He takes good care of that aunt of his.'

'Do you see Tom much?'

'Not as much as when it all happened. When Sue was first arrested I used to call in and check he and Annie were coping, but I got the impression Helen didn't like me interfering, so my visits grew less frequent, until they stopped altogether. I occasionally see Tom in Romsey when I'm shopping, and I say hi, but that's about it.'

'What about his sister Annie? When did you last see her?'

'I'm not sure I can remember. She seemed to take Ben's loss harder than Tom; I suppose it's because she knew him longer. She couldn't forgive her mum for what happened, and she took off as soon as she turned sixteen. I don't know if Tom or Helen are still in touch with her or not. Poor kid, losing both her parents like that. It's not right.'

He sensed she wanted to say something, so he

changed his approach. 'You have a lovely house. Have you lived here long?'

'Ten years or so, I suppose.'

'Where did you live before?'

'We were in Freemantle, three streets from the Dewis' house.'

'So this bungalow must be an upgrade on that place, right?'

'Oh yes. My husband was from Romsey originally, and the plan was always that we'd return here when the time was right.'

'Do you still work?'

'No, I retired five or six years ago. We weren't able to have children, so we managed to save more than most. My husband still acts as a Magistrate in Southampton to keep his mind occupied. I'm a lady of leisure these days.'

'You used to work in the textiles factory, didn't you?'

'Oh that was years ago, but yes I did. Sue and I both did for a time.'

'What did you do there?'

'We were both secretaries. Sue managed Ben's diary, and I managed George's.'

'What caused you to leave?'

'I think they realised they didn't need two of us. To be honest, we spent most of the day nattering, because there wasn't enough work for both of us to do.'

'So they sacked you?'

'No! Sue left voluntarily. She thought it was fairer for me to stay on, as I had a secretarial qualification from college. I think she got a job as a compliance inspector after that.'

'Oh I see. Were you there when all the troubles began?'

'I presume you're referring to the Inland Revenue audit? I wasn't around then. If you ask me, though, I'd say their troubles began long before that.'

'What do you mean?'

'Well, about six months before the audit, George hired this hotshot kid from university who wanted to revolutionise the business. He was hired as an office manager, and his role was to identify cost-cutting methods. Well, one of the first changes he suggested was to relieve me of my duties. He said they didn't need a secretary as there were computer programmes that could be used to manage the diaries, and he could handle any other administration duties for them. He had a way about him: he could be persuasive. George figured he was already paying an office manager, so why pay a secretary too? They were good about it, and offered a generous redundancy package. I didn't care. I wanted to set up my own business anyway.'

'What was the name of the office manager?'

'Kevin Lyons. He was moderately handsome, but had an inflated opinion of himself: reckoned he was God's gift, you know? He didn't do it for me, but then I was ten or so years older than him.'

'What troubles did Lyons cause?'

'It'll sound trivial now, but at the time, it made a big difference to the way things were run. Some of his cost-cutting schemes had an impact on the atmosphere of the place. Ben had always prided himself on treating staff like family. He always said happy staff work harder for you. Lyons suggested scrapping the staff canteen in favour of vending machines. It saved them thousands a year, but suddenly the staff had to bring their lunch in with them. There was nothing the union could do about it. He also proposed a reduction in the rate of overtime, from double to time and a half. Of course, people still worked the overtime when it was available, but the incentive was gone. Ben seemed to have a different member of staff in his office everyday complaining about one thing or another. He was fighting a losing battle as the changes were saving the company money, and that was all that mattered to George.'

'Do you know what happened to Kevin Lyons after the factory closed? I haven't been able to trace him so far.'

'No idea, I'm afraid. Once I left, I was too busy with my own business to pay attention to what was happening at the factory.'

'What was your business?'

'I set up a temping agency for secretarial staff and admin assistants. It's still going strong, but I don't run it anymore. I still enjoy my share of the profits though, which is good enough for me.'

'Do you think Ben stole the pension money?'

She freshened their tea cups. 'I honestly don't know. I don't believe he could have done, as he wasn't like that. I know Sue didn't think he took it.'

'What do you think happened to the money?'

'I have no idea I'm afraid. Why?'

'Tom and Sue both think whoever stole the money may have killed Ben.'

She rolled her eyes.

'What is it? You don't agree?'

She sipped her tea. 'It doesn't matter what I think. Now, if that's all your questions, I must get on. I have things to do, and places to go.'

He fixed her with a stare. 'I'm not going anywhere until you tell me what's on your mind. You've been hiding something since I arrived. Whatever it is: you can tell me. I'm only acting in Sue's best interests.'

'That's just it: is it in her best interests?'

'I don't follow.'

'Forget I said anything.'

'No, I want to know what you meant. You didn't answer my question earlier either: do you believe Sue didn't do it?' He saw her glance away. 'That's it, isn't it? You think she killed Ben.'

Her head snapped round. 'No...well, oh, I don't know. If she didn't do it, why did she ask me to lie to the police?'

'What did she ask you to say?'

She sighed. 'Oh well, she's the one who hired you, so I suppose she's anticipated the truth coming out.'

'I need to know.'

'Okay, okay. It's true Sue and I met on the Saturday night -'

'To go to the cinema,' he interrupted.

'Yes, well, that was the plan. I'd arranged to collect her at six, with the film's previews due to start at half past. I arrived five minutes early and she was already waiting for me. She got in, and we drove off, but I sensed something was wrong. She was quieter than usual. I asked her what was wrong, and she dismissed it, but I pressed, and she suddenly burst into tears. I pulled over and she told me it was about Ben. We decided not to see the film, and instead we went to a quiet pub where nobody would know us. We shared a bottle of wine. She eventually told me Ben had…that Ben had forced himself on her the night before. I couldn't believe it. She kept saying it wasn't his fault, and he was under immense pressure. I told her she had to report him, but she refused, saying he didn't need the additional stress. She said he hadn't meant to, it was just his way of trying to exert some control over his life. Things were bad at the factory. With the missing pension money, and his signature on all the paperwork, he was looking at a spell behind bars. I told her that was no excuse, and that he had no right to take his frustration out on her. That's when she told me it wasn't the first time he'd been violent towards her that year.'

'Violent how?'

'He'd hit her I think.'

'Did she show you evidence? Bruising, anything like that?'

'No. She said she'd been avoiding him, and he hadn't been violent for a few weeks until the rape. She said she wouldn't go to the police, but would sort it out in her own way. I wasn't sure what that meant, but I told her she was welcome to stay at my place whenever she needed.'

'That doesn't mean she was planning to kill him. She might have meant she was going to take him to some kind of counselling.'

'The thing is: I didn't drop her home at ten like we told the police. I dropped her home shortly after nine.'

'Why did you lie?'

'She asked me to. The film would have ended just

before, and ten was when she was due back, so that's what she told the police when they first interviewed her. She didn't want them to catch her in a lie, and suspect the worst, so she asked me to corroborate the story. What else could I do? She was my best friend, and I drove us home over the limit. If I'd have told them the truth I'd have incriminated us both.'

'Okay, so you lied about the time, but that still doesn't mean she killed him.'

'When she got out of my car, she seemed a lot more positive. I think it had been a relief to get it off her chest and to talk about things. She looked determined as she walked to her front door, like she knew what she needed to do. She never told me what happened between me dropping her, and the ambulance arriving. She had motive and opportunity to kill him. What if he tried to rape her again and she snapped?'

38

The three bedroom house in Valley Park looks like all of the others in the street. Built in the early nineties, it still looks new, despite the weather's gentle erosion of the brickwork. There is a warm, family feeling to the cul-de-sac. Beth could imagine living in one, and watching her children playing in the garden, from the kitchen window.

She knocked on the door. A moment later, she heard the door being unlocked. It opened with the latch firmly in place. A pair of terrified eyes stared back at her.

She raised her identification. 'Good afternoon. I'm Detective Sergeant Beth Taylor from Major Investigations. You called about an assault?'

The eyes stared at the identification, before the door closed, so the latch could be removed. The door reopened, and the terrified man stepped back allowing her to enter. Beth stepped through, noticing him scanning the street, before closing the door, locking it, and reapplying the latch. He pointed for her to walk through to the living room at the rear of the property.

The television was on, but the woman seated in the single armchair wasn't watching it. Her eyes were fixed firmly on the garden. She didn't even look up as

Beth entered.

The man turned off the television, and then sat on the remaining sofa. It was a large living room, with a dining table and chairs to one side. Beth noticed photographs of the couple, taken during happier times, hanging from the walls.

Beth waited for the couple to speak, but neither did. The woman continued to stare out of the window, and the man's gaze was now transfixed on the carpet.

Beth removed her notepad, and opened it to a clean page. 'I know this can't be easy for either of you, but I need you to tell me, in your own words, what happened to you last night?'

The woman turns her head to face Beth, and for the first time, Beth sees the thick bandage around the woman's ear. The woman's eyes are red raw from crying. 'We were out for dinner…Michael proposed…' Her voice trails off, and she pushes a fresh tissue to her nose.

'It was supposed to be the perfect night,' the man picked up. 'I spent weeks planning it. I booked a table at our favourite Italian. I told the manager what I had planned. He agreed to hide the ring in her dessert. Everything was going to plan, until…' He paused, and looked over at the woman. 'Until we returned to the car. That's when she…when she…she seemed harmless at first, but then…'

Beth's gaze moved between the two of them. 'Please, take your time.'

'She put a knife to my fiancée's throat, and made us drive her back here. She forced us in, and…'

'What did this woman look like? Can you describe

her for me?'

The man looked at Beth. 'She was big. I mean, she wasn't fat, but not thin. She was taller than me. I'm five foot nine, and she was at least five inches taller.'

Beth already knew the answer to the next question. It was the reason she'd agreed to come and meet the couple. 'What colour was her hair?'

'It was blonde, almost golden in colour.'

Beth wrote the description in the book. 'What happened when you got back here?'

The man looked back at his wife. Beth could see he wanted his fiancée to continue the story, but her gaze had returned to the garden beyond the window. 'She told us to go upstairs, and when we got there, she told us to remove our clothes. The knife was so big. I wanted to try and overpower her, but I froze. She had this look in her eyes. I don't know how to describe it…it was a look of pure evil. She -'

'She cut off my ear,' the fiancée interrupts, without turning. 'It stung; it still does. She said she would cut me up piece-by-piece if we didn't do as she said. She cut my bra off and made us lie on the bed. She told him to…to…' She can't bring herself to say the words.

The man's head is buried in his hands. The fiancée stares at him. Her look is a mix of empathy and disgust. She told Beth exactly what he did to her, and Beth's stomach turned as she recorded the details in her book. The man sobbed throughout the explanation.

At the end of the story, Beth showed them Kelly's printed profile picture. The man looked terrified again. He can barely look at the image, before passing it to his fiancée to confirm the identity.

The fiancée stared at the image with a look of pure hatred. 'It's her. That's the bitch who made him rape me.'

SATURDAY

39

'I want you to watch out for a black BMW,' Sanza said. 'Okay? That's what he drives. If you see one pull in, that's when I'm most likely to need you.'

Carmichael glanced at the reflection of the woman in the rear-view mirror. She was staring out of the window, chewing her nails. The purple bruise was spread across the right side of her face.

'Black BMW. Got it. Believe me, if I see him, you'll know about it.'

Sanza squeezed the woman's hand for encouragement and then the two of them slid out of the car. Sanza wrapped an arm around her shoulders as he tentatively led her back to the house she'd called home for seven years.

He hadn't recognised the number that woke him this morning. He answered it instinctively, and his first thought was that Sanza only used a different number because Carmichael was ignoring his calls. He expected a lecture, but something was wrong. He sensed it straight away.

There was fear in the cleric's voice as he spoke. 'I know you've been avoiding me, Johnson, but I need your urgent help with a matter. Please, don't hang up. This is important.'

He'd given Sanza the benefit of the doubt and

agreed to hear him out. The last time they'd spoken, Sanza had told him he would sleep better since he'd confessed, and the truth was, he had. The nightmares had stopped, and his mind was sharper, even without the Dexampex. Not that he would admit as much to Sanza. Despite everything he'd heard, there was still a nagging doubt in the back of his mind.

'I need some muscle,' Sanza continued. 'One of the church members came to me on Thursday. Her husband beat her. She's in a bad state. I've been looking after her, but now she needs to collect her things from their house. She can't go back there alone. I'm going to go with her, but I'm not…he should be at work, but in case he is there…look, I could do with your help.'

'What do you expect me to do about it?'

'I don't *expect* you to do anything, Johnson. It's just…you're the type of person that people think twice about fighting. I know you're handy with your fists, more so than me. I thought if you were with us, he'd be less likely to give us any hassle, *if* he returned. Please, Johnson? I wouldn't ask if I wasn't worried.'

What could he say?

'Okay, I'll drive you. What time do you want to go?'

'Thank you, Johnson. He should be at work from ten, but we'll go at midday to be safe. We'll meet you at the church. She lives in Highfield.'

The house was a standard three-bed semi, in a nice-looking neighbourhood. He kept the stereo on as he waited. The warm sun's rays were welcoming. The windows were down, and he could easily have fallen asleep. He didn't notice the BMW until it was on the driveway.

He tried to phone Sanza, but the phone went unanswered. He climbed out of the car and hurried over to the property. The front door was open and he could hear the husband shouting the odds upstairs. He took the stairs two at-a-time, and found the three of them in the main bedroom. The woman was huddled close to Sanza, like she was using him as a human shield. The husband was pointing his finger at them, demanding to know who Sanza was.

'Hey pal,' Carmichael said, slightly out of breath. 'There's no need for things to escalate. Let Elaine collect her things and we'll be on our way.'

The man turned and his frame filled the doorway. His arms were like tree trunks, and covered in tattoos. His neck was the width of his head. He was larger than Carmichael, and snarled at the interruption. 'And what the hell is it to you? Who are you two?'

Carmichael could suddenly understand why Sanza hadn't wanted to come alone. He stepped forward. 'We're here to look after Elaine. We don't want any trouble.'

'You're trespassing in my house, and you're interfering in things you don't understand.'

'Domestic abuse means the same thing in any language. Elaine wants us here, and so long as that remains, we're not trespassing.'

'Alright, smartass, seeing as you must be the brains of the outfit, how's this for you? You've got ten seconds to get out of my house. Me and Elaine need to talk about things.'

Sanza stepped forward. 'We're not going anywhere. Anything you want to say can be said while we're here. She's not safe to be left alone with you.'

'That's none of your damn business, pal. You've got no right to come between a man and his wife!'

'I have a right when that wife begs me to protect her from her abusive husband.'

The man snarled again, and stomped around the bed. 'Say that again. Go on, I dare you.' He pushed Sanza backwards.

Elaine whimpered.

Carmichael stepped into the room. 'Why don't you pick on someone your own size?' He rolled up his sleeves. 'You know there's nothing I hate more than a dickhead who thinks it's okay to lay his hands on a defenceless woman. It's evil.'

The man smirked. 'Okay, pal, you want a piece of me? Fine. I'll give you one chance to change your mind. When you're begging me to stop beating you, remember I gave you this chance.'

The man charged at him, wrapping those enormous arms around him and squeezing. He wriggled, but his arms were pinned at his sides. The man lifted him slightly, and then hurled him towards the bathroom. He clattered into the airing cupboard door, but was soon back on his feet. He looked for a weapon, and finding nothing but a small broom, he held it across himself defensively.

The man roared with laughter, and that was then he noticed the guy was missing several teeth. Carmichael gripped the broom like a sword and brought it crashing down on the man's head. The handle snapped, but the brute was temporarily stunned. Carmichael dipped his shoulder and charged at the man's gut. The barge connected, sending a shooting pain through Carmichael's spine, but the brute crashed to the ground.

'Now!' Carmichael yelled.

Sanza grabbed Elaine's hand and they tore out of the bedroom and down the stairs. The man was rising. Carmichael looked for something else to defend himself with, but it was just the two of them on the landing.

Elaine's husband was on his feet again, and he looked even angrier. 'I'm going to enjoy this even more.'

Carmichael threw a punch into the brute's gut, but he barely flinched, following up with a one-two to Carmichael's already bruised face. The detective crashed to his knees. The brute grabbed his arm and shirt and threw Carmichael into what must have been a spare room. He crashed into some cardboard boxes stacked in a corner of the room. The boxes toppled over, knocking over a bag of golf clubs. Carmichael grabbed a wood, and pushed himself back up. The brute took a step backwards when he saw the weapon.

'This ends now,' Carmichael roared at him. 'Apologise to your wife and let us out of here, or so help me, I will end you.'

The husband snarled and charged forward once again. Carmichael lifted the club into the air like a baseball bat and swung it into the approaching brute. He connected with the forehead, and the man stumbled to the right. Carmichael lifted the club again and brought it down on the man's back, sending him crashing into another stack of boxes. He hit him again, and again. The brute was making no effort to defend himself, but still the blows rained down.

'Johnson, stop!' Sanza yelled as he came running into the room. He grabbed the club, and Carmichael was about to hit him, but stopped when he realised who it was. 'Enough, Johnson. He won't give us any more trouble. We should get out of here. Elaine's got what she came for. You did well. He won't give her any more hassle.'

He blinked several times, before glancing at the bloody mess at his feet. 'Is he still…'

Sanza checked for a pulse, before smiling. 'He's still alive, don't worry. We'll call for an ambulance once we're on our way.'

He closed his eyes, and let out a relieved breath. 'I don't know what came over me…I…I -'

'You were doing God's work, Johnson. It's okay. I know it feels strange when God first takes control. You'll get used to it. He's chosen you, my friend. I told you the other night, he wants you to help battle the devil's slaves on this earth. Come on, let's get out of here. I'll wipe your prints off this club. We should celebrate.'

'No, I don't want to celebrate. I have things to do.'

He looked disappointed. 'Okay. Drop Elaine and me back at the church. I need to get Elaine into some sheltered accommodation. You should be proud of what you achieved here today.'

Carmichael followed him back to the car. He started the engine, and couldn't help the smile breaking out across his face.

40

Kelly pauses the video clip. Paul has been out all day, meaning she's been stuck in. With nothing to do, and only loneliness for company, she has been watching the small video she made on Thursday night. She didn't need to film the newly-engaged couple having sex, but she wanted a keepsake.

The look of utter defeat on the man's face as he forces himself inside his petrified and bloody fiancée is priceless. She can almost see the cogs turning in his mind. He wants to stop, to wrestle the blade out of Kelly's hand, but like most, his instinct is for life preservation. Everyone begs for a few seconds more in the end.

She doesn't believe in regret. When her time comes she is confident she will be the first person in human history to accept it without argument.

The man is crying as he climaxes inside his fiancée, but Kelly has replayed that part of the clip more than any other. It is only for the briefest of moments, but the man cannot hide the pleasure from his face, as he ejaculates. She has paused and studied his face. He looks repulsed by his own base instinct. It is the perfect image of man's sin: taking pleasure from dark acts. She is tempted to print the still and send it to him as a reminder of what he has done.

Leaving them alive was risky. It's possible they will report the incident to the police. They'd be able to give a fairly detailed description of her. She could have killed them. She could have run the knife across his throat while he sodomised his fiancée. He'd have bled out. The girl wouldn't have given her any trouble: she didn't have it in her. It would have been simple, but that would have given them the easy way out.

For Kelly, it's much better that they have to continue with their lives after what happened. She is confident they won't go to the police about the incident. It will be too painful for the woman to replay the events in her mind, and he won't want to admit he let someone like Kelly get the better of him. Even so, she knows it is wise to maintain a low profile.

Paul has been stomping around the house since his return. She cannot understand what is making him so angry. She can sense he is worried about something but he won't let her in. She has tried, but he isn't willing to share. She hasn't seen him like this before. His worrying is making her anxious. She refuses to accept he has found out what she did to Todd, Josh, and Claire. He would have reacted by now if he knew. Even so, he is keeping something from her.

She is looking out of the window at the sun setting in the distance. A large black spider is busy building a web on the other side of the glass. She watches as it carefully links each part of the web to the next. It moves across the window so delicately. It reminds her of the delicate way her father would tuck her in at night. He would carefully tuck the edges of the sheet under her body, so that she was cocooned and safe.

Their upbringing should have been something out

of a fairy-tale. Father was a surgeon, and mother was a midwife at the same hospital. Nobody was surprised when they married. They owned a big house and hosted fine dinner parties, but something was missing. They had everything in place to offer a child a good future: financially comfortable, a large house on the edge of the New Forest, and stability. They longed for a child to complete their family, but it seemed fate had other plans.

After years of trying, they finally conceived, but she miscarried six months into the pregnancy. Depression followed, but they resolved to try again. A little over a year later, she conceived again, but this time the baby arrived still-born. The trauma of losing one child during pregnancy can be enough to put anyone off, but twice was truly heart-breaking. The doctors warned she may never manage to carry full-term. Kelly knows she would have given up, but mother was determined to defy the odds.

Four years after they started trying, a little boy was born, and they were both delighted. Father had an heir to his kingdom, and mother had a little prince. They wrapped him in cotton wool. Mother always feared he would fall sick and that her heart would be broken all over again. Father worried about her state of mind, but he saw the joy their son brought her. She left her job, and chose to educate their son at home. Father's career continued to rise, and so did his hours. The son saw little of his father during the day.

Before Kelly came along, father would come into the boy's room late at night, and tell him stories about his day at work. Occasionally, father would bring him sweeties, but it was their secret: the boy was told not to tell mother. She would be sleeping in the bedroom down the hall, oblivious to her husband's late night visits. Kelly doesn't know whether mother chose to ignore the signs, or was too tired to care.

The late night visits became more regular, and father's treats became more lavish. Still, the boy was sworn to secrecy. Kelly would hear her brother gently crying himself to sleep after father had tucked him in. At such a young age, she didn't know why father made him so sad.

She discovered why, when father came to her room the first time. She pretended to be asleep, even as he gently shook her awake. He perched on the edge of the bed, rubbing her leg through the duvet. She heard him rustle his paper bag, before offering her a sweet. She sat up in bed and rubbed her eyes. She politely declined the sweet, as she could still taste toothpaste in her mouth. He told her she didn't need to worry, that he would take care of her. He told her to move over and then he climbed under the covers with her. She told him she was tired. He told her he'd had a hard day at work, and all he wanted was a cuddle. She placed her arms around him, and he squeezed her tight. He only held her that first night. She eventually fell asleep with her head on his chest.

He returned to her room the next night, and again gave her a sweetie. It was lemon-flavoured. He cuddled her tightly again, and then he told her what he wanted her to do. He explained that this was how people showed each other that they love them.

'You do love me, don't you?' he asked.

What else could she say? He was her father, and if he said this was 'love', who was she to disagree? Night after night he would come to her room.

Mother became withdrawn. Even with Kelly and her brother to talk to, she was lonely. She missed the warmth of her husband's body. They still shared the same bed, but their marriage was a shell. Mother self-medicated: she didn't want to know why her husband no longer made sexual advances towards her.

Kelly was a voracious reader as a child, and would read any book she could get her hands on. At age seven, she found a copy of Lolita in her father's bedside drawer. She read it in a day, and that was the moment she realised how wrong her father's love was. She couldn't talk to her brother about it. He was an automaton: a recluse who sought his parents' acceptance.

By this time, mother was barely functioning. She was awake long enough to feed them and refill her glass of gin. If there was no screaming, she remained locked inside herself.

Kelly felt her brother's sadness. She knew he couldn't do anything about it, and so she resolved to save him. One night after dinner, she secreted a kitchen knife under her clothes, and then snuck to her room and hid it beneath her pillow. When her father stopped by that night, he had no idea what was to follow. She tingled with nervous energy. Even now, the thought of him ignorantly climbing into her bed sent a shiver down her spine. He removed his clothes without a word, and ran a bony figure along her arm.

She waited for him to start touching himself before she reached under the pillow and coiled her fingers around the knife's handle. She didn't pull the knife out straight away, as a moment's panic washed over her. She'd killed plenty of bugs and rats in her time, but never anything bigger than a mole. She worried she wouldn't have the strength to do it; that she would fall at the final hurdle. His hand slowly moved up her leg, and in that split second, she knew she would rather die trying than to suffer the abuse any longer.

Lifting her hand high into the air, she thrust the blade into his neck. He spluttered in pained surprise, pressing the bed sheet against the warm, sticky blood as it gushed. She turned on the bedside light, and sat there watching, as the tone of his skin became paler. He didn't speak in the two minutes it took for him to bleed to death. He blinked rapidly throughout, as he stared at her. She couldn't remember whether he'd looked regretful, or whether her memory was tainted by imagination.

Making sure her brother was still asleep, she crept to her mother's room, and slowly opened the door. Mother was snoring; the bedside table littered with pill bottles. Mother didn't notice Kelly climbing onto father's side of the bed, nor did she stir when her eye mask was removed by her child. Kelly tried waking her: to demand how and why she'd allowed father to be so cruel, but she remained comatose. Kelly was less violent this time, drawing the blade's sharp edge across mother's exposed throat in one swift motion.

Mother's body jerked longer than father's, but the outcome was the same. Satisfied with her efforts, she cleaned the blade and returned it to the kitchen, before climbing into her brother's bed and going to sleep.

The spider's legs remind her of the hairs on father's arm as he clutched the bedsheet to his neck.

Her brother took the blame for what happened. The authorities tried to separate them, but their bond was now forged in blood, and there was nothing anyone could do to keep them apart. Due to the violent nature of the crime, her brother was sectioned at the secure wing of the Angel Hall Hospital near Dorchester. Kelly visited him regularly, and when the time was right, she helped him to escape.

SUNDAY

41

Carmichael didn't look up as Sue was escorted to the table. Tom was fetching tea and cake again. Visiting hours on a Sunday are 14:15 to 16:30.

'I was surprised to see you requesting a visit so soon,' she began. 'Does that mean you've made some kind of progress?'

He finally looked at her. 'Do you know what, Sue, I don't like liars. Never have. It's not good for business, and it wastes my time. It's a real pet hate in fact. So, you can imagine how angry it made me when I discovered you'd been lying to me.'

'I don't know what you're talking -'

'What happens in The Insider, Sue?'

Her lips moved, but no words came out at first. 'Well, it's, uh…it's…it's been a long time. Let me see, it's about a guy from the tobacco industry revealing secrets to a reporter.'

'Wow! Such a comprehensive review, but I could have read that on the poster.' His tone harsh. 'The thing is: I want to hear about it from someone who's watched it. Is it funny? Is it sad? Is there a twist at the end? I love a story that's packed with suspense and with a twist you never see coming. Is it like that, Sue? Will I enjoy it?'

'Well, it's based on a true story, I remember that -

,

'What happens at the end, Sue? I mean, you've seen it. That's where you were on the night Ben was murdered. Surely you can remember whether you enjoyed the film or not?'

'With respect, Mr Carmichael, a lot happened that night, you'll have to forgive me if my memory isn't so great.'

'But surely you'd remember if you'd seen the film or not? After all, that's what you told the police. That's where you said you were, and why you didn't arrive home until ten.'

Her eyes widened, as she realised what he was getting at. She opened her mouth to speak, but he cut her off with an accusatory finger. 'I met your friend Patricia Rankin.' A flicker of recognition in her eyes. 'That's right, good old Aunt Pat: the woman who drove you to and from the cinema that night. What do you think Pat told me?'

She glanced nervously in Tom's direction. He was still four people from the front of the queue. He smiled and waved at her. She looked back at Carmichael. 'Does Tom know?'

'I wanted to discuss it with you first.'

'You can't tell him. Please? If he finds out now that I lied to the police, I…I worry he won't believe the rest of what I said.'

'I wouldn't blame him! In fact, I'm struggling to believe a single word that comes out of your mouth.'

She leaned in closer. 'Okay, so I lied about where we were, but I didn't kill, Ben. I swear I'm telling the truth.'

'Pat told me that Ben…that he raped you. It's not

the picture you painted of him when I met you last week. You made out that he was a good man under pressure. Now I learn from your friend that he was abusive towards you on a number of occasions. It gives you motive, Sue.'

'I didn't kill him, Mr Carmichael. You have to believe me!'

'What time did you arrive home? I need to hear the truth, Sue. I need you to tell me exactly what happened that night. No bullshit! If you didn't kill Ben, I need to know everything.'

She glanced back to Tom again. He was two from the front. 'Okay, okay, but you can't tell Tom. He can't learn of what Ben did to me. It would destroy his good memories of his father. He idolised Ben. His desire to clear my name is to solve his hero's murder. I don't want that tarnished.'

'I won't tell him, but if I get even a hint you're spinning me a lie, I'll tell him everything and then walk away.'

She closed her eyes. 'Pat and I went to a pub. I assume she's told you that and what we discussed. It was good to unburden the pain. I still loved Ben despite what had happened, and I was certain he would never do it again. Pat and I shared some wine, and then she drove me home. I arrived back around nine o'clock. I went in to the house and Ben was in the lounge arguing with someone. I poked my head through the doorway, and saw he was on the phone. I was going to ask him if he wanted a cup of tea, but when he saw me he marched over and closed the door, shutting me out. He didn't want me to hear whatever or whoever he was talking to -'

'Was that unusual?'

'I didn't think so at the time. He often took calls with clients at the weekend, and the calls were confidential. I went through to the kitchen and poured myself a glass of water. I remember feeling cross as he hadn't washed the things from dinner. We'd had a casserole before I'd gone out with Pat, and the chopping board and knife were still on the counter, topped with a stack of our dirty plates. I thought about washing-up, but my head was pounding, and as Ben had said he would do it, I figured it could wait until morning. I think the mixture of crying and wine was causing the ache in my head, so I decided to head to bed and get an early night. I went upstairs, and checked on the children. They were both fast asleep. I remember kissing them both on the forehead and closing their doors. My head felt even worse, and I wondered whether I was starting to get a migraine. I suffer from them, you see. I went to the bathroom, and took one of my pills. They're pretty strong, and tend to knock me out quickly.'

Tom was now at the front of the queue.

'Something must have disturbed me, because I woke. I don't remember whether it was a noise or a light, or what, but something caused me to wake. I was still half asleep, but I saw it was nearly eleven. Ben hadn't come to bed, so I decided to go downstairs and see if he was okay. It was so quiet. There wasn't even any noise outside. I saw the kitchen light was on, so I assumed Ben was in there, maybe doing the washing-up. I walked through the door, and found him slumped on the floor immediately to my left. His chest was covered in blood, and the chopping knife was lying on the floor next to him. It was surreal. I thought I was having a bad dream. I remember pinching myself, and laughing hysterically. When I looked down and he was still there, I realised he must have been stabbed, and I panicked. He was still alive, so I put a tea towel over his wound, and pushed his hands on top of it. I remembered our next door neighbour was a vet, and stupidly thought he'd be able to do something to help Ben. I don't remember stumbling next door, but apparently that's what I did. The vet came round and an ambulance was called.'

'Why didn't you tell this to the police? I'm sure they could have tested your blood to confirm the presence of whatever pill you'd taken.'

'I was in shock. I didn't know what had happened or why. I'd discovered the man I shared my life with was fighting for his own. It was like a nightmare that I would eventually wake from. The calendar said I was going out with Pat to the cinema. When the police officer asked if that's where I'd been, I instinctively said yes, without thinking about what I was saying. By the time they interviewed me at the police station it was taken as gospel that I'd been to the cinema with Pat. I was trapped in the lie. I knew that if I told them the truth at that point, it would seem like I was fabricating a story. I kept thinking they wouldn't arrest me, because I hadn't done it. Then when it went to trial, I was sure I wouldn't be convicted because I didn't do it.'

'But why keep it a secret for so long?'

'After my appeal failed, I didn't see the point in speaking up. Again, it would look like the desperate act of a woman facing a life behind bars. Besides, what difference would it have made? If anything, it gives me more time to have done it.'

'Is that the whole truth? There's nothing else you haven't told me?'

Tom placed the tray on the table. 'Everything okay?'

'Everything's fine, dear,' Sue said, smiling at him. She shot a glare at Carmichael.

'Everything's fine, Tom,' he confirmed.

Tom sat. 'Good.'

'Sue, when you found Ben, was there anything out of the ordinary? Do you remember if anything in the kitchen looked out of place? Was the back door or kitchen window open? Did you hear any movement outside, like someone had just left?'

She shook her head. 'No, nothing like that.'

'The police used the lack of a break-in as a factor in accusing you. They said either the killer had access to the property or Ben had allowed his killer to enter the house. We need to establish who he might have let in so late on Saturday evening. Did Ben have any enemies you know of?'

'Ben was generally liked by most who met him. I wouldn't say he had any enemies as such, but with the embezzlement accusation hanging over him, he wasn't popular with staff at the factory. Those that knew Ben well knew he wouldn't have taken the money, but there were cynics as well. I suppose it's possible one of them could have done it.'

42

Beth exhaled, as she stepped out of the rickety lift. The smell must bother the residents, yet nobody had made an effort to clean it up.

She walked past Claire's old flat. The police cordon was still there, but it wouldn't be long until the council was ready to let it out again. She stopped outside Victor' flat. She knocked loudly on his door. She hoped he was home. She had brought a bag of Indian takeaway, and a large bottle of cider for him. She'd also brought the print outs of Kelly and Roxanne. She needed a formal identification of the blonde's presence at Claire's flat on the day of the alleged suicide, if she was to convince D.C.I. Payne of the connection.

She put the bag of food down, and knocked again, but there was still no answer. Beth bent down and looked through the letter box. 'Victor? Are you there? It's D.S. Beth Taylor. We spoke last Sunday about your neighbour Claire. Can I come in? I've brought food and drink for you. Please? It's really important.'

She couldn't hear movement inside, but she did notice the foul stench. It was a smell she recognised, and one that hadn't been there last week. 'Victor, if you're there, can you open the door? Otherwise, I'm going to force it open.'

Silence greeted her. She straightened up, and, after radioing in her suspicions, she barged the door with her shoulder. On the third attempt, the door opened, with the doorframe splintering as it did. The foul-smelling gas was even stronger inside. Beth instinctively covered her face with her jacket, and moved along the dark corridor. The food containers from the previous week were still littering the floor. The door to the main room was closed. She counted to five before slowly opening it. The stench erupted out of the room, and her jacket was no longer a suitable mask. She did her best to hold her breath and marched over to the window at the far side of the room, pushing it open. She sucked in fresh air, before turning back with a tissue over her mouth and nose.

Victor's lifeless eyes stared back at her from the single armchair. The dark skin on his face was paler. A line of dried blood joined together his nose and upper lip. His mouth was slightly open, frozen in a ghoulish grin. On the small table in front of him, she saw a foil packet, containing powdered crystals. In his hand, he was still clutching the hollowed out biro he must have used to snort the crystals.

She pressed her fingers to his neck, even though she knew it was pointless. The skin was cold. She leaned closer to examine the body for signs of a struggle, before heading for the front door. She radioed in confirmation of the death and requested the Medical Examiner on site immediately. Beth slumped down outside the flat, and a single tear escaped. She wiped it from her cheek with the back of her hand.

Why am I crying? I hardly knew him.

But her tears weren't for the loss of a close friend, they were pity for the waste of another life to Class A drugs. They were also for the loss of her one chance to tie Kelly or Roxanne to Claire Willis' sudden death.

MONDAY

43

Melissa was chewing her fingernails when Carmichael arrived. She didn't wait to be invited in to the room.

'How was your trip to the prison yesterday?' she asked.

He sighed as he sat. 'Well, she admitted to not being at the cinema on the night Ben died, but there was little else she could say: I'd caught her in a lie.'

'So do you think she's lying about the rest?'

He considered the question for a minute. 'My gut says she's not lying, but I'm certain there's something else she's holding back.'

'Like what?'

'That's just it: I don't know.'

'Do you think she knows who did it?'

He shook his head. 'If she knew who killed Ben, she would have said something much sooner, right? You wouldn't spend sixteen years of your life behind bars if you knew who'd done it. Besides, I gave her plenty of chances to come clean. She swears she's not hiding anything else.'

'What does her son think about his mum's lie about the cinema?'

'He doesn't know. She asked me not to say anything to him. I don't think it would matter anyway.

He refuses to accept the possibility that she might be guilty anyway. Have you made any progress tracking the mysterious Kevin Lyons yet?'

'That's what I wanted to speak to you about. I've found him.'

'You have? That's fantastic.'

She scrunched her nose. 'You're not going to like what I have to say, Johnson.'

'Why not? He isn't dead is he?'

'Not exactly…' She trailed off as she tried to find the words to tell him the truth.

'Melissa, spit it out.'

'Okay, okay,' she relented. 'I spent a couple of days looking for any newspaper articles mentioning him. There were a couple up north where the name Kevin Lyons appeared, but neither subject matched the age range or description of our Kevin Lyons. So, I decided to go darker.'

'Darker? What do you mean?'

'You know what the dark web is, right? If you imagine the internet we use day-to-day as a three dimensional map, the dark web is what lives in the shadows and beneath the surface of the map. It's hidden from everyday view, but can be accessed using certain software, if you know where to look.'

'I know what the dark web is. It's where people go to buy drugs and guns -'

'And to cheat on their partners, that's right. Those hackers who stole the database of users from the Ashley Madison site last year, published the names and addresses on the dark web. However, it can also be used to find people who don't want to be found. Armed with the right information it's possible to track virtually anyone.'

'What kind of information?'

'I managed to get hold of a copy of Kevin Lyons last payslip from the Dewis' factory. That gave me his name, address, and national insurance number. I entered the details into a dark net search engine this morning and found him. Well, sort of.'

'What do you mean?'

'I mean, I found the person who went by the name of Kevin Lyons sixteen years ago. His real name is Steven Preston.'

'His real name?'

She nodded. 'Steven Preston, born 1976, spent some years at a secure facility as a child. He was imprisoned at the age of nineteen for conning elderly pensioners out of their life savings. From what I found, his victims were all living at a retirement home in Bournemouth, where Preston volunteered. He was a fitness instructor who visited the home twice a week. By the time he was caught, he'd swindled close to three hundred grand through complex pyramid schemes. He was released to an address near Cadnam at the age of twenty-three, before changing his name to Kevin Lyons. Presumably he faked the degree certificate he used to secure his job at the factory.'

'That's incredible! Is he still at the address now?'

'I'll come to that. He is registered at the property as Kevin Lyons from 1997 to 2000. He paid the council tax during that time, but was not included in the UK Census carried out in April 2001. In fact, I cannot trace any record of him post May 2000, which is -'

'Two months after Ben died,' Carmichael finished

for her.

'Exactly! He disappears, and I cannot find him anywhere since.'

'You think he died?'

'If he did, his death was never registered formally.'

'You think he was killed and his body never discovered? Like a hit?'

She shook her head. 'Bear with me, as this is a stretch, but I think he changed his name again. In June 2000, a new name appears on the council tax records for the address in Cadnam. Ordinarily that wouldn't make me suspicious. My first assumption was that Lyons moved out and a new tenant or property owner arrived.'

'I sense a 'but' coming here.'

'A big 'but' as it goes. I recognised the name of the new council tax payer, so I did some digging. I checked the history of the new name against the address and National Insurance details I had been checking for Lyons and Preston. It's the same person. The new name has been using the same National Insurance number since June 2000, one month after Lyons disappeared.'

'Hold on, so what you're saying is Preston became Kevin Lyons, and then after Dewis died, took a new name again?'

She nodded grimly.

'So who is he?'

She gulped. 'Paul Sanza.'

He opened his mouth to speak, but no words came out.

'I know what you're going to say,' she said eagerly, 'but I don't have an agenda here. I can show you all the paperwork. It's him. Lyons *is* Sanza. Sanza is Lyons. I was as surprised as you.' She placed a printed image in front of him. 'I got this copy of Lyons' photo card driving licence on the dark web.' She placed a second image next to the original. 'And this is Sanza's. He hasn't even changed the photograph!'

Carmichael lifted the papers closer to his face, before scrunching them and throwing them at the wall in rage. 'Son of a bitch!'

Melissa passed more pages over to him. 'This is Preston's arrest record. It seems he was an astute conman in his day.'

'There's no history of violence though. It's a stretch to go from hustling someone to butchering them with a knife.'

'I agree, but it's not much of a stretch to suggest Lyons might have been involved in the embezzlement. From what we've heard, he had access to the office. He has experience of forging credentials.' She shrugged. 'Is it so impossible to believe he might have been the one to take the money? You said yourself that George Murphy hardly looks like someone with a million in the bank.'

'Neither does Sanza though.'

'You don't think? It's the perfect cover though, isn't it? He doesn't have a proper job, but manages to get by well. I'm just saying: it warrants further investigation.'

'I can't believe he could be involved in something like this. He seems so -'

'Listen, I know you're close to him, so if you want me to step in and ask him about it, I'll understand.'

'No! I'll speak to him. I need to look in his eyes

when I ask him about it.'

'I can go with you if you want? You know, two heads are better than one.'

He shook his head. 'No, I don't want him to think we're ambushing him. I'll approach him about it as if I'm tipping him off. Maybe he'll think I'm being friendly and tell me about it. There's no reason for him to suspect I'm working on proving Sue's innocence.'

'What do you want me to do?'

'We don't know for certain he took the money. See what evidence you can find. Can you use the dark web to trace historic bank account records?'

She considered the question. 'Probably not, but there are hackers who lurk in the dark who might be able to find what we need. Leave it with me, and I'll see what I can find.'

Carmichael reached for his car keys.

44

Kelly cannot contain her excitement when the doorbell rings and she hears Carmichael's voice. Has he come for her? Are they to meet at last? Paul beats her to the door. She ducks out of sight but watches as they go into the living room. She will stay out of sight, but it is time to hear what Paul is hiding from her. He has been so closed off recently. She needs to know what is happening.

Carmichael seems anxious. She can hear him pacing, while her brother sits. Paul offers him a drink, but he declines.

'It's my assistant,' he says. 'She showed me something today, which frankly, it leaves me speechless.'

'What's the matter?' Paul asks.

Carmichael passes him a piece of paper, but she cannot see what it is. 'Can you explain this?'

Paul looks at the paper. He sounds nervous when he speaks. 'So now you know my secret.'

'So you don't deny it, then? You are Kevin Lyons?'

Kelly is distraught. If he's found that out, what else does he know?

'How can I deny it?' Paul continues. 'You've shown me your evidence. What do you expect me to say?'

'I thought you'd try and deny it, or to convince me I'd made a mistake.'

'You've been honest enough with me over the last week, it's only fair I return the gesture. Besides, I don't treat my friends like that, and I now consider you a friend. We will have many challenges to face together, and this is the first of them.'

'My assistant tells me your real name isn't even Lyons. It's Steven Preston.'

'What does it matter what name my parents gave me, or I chose to adopt. A name is nothing more than the envelope we inhabit on this earth. It's not a crime to change your name or assume a new identity.'

'It is when you steal the identity.'

'I haven't stolen any identity. Your records should show that I still use the same national insurance number, and this has been my address since I moved to Hampshire. I have adopted a new name, but I haven't stolen it from anyone else. This isn't anything that should trouble you.'

Carmichael stops pacing. 'I've been looking for Kevin Lyons.'

'How come?'

'You knew Ben Dewis.'

'Of course I did. I used to work for Ben, some…let me see…ten or so years ago.'

'Try sixteen.'

'Has it been that long? Well, you know what they say about time flying.'

'Ben's son Tom hired me to prove his mother didn't kill Ben.'

'After all this time? Wasn't she convicted of the crime?'

'She maintains she had nothing to do with it.'

'Good for her. I don't see what this has to do with me.'

'Did you kill Ben?'

Paul laughs. 'Are you serious? Of course I didn't kill Ben. What do you take me for?'

'I don't know what to think anymore. You seem like a good guy, yet these questions keep coming up about you.'

'Johnson, look me in the eye, and check my pulse. I had nothing to do with what happened to Ben.'

'Before Ben died, he was accused of embezzling a million pounds from the company's pension fund. I suppose you're going to claim you know nothing about that as well.'

'I'm a little offended you would even suggest that.'

'It's a reasonable conclusion to draw. You have a criminal record for conning people out of money.'

'Just because I did bad things once, doesn't mean I will repeat them. You should know that better than most.'

'Why didn't you tell me any of this before?'

'I did. The first time we met I told you I was in a bad place when I first heard God's call. The truth is, I was in prison. It was while I was serving my punishment for conning those old folks. That was the moment I decided to turn over a new leaf and go straight.'

'So you became Kevin Lyons?'

'Yes I did. It sounded like such a wholesome name. I managed to get the job at the factory, and things were going so well, but then Ben died and the factory went into administration.'

'How did you manage to get a job at the factory with your record?'

'I took a chance. I made my C.V. sound appealing and I gave false referees. I knew if they bothered to do their homework they'd learn the truth, but I gambled on them cutting corners and they did. My intentions were pure. I wanted to turn over a new leaf.'

'By lying to get there.'

'No harm was done.'

'So why change your name again?'

'God called to me in prison, but I wasn't willing to admit what I knew he wanted me to do. I thought going straight, and treating others well, was enough. It was only after the factory closed that I finally accepted he wanted me to do so much more. I needed a fresh start: to finally get things right. Paul turned over a new leaf on the road to Damascus, so I chose that name. It seemed fitting.'

'I don't remember him stealing after his conversion.'

'He didn't, and neither did I.'

'Who stole the pension money?'

'How would I know? It was Ben for all I know. He had access to the money and he knew how much was there. I was only a junior colleague in the office. I couldn't access that kind of stuff.'

'So it's just a coincidence then?'

'Yes, an unfortunate one. You know I haven't thought about that time of my life in years. I don't know who pointed you in my direction, but they're leading you along the garden path.'

'Do your followers know about your past?'

'No they do not, and I would prefer it stays that way.'

'Surely they deserve to know the real person who preaches how they should live their lives.'

'It would only complicate matters. I have buried Steven's crimes in my past, and that's where they should remain. I am clean. I don't drink, smoke, or take drugs. I dedicate every day to undertaking God's work. If that part of my life becomes public knowledge, it will undo everything I have worked so hard for.'

'They deserve to know.'

'Maybe they do, maybe they don't. Everyone deserves a second chance, Johnson. Think about how things would change for you if your involvement in Lennon's and the Russian's deaths was exposed.'

'Are you threatening me?'

'Not at all, I'm trying to encourage you to empathise with my situation. Are you a killer or someone who crusades for justice? Am I a thief, or a man interpreting God's message to those who crave it? We all have two sides, Johnson.'

Kelly isn't sure she can listen to much more. She can hear her brother is struggling to convince him. They are so close to putting all this behind them. She will not let anyone destroy their plans.

'What would Tom want you to do?' Paul asks.

'This has nothing to do with him.'

'Maybe not, but he's a level-headed man, someone we both trust. What do you think he would want to happen? The two of us exposed for our past mistakes, or for the future to be safe and secure?'

Carmichael sits. When he speaks, he is quiet and

pensive. 'I need to hear the truth from you, Paul. I won't be angry, but if we are to remain friends, I need to know that you've been honest with me: did you take that money and kill Ben?'

'With God as my witness, I did neither of those things. Now, can we put all of this behind us?'

'Okay. I believe you, Paul. I'll keep your secret. I hope I don't live to regret that decision.'

TUESDAY

45

Helen Dewis' small bungalow in Milford on Sea was a stone's throw from the Solent. It was a clear day, and Carmichael could see the Isle of Wight in the distance as he parked outside the bungalow. It was some view.

He'd briefly met Helen when Tom had introduced them at his house the week before. She looked equally as flustered opening the door to him now. She was wearing the same checked tabard as before, and her straggly, fair hair still looked as though it hadn't been brushed. Her frequent blinking was a noticeable tick, but he tried to ignore it. Tom had phoned to advise her that Carmichael would be over to ask some questions. She led him into the living room at the front of the house. The large window captured the view of the beach.

'You have a lovely home,' he offered, to put her at ease. 'And that view: it's to die for. Have you lived here long?'

'Long enough.'

'Did Tom explain why I've come over?'

'He said you had questions.'

'That's right. Do you mind if I sit?'

She shrugged.

'Did Tom explain he's hired me to find the truth

about what happened to Ben?'

'He was a great brother. Bought me this place, he did. We were close.'

'You must miss him.'

'I do, deeply. It's not been the same since he passed.'

'I understand you were close to Sue as well.'

She grunted.

'Is that wrong? Were you not close to Sue?'

'That harlot killed my brother. I don't like her name being mentioned in this house.'

'Before that night, though, Tom showed me photos of you at their place for family barbeques. You seem to be getting along well with Sue.'

Another grunt. 'He should never have married that two-faced snake. He was never the same after he met her. Me and him were like two peas in a pod as kids, but when she came along, he changed. I saw him less regular, like. I tried to tell him, but he was smitten.'

'So you resented Sue from the start?'

'No. I made an effort. I tried to get to know her, but I wish I hadn't bothered. I obviously didn't know her that well, because I never realised she was capable of killing him.'

'Tom believes his mum didn't do it.'

'Well he's always been a soppy sod. I've tried to warn him about her, but he's like his father: he thinks the world of her in spite of what she did.'

'What makes you so certain that she did it, Helen?'

'It was proved, weren't it, in a court of law. Them jurors convicted her. If she was innocent, she'd be out now, wouldn't she?'

'You appeared in court as a witness for the

prosecution, claiming Sue threatened you with a knife. Can you tell me when that was and what happened?'

Helen stood. 'Do you want a cup of tea or something?'

'Sure.'

'How do you take it?'

'Milk and two sugars.'

'Will sweetener be okay? Haven't had sugar in this house since I was diagnosed with diabetes.'

He nodded, and watched her leave, before standing and moving to the unit in the opposite corner of the room. The real reason he'd stopped by was to try and find a clue to the whereabouts of Tom's estranged sister, Annie. He sensed that if he asked her outright, she'd clam up. Tom had said he hadn't seen his sister in several years, but he was certain Helen was still in touch with her. The unit didn't contain an address book as he'd hoped. He returned to his seat when he heard Helen coming back. She handed him a mug.

'So, Helen, you were about to tell me about the day Sue threatened you with a knife.'

'It's hard to remember. It was a long time ago, and my memory's not what it was.'

'Sue claims you fabricated the whole -'

'Well, she would say that, wouldn't she?'

'I'm not saying I don't believe you, Helen. It's your word against hers. Tell me what happened.'

'I was over there, and we was in the kitchen. She grabbed the knife and waved it at me, threatening like, and that's it.'

'What led to the threat? Were the two of you arguing about something?'

305

'I don't remember.'

'Did she say anything when she waved the knife?'

'I don't remember.'

'I've read the coverage of the case in the newspaper. You told the court the two of you had been arguing and she'd threatened to kill you when she pointed the knife at you. So which is it? Did she wave the knife or point it at you?'

'If I said she pointed it, then that's what she did. I told you, I don't remember.'

He decided to change tack. 'It was brave of you to take guardianship of the children. It must have been hard on you.'

'What else could I do? They had no one.'

'Even so, Tom was what, seven? How old was Annie again?'

'Fourteen.'

'That's right. Fourteen. That's a tough age, isn't it? Particularly for girls. With their hormones raging, and self-conscious about body shape and size. It must have been hard for you to take on such a challenge.'

'I coped.'

'You must have had to work your socks off to earn enough to feed them though, right?'

'I received their benefits money, and Ben had left me some money in his will. I managed.'

'Well clearly! Tom's a good guy. You must be proud.'

'I am. He turned out well, despite his mother.'

'What about Annie? I'd love to speak to her about what she remembers from that awful night. You know, whether she heard anything or saw -'

'I don't know where she is.'

'So you're not in contact with her?'

'No.'

'When did you last see or speak to her.?'

'I don't remember.'

'Tom told me she only stuck around for a couple of years before leaving. Is that right?'

She finished her tea and placed the mug on the unit. 'Ben's death hit Annie the hardest I think. She was a real daddy's girl. She hated her mother for killing him. She'd been such a happy and well-adjusted girl, but something in her died with Ben. She became withdrawn. I don't think it helped that she had to change schools, but there was no way I could have got her to the old school every day. She made some new friends here I think.'

'What about boyfriends?'

'She finished with the boy she'd been seeing when they'd lived in Highfield. There were a couple of boys I saw her with when she lived here, but nothing serious.'

'Why did she leave?'

'She always thought people were judging her for being the daughter of a murderer. She was desperate to put the past behind her, but didn't think she could do it here, even in a new school. She completed her G.C.S.E.s and then she moved away.'

'Where did she go?'

'I didn't know at first. The day after she received her exam results, she was gone. She left a note thanking me for making life bearable, but she needed to venture out alone to get her head straight.'

'Weren't you worried about what might happen to her? The world is a scary enough place for grown-ups.

I can't imagine how fearful it is for a child.'

'Of course I was worried, but she was mature for her age; she'd had to be. Losing both parents so young has that effect on people. She got in touch on the anniversary of Ben's death and told me she was well, and living under a new name. She'd met a guy and they were renting a place together.'

'Whereabouts?'

'It was up north somewhere. Far away from anyone that might recognise her.'

'And is she still living in the same place?'

'No, no, no. She's lived all over since.'

'Like where? I'd like to track her down. If you can tell me some of the places she's lived in, it'll give me somewhere to start.'

'I'm not sure I can remember. She was in Edinburgh for a bit, and then Marseille.'

'Where was she when you last heard from her?'

'I don't remember.'

'Was she in the UK?'

'I think so, but I'm not sure.'

'Do you have a mobile number for her? How do you contact her?'

'I don't. She contacts me from time to time, to let me know she's okay.'

Carmichael drained his mug and stood. 'Can I use your toilet before I go?'

She carried the mugs out to the kitchen. 'It's through the kitchen, the door to the right.'

He made his way to the small bathroom, and waited until he heard her leave the kitchen before coming out. Every surface of the kitchen had been scrubbed clean, and there was no crockery on the drainer. She'd even washed, dried and put away their mugs. He carefully opened each of the three drawers beneath the counter. One contained cutlery, the next other utensils, and finally a drawer with batteries and a torch, but there was still no sign of an address book. He quietly closed the drawer, and was about to return to the living room when a picture on the fridge caught his attention. He removed the magnet, and looked at the postcard. It was a tourist card from Cowes, but the post mark was from Devon. Curious, he turned the card over and read the message. It was signed by "A", but there was no return address. The card was dated a month earlier. He pocketed it, as he heard Helen moving around in the living room. He thanked her for her time and asked her to get in touch if she heard from Annie.

46

'Ma'am, I'm telling you, it's Roxanne: *she's* the woman we're looking for.'

Payne looked at the three blow-ups on her desk. 'I'm sorry, Beth, I'm not seeing it.'

Beth tried to keep her frustration in check. 'Please, Ma'am, look at the shoes in the images from the café and the club. Both women are wearing high-heeled stilettos. Spinks has confirmed such a heel may have been the weapon used to kill Josh outside the club.'

'There's no denying the blondes in the images are of a similar build, and share a taste in shoes, but that's all you've got. Even if we made the leap – and it would be a leap – and said the woman seen in the café in Totton killed Todd *and* then went out and killed Josh, you're still no closer to identifying who she is.'

'Roxanne has a record of aggravated assault, shoplifting and prostitution. She's only been on release for eight weeks. Maybe she lost a few pounds inside.'

'But other than your gut feeling, you have no proof she's guilty of anything.'

'But, Ma'am -'

'But nothing, Beth. You know better than that. You need a chain of evidence, and you've got nothing. For all you know, Roxanne has turned over a new leaf and joined a convent.'

Beth rolled her eyes. 'Let me bring her in. I'll ask her to come in voluntarily, so I can get a sense of where she's been and what she's been doing since she got out. There's no harm in that. I won't be formally accusing her of anything.'

'*If* she agreed to come in and *if* she even agreed to answer your questions with more than a "no comment", you still won't have enough to entice the CPS.'

'What about Claire Willis? I have a witness who saw a blonde entering Claire's flat shortly before she decided to hang herself.'

'You *had* a neighbour, who was high on meth, who thought he saw a blonde woman near Claire's flat at some point on the day she died. He couldn't confirm a specific time, and he was off his face. I can't believe you're even bringing this to me. It's not enough, Beth.'

She was banging her head against a brick wall, but what was frustrating her most was she knew Payne was right.

'Is everything okay, Beth? I know how hard you've been working in White's absence, and don't think all the overtime you've been clocking up has gone unnoticed. I heard about what happened on Wednesday night.'

'Ma'am?'

'If it's any consolation, I didn't know Harris was gay either. It seems so obvious now when you think about it. I know you want to make a name for yourself in this unit, and believe me, you're doing the right things to earn progression up the ranks, but you need to let this one go. Okay? I'm speaking to you as a friend rather than as your D.C.I.'

'What if I can find something or someone who confirms seeing Roxanne in a blonde wig?'

'You still don't have anything close to resembling motive, but, yes, if you can prove Roxanne has been wearing such a wig, then I'll take another look at it.'

Beth leapt to her feet. She knew what she had to do. She gathered the images, thanked Payne for her time, and raced from the office. She was behind the wheel of her car within minutes. She drove the short journey to Freemantle, and parked around the corner from the address Roxanne had given to her parole officer. It was nearly lunchtime, and she hoped Roxanne wouldn't be home.

She rang the buzzer to the flat. There was no answer. She rang it again, but still no answer. She pressed the buzzer of the next flat.

A gruff man's voice answered. 'What?'

'Hiya, it's Roxanne from flat five. I've locked myself out, are you able to buzz me in?'

There was no answer but the communal entrance buzzed open a moment later. Some people were far too believing for their own good. Beth entered and climbed the single flight of stairs. She knocked on the door of flat five, in case Roxanne had been ignoring the intercom. There was no sound of movement inside, so Beth pulled out the small spindle of picks White had once given her as a Christmas present. She'd been appalled at the time, but he'd winked and said 'You never know when they might come in handy, like.' She wished he was here now. She knew he'd back her gut feeling without question.

She fiddled with the lock, until she heard the catch click, and then she carefully pushed the door open with her shoulder. She put on a pair of latex gloves and entered.

The flat was tiny compared to her own. There was a kitchen-living space, a box room containing nothing more than a double bed, and a bathroom big enough for a shower cubicle and toilet. The ceiling had large brown patches of damp, and the walls looked like they hadn't seen fresh paint in years. The air smelt stale, and it amazed her that anyone could live like this. There was a drawer unit next to the sofa in the living room. She opened the top drawer. It was crammed with knickers and bras. She rummaged about, finding a small bag of weed. She put it back where she'd found it, so as not to alert Roxanne that she'd been in the flat. The next drawer contained vests and t-shirts, and the bottom drawer contained pyjamas and more lingerie. Where were the rest of her clothes?

She stepped into the bedroom. There was an eight inch gap between the bedframe and the wall at the foot of the bed. A door in the wall revealed a small built-in wardrobe. She banged the door on the bedframe as she opened it. She found several pairs of trousers, a dozen or so dresses, and a fur coat. She compared the dresses with the images from the club and café but couldn't find an obvious match. She cursed as she closed the wardrobe door.

Where could she be hiding the wig? Beth headed to the bathroom but returned to the living room when she still hadn't found anything. Maybe Payne was right; maybe Roxanne had nothing to do with it.

She looked out of the living room window. The

world was still turning below her. Cars drove past, people nattered as they walked along the street. All of them were oblivious to the killer living in their midst. Beth lifted the net curtain as a flash of something caught her eye: blonde hair, and it was moving quickly. Before she could get a better look, the hair was out of sight.

She turned and rushed from the flat, down the stairs and into the street. A hundred or so yards to her left she saw a woman in a dark coloured dress moving quickly along the street. The hair was almost white. It was impossible to judge if it was a wig from this distance, but it was too much of a coincidence that Beth should see her from Roxanne's window. Perhaps Roxanne had seen her looking out, and had decided to scarper rather than confront her. That would explain why she hadn't found the wig in the flat. Beth broke into a jog.

The blonde was still some distance away, and she hadn't looked back. It had to be Roxanne. If Beth could catch her in the wig, she'd have enough to expand her investigation.

The blonde turned onto a road to the right. Beth increased her pace, her forehead veiled in sweat. She wasn't dressed for a chase on such a warm day. She reached the corner and looked right. There was no sign of Roxanne. She ran to the bottom of the new road, which was then bisected by another road. She looked left, but the street was empty. She looked right, and the street was also empty. She rested her hands on her knees and sucked in breath.

How could she have disappeared? She had to have gone into one of the houses, but which one? The road was lined with nothing but houses as far as she could see. She couldn't search every property in the hope of finding Roxanne. She'd come so close. She looked both ways again, but the street was still empty.

She was about to turn around and head back to her car, when a building caught her eye. It stood out because it was set further back from the road, and was larger than any of the other properties. It looked more like a business than a residence. She approached it slowly, and, as she grew closer she saw a cross erected on the roof, beneath which hung a sign reading: Church of Eternal Light. It was an odd place to see a church, even if it was one of those new-age places that were becoming more common.

She wiped her forehead with a tissue, and removed her jacket, folding it over her arm. There was a car parked in front of the building. Beth approached the door and rang the bell. Two minutes later a man opened the door.

Beth raised her identification. 'Hi, I'm D.S. Beth Taylor from the Major Incident Team, and you are?'

'I'm Paul Sanza. I run the church.'

'Hi Paul, I'm hoping you can help me with something.' She showed him Roxanne's mugshot. 'I'm looking for this woman. She lives in the area, and I was wondering whether you've seen her at your church.'

Sanza took the photo and studied it, before passing it back. 'I can't say I recognise her, I'm afraid. Is she in some kind of trouble?'

There was something strange about his demeanour she couldn't place. 'Oh no, nothing like that, I'm looking to speak to her about something she may have witnessed. Are you certain that you don't know her?'

'I'm certain, detective. Although we have a number of followers at the church, I'm pretty sure I'd remember her.'

Beth passed him the image from the café. 'What about now? We believe she sometimes wears a bright blonde wig like this one in the picture. She has a distinct body shape. Can you look again, and make sure you don't recognise her? She was on this street moments ago, and I thought it might be possible that she's come here seeking sanctuary. It is important I speak to her.'

A single bead of sweat trickled down the side of his face. He quickly wiped it away with his hand. 'I'm sorry, detective, but I've never seen that woman. Now, I must get on. We have a service this evening that I need to prepare for.' He closed the door before she could say anything else.

Beth walked away, not noticing the pair of eyes staring at her through the church's main window.

47

Melissa placed a mug of coffee on his desk, before sitting across from him. 'So, where do we go from here?'

Carmichael sighed. 'I've been looking at this case for over a week, and I still don't feel like we've made any headway.'

'Maybe you need to get away from it. Why not take the day off and simply forget about it? Sometimes that can be enough to gain perspective.'

'Take the day off? What would I do? I need to keep focused.' He sighed again. 'Right, let's start at the beginning. What do we know?'

Melissa reached for her notes. 'Ben Dewis was stabbed to death in his home, but there was no sign of a break-in. Sue and the children were fast asleep in bed when it happened. Sue was woken by some kind of disturbance and found Ben.'

'Good. Who are our suspects?'

'George Murphy: two people have pointed the finger at him for stealing the pension monies. Maybe Ben found out the truth and Murphy killed him to keep it quiet.'

'If he did take it, what happened to it? I saw him; he's hardly living the high life. Who else?'

'Kevin Lyons, or Sanza, or Preston, whatever you

want to call him. He was working at the factory at the time the money went missing. He has a conviction for theft too, so for me, he's the prime -'

'But if he took the money, why did he kill Ben?'

'To cover his tracks, like we said for Murphy.'

'I don't buy it.'

'You're biased.'

'No, I'm not. I don't buy that he did it. You've been spending too much time with Wendy Barlow.'

'I'm leaving his name on the list. You mark my words: there's something not right about him and his church.'

'Move on.'

'Okay, what about Ben's estranged son, from his first marriage? Sue said he turned up demanding money a few weeks before the murder. Maybe he demanded more and reacted when Ben said no.'

'He couldn't have taken the million though; it was already missing when he arrived on the scene.'

'Have you managed to get hold of him?'

'He's away on holiday apparently. He's due back on Sunday night, so I'll pay him a visit first thing on Monday. Have you managed to dig up anything else on him?'

Melissa turned over the page. 'He's married and his wife is pregnant with their first child. He's working as a mechanic at a garage in Poole, where they live. No criminal record, but his credit rating isn't great either.'

'Is that it?'

'Yep, I'm afraid so. It could be any of them.'

He rubbed his eyes. 'Or none of them. I still can't believe the investigation ended without finding the money. It has to have gone somewhere. Wait a second, are you still friends with that fraud guy in the Met?'

'You mean Gavin? I haven't spoken to him in more than a year. Why?'

'The guy who came to see me from HMRC said the police weren't involved in the investigation as the regulators were still investigating matters. Would you mind giving him a call and running the details of the case by him? I want to know if there's a particular type of person we should be looking for. If he's an expert in his field, maybe he can give us some direction.'

'Okay. I'll see if he can help. How did you get on with the aunt this morning?'

'She claimed not to know where Annie is, but I'm sure she was lying.' He passed Melissa the postcard he'd taken from the fridge. 'I found this. I'm thinking it's from Annie. It was posted in Devon but it's from the Isle of Wight. Can you use those locations to do a dark web search to see if you can trace her whereabouts?'

'Sure.'

'I find it hard to believe a sixteen year-old girl can disappear like that.'

'Are you thinking she had some help?'

'Maybe. I don't know, something doesn't feel right about it. She refused to visit her mother after the arrest, and from what Helen told me, Annie was certain her mother did it. Maybe she witnessed something. What I do know is, it's vital we get hold of her as soon as possible.'

'Of course, there is one suspect we haven't talked about yet, and that's Sue herself. Are we certain she didn't stab Ben? She had opportunity and motive, and her fingerprints were all over the murder weapon.'

'Don't! I can't stop asking myself that same question. What if we were hired under false pretences? I have to assume she's telling the truth. For now.'

48

Kelly watches the detective walking away from the church. She breathes a sigh of relief and steps back from the window. That was too close for comfort.

It was a risk to go outside, but she didn't imagine she would run into the woman hunting her. It was Paul's fault. She'd needed something to eat, but he wasn't willing to get her anything. She only stepped out for ten minutes. She went to the local shop and bought a chocolate bar. Where the detective emerged from was beyond her.

How long has Beth been following her? How long has she known Paul has been hiding her?

She regrets going to the shop, but at least her hunger pangs are gone, for now. She knows she cannot risk showing her face outside again, and will have to be careful when they leave here to return home.

Of course Paul didn't turn her over. How could he? They were family, and family doesn't do that kind of thing. He'll be connecting the dots now. She knows she is going to have to talk to him, and explain everything that has been going on. He won't be happy, but she is sure she can convince him of her plan for their future.

The net is tightening. First it was Carmichael

confronting Paul, and now Beth. She's been so careful until this point, but it is only a matter of time now.

She didn't expect the police to find them so soon. The detective showed him some photographs. They can't have been too revealing, otherwise the detective would have made the connection sooner. At least Beth didn't seem to notice the familial resemblance. That should buy Kelly at least another day. But once Beth digs into Paul's background, the game will be up.

The detective is quite attractive in the cold light of day. She can see why Carmichael is attracted to her. But there is something about her: a quiet determination. Kelly can tell that Beth is going to figure it out.

She needs to bring forward their escape. Tomorrow night will have to be the day instead. What other choice does she have? If Beth finds her, the game is up. There is no way she'll be able to explain why she did what she did.

Kelly glances back out the window to make sure Beth has gone. She is relieved to see the detective isn't skulking. She can tell Paul is quietly seething. She takes a deep breath and goes to find him. It is time for her to come clean. She needs to explain why they need to leave. She must convince him that Beth has to die.

WEDNESDAY

49

Carmichael was pacing the floor of his office when Melissa eventually arrived. 'What the hell time do you call this? It's nearly lunchtime. Where the hell have you been?'

She was breathless, and flung her bag into the far corner of the room. Her eyes were wild. 'You wouldn't believe me if I told you,' she panted. 'I think I've cracked our case though.'

'Okay, you've piqued my interest. I'm listening.'

She raised her hand to buy a moment to compose herself. 'Right, you asked me to consult my friend Gavin in the Fraud Squad. I managed to get hold of him yesterday evening. I wasn't sure he'd be willing to even discuss it with me, but it turns out he's had a crush on me since college, and once I'd agreed to go out for dinner with him, he was only too happy to help.'

Carmichael raised an eyebrow.

'Relax, boss, it's just dinner. I've not prostituted myself…well, not yet anyway.' She winked. 'Anyway, he asked me to summarise what we knew about the embezzlement, and who the factory's main players were. We must have been on the phone for nearly two hours. Anyway, long story short, he points the finger firmly at George Murphy's door.'

'Okay. Why?'

She opened a can of energy drink, and drank half the can. 'He said in his experience, such crimes can only be undertaken by those at the top of the power structure. Ultimately, it had to be Murphy, or Ben, or both.'

'Both?'

'Sure, it's possible. Everyone said Ben's behaviour changed once the accusations hit the papers. We've all assumed it was because he was feeling the pressure of proving his innocence, but what if we're wrong? What if his behaviour changed because he was complicit in taking the money and he feared the truth emerging?'

Carmichael's eyes darted left and right as he processed the possibility. 'I don't buy it. If you're right, what happened to the money? It's not easy to hide a million quid. They were small-time entrepreneurs. Something on this scale would involve someone with good street sense.'

'Oh, you mean like a convicted confidence trickster perhaps?'

'I didn't say -'

'No, but if the cap fits.'

Carmichael shook his head. 'I've been to Sanza's house. I don't think it was him.'

'I didn't say it was. It was you that leapt to that conclusion.'

Carmichael frowned. 'What else did your friend have to say?'

'I asked him whether it was unusual for the pension regulator not to pursue this kind of case to a conclusion. He said not in his experience. He was surprised the police weren't invited to support such a major investigation. He offered to phone the regulator first thing to understand why everything ended when Dewis died.'

'Okay, so next step, we need to prove Murphy or Dewis were involved.'

Melissa raised a finger and took another gulp from her energy drink. 'Where do you think I've been all morning? After I got off the phone with Gavin, I phoned Tom. I told him I wanted to look at all of the factory's accounts from the twelve months prior to the Revenue's tip-off. He told me hardcopies of all the statements and files were in storage, and I managed to persuade him to meet me at the site so I could look at them last night.' She crushed the empty can and threw it towards the waste bin. She punched the air when it landed perfectly in the bin.

'Wait a minute. You were awake all night?'

She nodded.

'How many of those drinks have you had?'

She grinned sheepishly. 'I've lost count. It doesn't matter anyway. So, we looked at the company's bank statements. Your contact at HMRC was right: Ben ran a tight ship. The files were immaculate, clearly sorted into expenses, income, salary and benefits folders. Once we figured out his system, it was easy to track what went where. We managed to track every payment from January 1999 to September 2000, but -'

'Wait, who's we?'

'Oh, Tom and me. He offered to stay and help me out. You know, he's a nice guy. I think once we're done with this case, I might ask him out for a drink.'

'What about your dinner date with the detective?'

She shrugged. 'What, a girl can't play the field?'

He rolled his eyes. 'You said you only managed to track to September?'

'Oh yeah, so that's where things went a bit strange. We couldn't find the paperwork relating to the payments from the company into the pension scheme.'

'You mean they'd stopped paying into it?'

'No, no, I mean the paperwork was missing. It was like someone had removed the documents.'

'Maybe the pension regulator people took it?'

She snapped her fingers. 'That was my first thought too. Isn't it awesome when great minds think alike?'

'Well?'

'Oh yeah, I don't know where my brain is today. So, I suggested it to Tom, but he said they would only ever remove copies of documents and that it had to be there somewhere. We went through all of the boxes in case the statements had been misfiled in error, but there wasn't a trace of them. We thought we'd hit a brick wall, but then Tom had an idea.' She paused and opened a second can of energy drink. 'Tom said he recognised the style of boxes all the files were being stored in. He said his dad's stuff had been packed in the same boxes and were in the loft at the family home. We left the storage facility and headed to his place, and sure enough, we went through his dad's things and found the missing paperwork.'

'So Ben had it all along? Did you find where the money went?'

She sipped her drink, and belched. 'Hold on, hold

on, I haven't finished yet. Somebody had highlighted particular payments on particular dates with a fluorescent highlighter.'

'The regulator?'

She shook her head. 'I told you, they would have taken copies. These were the originals. I think it was Ben who made the notes. I think he found out that somebody had been fiddling the accounts, and that would mean -'

'He knew who took the money,' Carmichael finished.

She nodded. 'What if he discovered who had taken the money and confronted them about it? Sue said he was having a heated discussion on the phone with someone when she arrived home. What if he was talking to the culprit, who then came round and stabbed Ben to cover his tracks?'

Carmichael considered the theory. 'It would explain why Ben had let his killer in. So did Ben leave the name of the real culprit on the paperwork?'

'Unfortunately not.'

'So we've hit another brick wall.'

Melissa couldn't contain her excitement any more. 'Tom and I looked closer at the transactions that were highlighted. Do you understand how a pension fund works?'

'Vaguely.'

'Right, well, without wishing to bore you with too much detail, monies or contributions are collected in a pot. Think about it as like having a piggy bank on a shelf. Each month you pay an amount into the piggy bank that you can't reclaim until you reach retirement age. Your employer might contribute a monthly amount into the pot as well, but you don't ever receive what has been put into the pot.'

'I don't?'

'No. Instead the money in your piggy bank is added to the piggy banks of every other employee at the company and the whole amount is stored in a much bigger pot. This is known as the pension fund. In order to make everyone's contributions worth more, the pension fund is invested into the stock market. When the time comes for you to retire, your personal piggy bank is refilled with what remains from your contribution to the larger fund. If you've been lucky your piggy bank is now worth more than the combination of yours and your employer's contributions.'

'And that's what I'd then receive when I retire?'

'Not exactly. There's a whole other conversation we could have about annuity thresholds, but that's not relevant for what you need to know for this case.' She sipped from her can. 'So, the total pension fund for the factory was estimated at a little over a million in September 1999. That's what the last statement at the storage facility had recorded. In November 2000, the pot took a sudden drop. Not a massive drop, but the estimated value had dropped by twenty per cent. Now, what you need to understand is that pension money cannot be removed. It's not like you can walk into a bank and just withdraw it.'

'So where did it go?'

'This is the complicated bit.' She crushed her can and threw it at the bin again. 'Amongst Ben's things we found a letter from an independent accountants firm confirming the Dewis-Murphy Pension Trust, or the DMPT, had successfully purchased shares in a third-party company called Future Telecoms. The letter was dated September 1999. The entire pension fund had been used to purchase shares in Future Telecoms. Each share was valued at two pounds, so they'd effectively bought half a million shares in the company. On its own, this isn't necessarily unusual activity, however, Future Telecoms doesn't exist, or to be more accurate: never existed.'

Carmichael frowned. 'How is that even possible?'

'I spoke to my friend in the Fraud Squad again. He was able to check the Companies House register and there has never been a company with that name registered.'

'So how did the trust manage to invest in them?'

'My best guess is somebody with forging skills created the letters of administration and the like, and created a fictional company for the scheme to buy shares in.'

'You're hinting at Sanza again.'

'Am I? Again, it's you who suggested it.'

'Well who else could have done it? Murphy? Dewis?'

'If Sanza, or Kevin Lyons as he was then, was the one who created the Future Telecoms shell, I still think one of the factory's directors had to have been involved too. Sanza had access to the office, but not necessarily to documentation relating to the pension scheme. My friend at the Fraud Squad thinks at least one of Dewis or Murphy must have been in on the scam too, if not both of them.'

'So what happened to the money then?'

'From what I can ascertain from the files we found

amongst Dewis' things, the Future Telecoms business had valued itself at five million pounds, meaning DMPT bought a ten per cent stake in them. The initial twenty per cent drop in the pot followed a revaluation of the shell company. In January 2000, there is a letter on Future Telecoms headed paper declaring itself bankrupt, but assuring DMPT they will be first in the queue to reclaim lost monies at an insolvency court. Basically, the person who created Future Telecoms pocketed the million pounds, and then disappeared. DMPT was left with no way of getting the money back because the company never existed to begin with.'

'DMPT must have had trustees in place right? The people that would have had to confirm the purchase of the shares?'

She put a document on the table in front of him. 'This was in with Ben's things. It is confirmation of the share purchase signed by four trustees: Ben Dewis, Terry Hunter, John Dresden, and…Sue Dewis.'

Carmichael spat out his tea. 'Sue was a trustee?'

'Apparently so.'

'And she gave consent to buy the shares? Wait till I see her tomorrow. She knew what happened to the money?'

Melissa scrunched her nose. 'I'm not so sure, to be honest. Tom was in shock when he saw her signature, and said it looked like hers, but then we compared it to some old correspondence we found of hers in a filing cabinet. The signature is almost a perfect match, but not quite. If you look at the signature on the document in front of you, you might notice there is a blob of ink on the 'e' of her surname, like the writer paused while writing the letter. On all the other correspondence we found, she never pauses on the 'e'. I'm no expert, but I think it warrants further investigation with a forgery expert.'

'What about the other two signatures?'

'I'm not sure who Hunter and Dresden are, but if we can find them, it would be worth comparing their signatures too. Best guess: all four were forged in order to authorise this transaction.'

'Wouldn't this have been discovered in the regulator's investigation?'

'The transaction looks above board. As far as they would have been concerned, the pension fund was simply invested badly in an insolvent company. Case closed. I'm speculating of course. At least it gives us a direction to go in.'

'Surely the accountancy firm would have done some kind of due diligence on the transaction?'

'That's just it: they never existed either. I think they were a front to verify the business. None of this was above board. It looks genuine enough on the surface, but delve deeper, and it's an obvious fraud.'

He looked out of the window. 'What's your best theory? Who was involved?'

'I think Murphy and Lyons undertook the fraud, Ben found out, hence the highlighted documents we found, and threatened to blow the whistle. One or both of Murphy and Lyons killed Ben to cover their tracks.'

'Why didn't Dewis go to the police if he suspected all this?'

'How could he? His forged signature is on the

paperwork too. It would have looked like he'd got cold feet, and he'd have still faced prosecution. Maybe he tried to reason with the pair and get them to return the monies.'

'So you've been awake all night looking into this?'

She stifled a yawn. 'Yup. I'm wired right now. God knows how much caffeine is clogging my system.'

'This is fantastic work, Melissa. I mean that. Thank you for your efforts. You should get yourself home and try and get some sleep. In fact, you're probably not safe to drive. Grab your bag, I'll drive you home now.'

'No chance! I'm still wired on caffeine and sugar. Even if I went to bed, I'd lie awake for hours. It's better if I stay here. I can keep looking for Annie. What are you going to do? Are you going to confront Sanza?'

'Not yet. I'll get hold of Murphy again first. I reckon if I apply the right kind of pressure, I can get him to admit the truth.'

'You think he killed Ben?'

'Yes I do.'

'If that's the case you need to contact the police.'

'It's okay. I'll give Beth a call on the way, and have her come with me.'

50

Beth looked at the rap sheet she had printed out. Paul Sanza, also known as Steven Preston, served four years at Her Majesty's pleasure for conning a group of pensioners out of their life savings. It was the same man she'd met at the church yesterday afternoon. She'd run the plate of the car outside the church, and it was registered to him.

What was an ex-con doing running a church? In her experience a leopard never changed its spots and, in the same way, criminals never went clean. The trouble was, they could never resist that one last job. That final chance to stick up two fingers at society and secure their future away from the boredom of working life.

Sanza had to be operating a long con of some sort. Maybe he was encouraging his church members to donate their savings to support the church, while pocketing everything on the collection plate. It was a guess, and not one founded on anything more than instinct. It could wait until tomorrow. She returned the rap sheet to the paper wallet on the seat next to her.

Right now, she had more important matters to resolve, like, why he was harbouring Roxanne? Beth had determined that Todd's murder was a botched robbery attempt. Something must have disturbed Roxanne, and she fled the scene in a panic. It was a reasonable assumption to make. Josh's murder, on the other hand was still a challenge. Maybe she got him outside and away from his friends because she thought she could rob him, but things got out of hand. Spinks said he found bruising to the victim's face and abdomen, suggesting she beat Josh before stabbing him in the ear.

That left the supposed suicide.

She hadn't managed to connect Roxanne with Claire in any way. They went to different schools, and lived in different parts of the city. Why would Roxanne either aid or cause Claire's suicide? This was the question that had been plaguing her all morning, and why she was now sitting in the home of Claire's mum.

'You want a cuppa, love?' the woman asked.

Beth smiled. 'No, I'm fine.'

Claire's mum looked every bit of her fifty-nine years. Her cheeks sagged, as did her double chin, and it was clearly a struggle for her to squeeze herself into the armchair opposite Beth.

'Are your lot gonna release our Claire anytime soon, or what?'

'I'm afraid we can't release her for burial until I close the case. I can appreciate how difficult this must be for you.'

'You know who did it yet?'

'I'm still trying to trace Claire's final movements last Saturday. Her manager confirmed her shift finished at midday, and that she was seen walking back to her flat, but it's not clear what happened next.

We believe her time of death was somewhere between midday and one p.m., but that's still a reasonably large window. It would have taken her between five and ten minutes to get back to her flat, if she walked straight there, but I'm wondering whether she stopped off on the way to meet anybody.'

'Like who?'

'That's just it: I'm not sure. I was hoping you might have some idea.'

'Haven't got a clue, love. The only thing I know is that our Claire wouldn't have topped herself. She wasn't the sort, you know? That girl was a lot of things, but she was a survivor.'

'And that is why I'm inclined to think something happened on her way home. Her colleagues said she was in a good mood when she left work.'

'Finally, you lot have got something right. It's about time!'

Beth resisted the urge to defend the hard work of her fellow officers. 'One of Claire's neighbours said he saw a woman with blonde hair at Claire's flat on the day in question.' She passed over the security camera images from the café and club. 'Do you recognise the woman in these pictures? Perhaps she was a friend of Claire's, or someone she didn't get on with?'

The woman put on her glasses, and looked at the images, before passing them back with a shake of the head. 'She doesn't look like any of Claire's friends, and I know everyone she was close to.'

'We think the woman in the picture is wearing a wig. Does that make a difference? Does she look like any of Claire's friends, minus the hair?'

The woman lit a cigarette and looked again. 'I'm sorry, I don't recognise her. Who is she?'

Beth passed Roxanne's mugshot over. 'I can't be certain, but I believe it might be this woman.' Beth knew she shouldn't be sharing information about a possible suspect, but desperate times called for desperate measures. 'Do you know this woman? Do you know if Claire knew her?'

Ash from the cigarette dropped onto the photograph. 'Sorry about that.' She quickly brushed it off. 'I can't say I recognise her. She's looks a bit older than Claire. Most of her friends were the same kind of age. She went to school with all her friends, so I can't see how or why she would know this person.'

Beth silently cursed. She'd been certain Claire's mum would identify Roxanne for her, and give her reason to bring her in. 'Are you certain?'

The woman passed the three images back. 'Sorry, love, I don't know her.'

Beth opened the small paper wallet and placed the photographs in the back.

'Who's that?' the woman asked, pointing at the rap sheet on top.

Beth lifted it. 'This man is Steven Preston. Do you know him?'

The woman leaned closer. 'What did you say his name was?'

'Steven Preston, but he also goes by the alias Paul Sanza.'

The woman snapped her fingers. 'Of course: Paul. I thought I recognised him.'

Beth couldn't hide her excitement. 'You know this man?'

'Yeah, him and Claire had a thing a couple of years back. I thought she was gonna manage to keep that one.'

'I'm sorry, you're saying Claire used to go out with this man?'

'Yeah. He wasn't her usual type. She brought him round here once. He was polite, but so...what's the word...he wasn't like the usual rough blokes she hooked up with.'

'He was what, more...conservative?'

'Yeah, I guess so. He knew how to use a knife and fork and he always said please and thank you, like he was brought up proper. I told her he was too good for her and she should do whatever she could to hold onto him, but they broke up in the end. Such a shame.'

'When did they break up?'

She stubbed out the cigarette. 'Must be a couple of years ago. I can't remember.'

'Do you know whether Claire had seen him recently? Did she mention she'd seen or heard from him?'

'She didn't mention it to be honest.'

That was it: the connection she'd been looking for. Claire didn't know Roxanne, but she knew the man who was protecting Roxanne. It was tenuous, but it gave her another lead to follow. She thanked Claire's mother for her time, and promised she would be in touch once she knew more.

She left the house and walked along the road. She had been forced to park further away, as there had been no space outside the property. She saw she'd missed two calls from Carmichael, but she didn't have time to speak to him now. She climbed into the driver's seat and started the engine. She didn't see the hand reaching out from the back seat, until the chemical-soaked rag was pressed over her nose and mouth. Her panicked eyes looked at the rear-view mirror in a desperate attempt to see who was attacking her. The last thing she saw was the sunlight reflecting off the platinum blonde wig.

51

Carmichael ended the call when he heard Beth's voicemail kick in again.

Where is she?

It was unusual for her not to answer her phone, let alone to leave him in limbo. He returned the phone to his pocket and stared at the headquarters of George Murphy's online dating agency. It was no wonder the company hosted its party evenings in hotels. The office was barely noticeable above a late-night takeaway. He'd managed to find the address online, but it had taken several minutes to work out the office was above the shop, rather than its own building. How could someone who stole a million pounds be running a business from such a small and insignificant base?

He had left Melissa at the office. She'd needed to sleep, but he knew better than to argue with her. He'd had doubts about taking her back on as an apprentice, rather than as his assistant, but she'd proved him wrong. She had the knack for investigative work, and, assuming she achieved her licence, she would make a formidable partner.

The entrance to Murphy's office was through a narrow door to the left of the takeaway. According to the directory on the wall, it was one of three businesses that occupied the floors above the shop. He was going to use the buzzer to ask Murphy to let him in, but when he tried the door, it opened. He charged up the two flights of stairs, and having turned the corner, found a door with a paper sign stuck to it, highlighting he'd reached his destination. This door didn't open, so he knocked instead.

Murphy appeared at the door a moment later, phone pressed to his ear. He opened the door, and initially looked confused, but then a moment of recognition, and he allowed Carmichael to enter. The office, if you could call it that, was a tiny box room, barely large enough for the makeshift desk and the chair Murphy was sitting on. It made Carmichael's own tiny premises look like a palace. A topless girl adorned a calendar hanging from the wall behind Murphy's head. The empty mug on the desk was stained brown, and looked like industrial-strength cleaner would be needed to ever see the original veneer again. Two empty polystyrene takeaway containers lurked on the corner of the desk. Murphy held up a finger while he finished his call and then asked what Carmichael wanted.

'I know the truth, George,' he began. 'I know what you did, and when you did it. I even know how you did it. What I don't know is why. How could you rip off your employees, and leave them without futures? I mean, what drives someone to stoop so low?'

Murphy shifted awkwardly in his chair. 'This again? I told you the other night, I had nothing to do with what happened.'

'Save it, George. Ben knew didn't he? He found out what you'd done. We discovered a paper trail amongst his things that points to the embezzlement. I have to applaud you for the clever way you managed to get the money out of the pension fund. Dummy corporations, false accounting, it was clever. It must take a pretty smart individual to devise that kind of scam. What's your plan with this place? Encourage your subscribers to invest in shares before scarpering?'

'How dare you! This is a legitimate business. I've started this from ground-level -'

'Doesn't look like you've got too far yet. Is that why you don't include a photo of your premises on your website? I had to find your address on the Companies House register. I assume you don't have many visitors?'

'It's an online business. That's what people want these days. They don't want to use the phone, let alone meet face-to-face. Everything's done by email and text message.'

'Sadly, I think you're probably right. Still, this place is a shithole. Why haven't you used some of the million to buy better headquarters? I think I need a hepatitis shot just for being in here.'

Murphy lit a cigarette, and opened the tiny window behind him. 'So, what is this? You think you can strong-arm me?'

Carmichael smiled thinly. 'Future Telecoms: was that your idea? Who thought of the name? Oh, and the fake accountants who verified the purchase of shares, was inspired! You're obviously much smarter than I gave you credit for, George.'

'This is all bullshit. I had nothing to do with money going missing, and you can't prove otherwise.'

'Maybe you're right, but you see, I don't have to prove you did it. That's not my job. I wasn't hired to prove who stole the money, only to find who killed Ben. All the paperwork that Ben left, well, I'll turn that over to the police and the pension regulator. They can do the necessary digging. I'm sure we've only scratched the surface. They'll catch you eventually.'

Murphy took a long drag on the cigarette. 'What do you want? If you're looking to blackmail me, you're wasting your feckin' time. I have no money.'

'That's how you people think isn't it? You assume the rest of us are as bent as you! You're wrong, George!'

'What the hell do you want then?' Murphy shouted.

'To know the truth! Who killed Ben?'

'What? How the feck should I know?'

'Was it you? Did he confront you about what you'd done? Did you plan to kill him when you went round there, or was it an impulse to grab that knife? I mean, how could you? His kids were sleeping upstairs!'

'I told you the other day: I didn't kill Ben. I wasn't even in the feckin' country when it happened!'

'What?'

'That's right. I wasn't here. I was on a plane and there are records to verify I was in the air when he was stabbed. Ha! Bang goes your theory there, matey!' He squashed the cigarette against the wall, and then flicked the butt out of the window.

'You can tell it all to the police.'

'You're bluffing. I can tell a bullshitter when I meet one. If you were going to go to the police, you'd have done it already and it would be them here, and not you. What's your angle?'

'I will be going to the police. In fact, there's a detective on her way over here now. I wanted to give you the opportunity to cut a deal, but as you're not interested -'

'Deal? What kind of deal?'

'I know you were involved in the embezzlement: your guilty face gives it away. But I don't think you acted alone, George. In fact, I'd go so far as to say it probably wasn't even your idea. It was Kevin Lyons wasn't it? It was his idea to steal the million pounds? What did he suggest? A fifty-fifty split? I bet he told you to pin all the blame on Ben too, didn't he?'

'Are you wearing a wire? Are you trying to trick me into confessing something? If you're wearing a recording device, and I ask you, you have to admit it, or any recording will be inadmissible in court.'

Carmichael stood, raised his shirt and turned in a circle. 'No wire, George. It's only me and you. For now. When the police get the evidence they'll arrest you and Kevin. The first one of you to speak about the other will be most likely to get some kind of reduction in sentence. If it was me, I know I'd be first to speak. It makes sense.'

Murphy lit a second cigarette, and smoked it to the butt, before speaking again. 'Okay, okay. Look, it wasn't my idea. It was that snake Lyons. He suggested it, planned it all out, and supplied the paperwork. All I had to do was give him access to what he needed, and then turn a blind eye. He said nobody would be any the wiser for at least six months. He said we had time to get away, and that when the truth was discovered, Ben would take the fall. I nearly fired Lyons when he first suggested it, but then I started to think, as you do. I spent the money in my head. Half a million quid is an incentive.'

'How could you allow Ben to take the fall for it? I thought you were best friends?'

'The business was already failing. It wouldn't have been long before we'd have had to close the factory anyway. I planned to cut Ben in on the deal, but he never would have gone for it. I invested time and money in building that business. We both did. But then that bastard company in the US pulled the rug from under us. We didn't deserve to lose everything. Reclaiming the pension fund seemed like the fairest thing to do.'

'But you were stealing from your workers. What about them?'

'I planned to use my cut of the money to start a new company. I was going to re-employ all of them. I was securing their future. They would have been able to start saving again, and when the new business was profitable, I was going to bump the pension fund back up. They would have got it all back. It was a gamble I knew I could pull off. It made sense to do it. Lyons was persuasive, and the paperwork he produced was impeccable.'

'So what happened? Why didn't you start the new company?'

'That snake Lyons took *all* the money, that's why, and then he disappeared without a trace. He's probably living the high life in a country without an extradition treaty.' He lit another cigarette. 'Lyons suggested we open a Swiss account to transfer the money into. He said it was easy to do, and that the Swiss authorities were less stringent with documentation. He opened the account, and he explained we both had to sign to take the money out, so it was perfectly safe. That brought me comfort, but then Ben found out the truth. He cornered me one night, about a week after Christmas. He showed me all this paperwork and said he'd rumbled what we'd been doing. He said he was going to go to the authorities. I told him if he did, he'd be in as much trouble as his signature was on the transfer paperwork. I explained what my plan was: how we'd start the new company and fix everything with the pension money. I told him it was the only way to fix things. He knew the business was in trouble, and it would be weeks, rather than months before it folded. I told him to think about it, before doing anything rash.

'We didn't see much of one another in January and February, what with the auditors about the place. I think we were taking it in turns to avoid each other. I thought he was coming round to the idea.' He paused. 'But then… he phoned me. I remember it was late on a Saturday night. I was out for dinner with my ex-wife. He said he couldn't allow us to go through with it. He said he didn't care about the consequences, he was going to go to the police first thing on Monday morning, unless we returned the money to the fund. I said it was impossible. The way we took the money…to return it would have raised too many questions. He was adamant: return the money or face prison. I did the only thing I could.'

'You killed him.'

'No! I booked a flight to Geneva.'

'Geneva?'

'Yes. I went to the bank to try and get the money out.'

'But you said it required you and Lyons to both sign for it.'

'I know, but I thought if I showed willing, it would buy me some more time with Ben. I kept phoning Lyons from the airport, both here and over there, but his line was dead. I thought if I told him what Ben was threatening, he'd join me and we could work out a way to return the cash. The last thing I wanted was to go to prison. I was sure he'd feel the same way, but when I got to the bank I realised why he wasn't answering his phone.' He stubbed out the cigarette. 'It was gone. All of it. He'd cleared the account.'

'Wait, how? He would have needed your…'

Murphy nodded. 'My signature, aye. I demanded to see the withdrawal confirmation, and there it was: my signature. Well, a good forgery of my signature. To this day, I don't know how I didn't see it coming. Too trusting, that's my problem.'

'How did Ben react to the news?'

Murphy frowned. 'I never got to tell him. I arrived back in Southampton the next day, to learn he'd been killed. I couldn't believe it! I'd known him longer than anyone else. A part of me died that day too. I wondered whether Lyons had done it, but then when the police arrested Sue and the press reported her fingerprints were on the weapon, well, I assumed she'd done it. I knew he'd beaten her before, and figured she'd retaliated in the worst way.'

'Did you ever find Lyons?'

'No. I tried to trace him, but without any luck. It was as if he'd disappeared off the face of the planet. I couldn't go to the police about it, because they'd have thrown me in jail, and they'd have still not caught the bastard. In the end, I drew a line in the sand, and I've been trying to get back on my feet ever since.'

'You said Ben first confronted you in December. Why didn't he go to the authorities straight away? Why wait three months before taking action?'

Murphy threw his empty cigarette packet on the floor, and popped two pieces of gum into his mouth. 'Lyons blackmailed him into keeping quiet.'

'Blackmailed him? With what?'

'I never found out to be honest. It was to do with something from Ben's past. Lyons found out and threatened to spill the beans if Ben spoke out.'

'What do you think it was?'

'To this day, I still don't know. Whatever it was, I sensed it was something pretty volatile, as it stopped Ben from taking any action.'

'Do you think Lyons killed Ben, and left Sue to take the blame?'

Murphy lowered his head in defeat. 'I honestly don't know. The possibility haunts me to this day. If he did kill Ben, what's to stop him coming after me one day too? That's why I stopped searching for him: better this shit than being dead.'

Carmichael stood, and straightened his shirt. 'I'm giving you until the end of the day to get your things in order, and then I'm turning everything over to the police. I have a lead on where Lyons might be, so take my advice and be the first one to confess. It'll be easier for you in the long run.'

52

Kelly smiles as she secures the detective's wrists behind her back with nylon cord. It won't be long until Beth wakes. She is starting to moan, which means she's regaining consciousness.

She can't believe how easy it was to get to the detective. She's been following her all day, and when she saw Beth go into the whore's mother's house, she knew it was time to act. If Beth has linked her to Claire's death, then it is only a matter of time before she joins the final dots, and that will be bad news for Paul and her.

It seems fitting that Beth's final moments should be spent in the place where Kelly first determined their escape plan. It's almost poetic.

Paul was less receptive than she'd hoped when she confronted him at the church after Beth's visit. He didn't react well to the truth, and that is why she has locked him away. If he could see that she has tied up Beth, he would want to take control of the situation and set the detective free. She can't allow that to happen. It is time for her to step out of the shadows. It is for his own good. He'll see that eventually. Sometimes tough choices need to be made for those you love.

She has Paul's phone. She drafts a text message,

and then deletes it.

She has been racking her brains for an alternative conclusion that doesn't result in her killing Johnson. She has thought about phoning him and explaining who she is, and why she did what she did, but every time she has played the conversation in her mind, he rejects her. She desperately wants to win him over. Her feelings for him are like nothing she has ever known. She thinks she loves him, but having never been in love before, she isn't sure she can trust her heart.

She types the message again. If she can get him here, if she can *show* him who she is, and how much he means to her, then maybe…just maybe…

Beth groans, and her head sways. It is a pity: Beth is pretty, and in another set of circumstances, things might have been different.

Kelly leans in and checks Beth's pulse. It's faint, but she is still alive for now. Her hand lingers near Beth's neck. She knows it's wrong, but she allows her fingers to unbutton Beth's blouse.

What am I doing?

She ignores the voice in her head and cups one of Beth's breasts. It is warm and soft. She's been with women before, but that was always as a means to an end. This is a different feeling. She is drawn to Beth. No, it's more than that: she wants Beth for herself. She is disgusted, and yet she cannot stop staring at her. Beth looks so helpless.

What is wrong with me?

She forces her hands away and she stands and moves to the mirror hanging from the wall. She stares at her reflection and then slaps herself hard across the face. Her cheek warms. She slaps herself again.

Get your shit together.

This is her brother's influence. She looks back at Beth. That svelte body, the shape of those breasts. She's still not conscious. She wouldn't notice if Kelly kissed her. She closes her eyes and takes a deep breath. She needs to regain control.

This bitch will ruin everything. She will take Johnson away from you. Do what you need to do!

She crouches and checks the restraints around Beth's legs. Beth's head is swaying again. It won't be long now.

Beth's complexion is smooth, and she has only used minimal makeup. One kiss won't hurt. It will get it out of her system. Kelly leans in. Beth groans and her eyes flicker open. Kelly stops, and recoils in panic. Beth's eyes open, and there is a moment of recognition. Beth's screams are muffled by the tape over her lips.

Kelly breathes a sigh of relief. She's never been so close to losing control like that before. She doesn't have time to worry about that now. She smiles. 'I bet you didn't expect to see me.'

Beth's eyes widen as she becomes aware of the ropes pinning her limbs to the chair.

Kelly presses send on the phone, and then puts it in her pocket. 'Don't worry, our brave man will be here soon. He has an important decision to make.'

Kelly disappears off to the kitchen and returns a moment later. She places the plastic container on the floor next to Beth. The smell of accelerant is overpowering. 'I need to prepare everything for his arrival.'

53

Melissa was half asleep by the time Carmichael made it back to the office.

'Are you sure you're alright?' he offered. 'You don't look so good.'

She yawned. 'I'm fine,' but she could barely keep her eyes open.

'I think I should take you home. You've done more than enough for today.'

Her heavy eyes began to close, but then she jolted awake. 'Wait, no, not yet. I need to tell you something.' She blinked rapidly to kick-start her memory. 'I haven't managed to track Tom's estranged sister yet. She did a good job of hiding her past. While you were out, I did a little more digging into Sanza's background. We already know Sanza was Lyons, and prior to that he was Steven Preston, right? I ran a dark web search on Preston, and on the sixth page of the search engine, I found a redacted document. It looks like it is a medical assessment, but it's impossible to make out what the assessment relates to, as all the words are blacked out apart from Preston's name and age, the signature of the doctor who completed the assessment and the name of the hospital. I said to you earlier that Preston had spent some of his childhood at a secure facility, well this hospital is that facility. It is Angel Hall Hospital, and it is near Dorchester, further along the coast. The hospital is still there, but it's now a facility specialising in treating patients with personality disorders and depression. Back in the late seventies Angel Hall was a secure hospital for disturbed children, that is, children with significant mental disorders. They also housed children deemed unfit for borstals. I can only imagine the kind of crime a child would need to have committed to end up there.'

'The document doesn't say anything else?'

She shook her head. 'Every line of the report has been inked out with a marker pen. I suppose it was for the protection of the children held there.'

'But he got out, right? So surely he was cured of whatever he was suffering with?'

Melissa shrugged. 'Your guess is as good as mine. I couldn't find anything else online, but, yes, presumably he was released at some point, as he then pops up at the old folks home conning the pensioners in 1995, aged nineteen.'

'Murphy claimed Lyons was the one who perpetrated the fraud at the factory. He said it was all Lyons' idea and work, and that all Murphy did was turn a blind eye, in exchange for a fifty per cent cut of the stolen money. The thing is, Lyons disappeared without trace before the money was split. Murphy claims he never saw a penny of it, and I'm inclined to believe him. We know Lyons became Sanza within a month of Dewis' death. The question is: what happened to the money? He hardly lives like a man with a million pounds in the bank.'

'Maybe he has a gambling addiction we know

nothing about.'

'Maybe...Murphy says he was on a flight to Switzerland when Dewis was killed, and although the police will need to confirm that, it leaves Lyons as our prime suspect for the murder.'

'I think it's time to get the police involved. You're too close to this, Johnson. I know you can't believe Sanza could be the same person that conned those pensioners, and defrauded the pension fund, but all the evidence points towards it.' She yawned again. 'He's manipulated you, so it's time to step away.'

Had Sanza been manipulating him this whole time?

He rubbed his eyes. 'I've been trying to get hold of Beth since I left here earlier, but now her phone is switched off. It's unlike her. I'm worried.'

'Have you tried the station? Maybe her phone's battery is dead.'

'I tried there and they said it's her day off. I left a message for her to call me ASAP. Have we had any calls here?'

'Nothing.'

Carmichael's phone beeped. He opened the message, hoping it was Beth. 'It's Sanza.'

'What does he want?'

'He wants me to meet him. He says there's something he needs to speak to me about urgently. He's at the farm where the church was established.'

'You think he's going to admit killing Ben?'

'Your guess is as good as mine.'

'I don't like it, Johnson. You need to leave this to the police to handle.'

'Keep trying Beth. When she answers, tell her to

meet me at the farm. This ends tonight.'

'Wait, Johnson, he has an unhealthy control over you, what if he -'

'That's a chance I have to take. Get hold of Beth, and get her to the farm.'

54

The smell of the paraffin was making Beth cough, which was hard to do with her mouth plastered shut with gaffer tape. Kelly disappeared upstairs half an hour ago, and she heard her arguing with someone up there.

The room was dark, the sun having set behind a hill in the distance. She had been trying to wriggle her wrists free of the rope, but they are stuck fast. If she could only find something sharp, she could cut her way out. That was her only chance of escape.

Beth heard footsteps on the stairs. Kelly was returning. An orange glow preceded her into the room. She was carrying a candlestick. Beth's foot was inches from the container of paraffin, but she could do nothing to push it away.

Kelly has changed: she is now wearing a bright red cocktail dress. She placed the candlestick on the table to Beth's left. She was about to speak, when the sound of a door being barged open shattered the silence.

'He's here,' she said excitedly.

Beth heard Carmichael calling her name. She tried to shout out, but her screams were little more than a whimper.

He stomped through the kitchen and appeared in the doorway behind her. 'Beth, oh my God, what are you -'

'Welcome, Johnson,' Kelly said, stepping out of the shadows. 'You're right on time.'

He squinted through the darkness. 'Do I know you?'

'My name's Kelly. We met a week ago, but you probably don't remember it. I've been waiting for the chance to introduce myself properly.'

There was something familiar about her voice, and he couldn't shake the feeling he had seen her before. 'Listen Kelly, I don't know what's going on here, but this woman is a police officer, and a friend of mine. You need to let her go.'

'I can't do that.'

'Listen, the room upstairs is on fire. I could see it from outside. We need to get out of here.'

'Don't come any closer, Johnson. It's not time to leave yet. We have work to do.'

There was a large crash as the ceiling fell in the vestry behind him. A cloud of smoke burst into the room.

Carmichael covered his mouth with his sleeve. 'This place isn't safe. We need to get -'

'No!' Kelly screamed, lifting the can of paraffin and pouring it liberally over Beth's head. Beth screamed beneath the tape. Carmichael stepped forward, but Kelly showed him the lighter in her left hand. 'Stay where you are.'

He looked around the dim room for something he could use to cut Beth free. 'I don't understand what's going on here. Where's Paul? He told me to meet him here.'

'Paul is gone. *I* sent you the message.'

The smoke from the vestry was becoming denser. Carmichael covered his mouth with a handkerchief, and then charged at her, grabbing the wrist holding the lighter. He twisted it behind her back. She lifted her other hand, and splashed them both with the paraffin. The liquid stung his eyes, and he let her go. He wiped at his eyes with the handkerchief.

'Stay back, Johnson. If you try something like that again, I'll torch the lot of us.'

He blinked against the stinging, staring at the crazy woman in front of him. His mouth dropped when he saw who it was beneath the wig. 'Paul?'

'I told you, Johnson, Paul is gone. He served a purpose, but I had to silence him.'

'I…I don't understand,' he stammered. 'Is this some kind of joke?'

'It's no joke, Johnson. This is who I am.'

'Don't be ridiculous, Paul. Why are you wearing a dress? And that wig?'

'I'm not, Paul. My name is Kelly. Paul was an aspect of my personality; he was my brother. I loved him dearly, but he reacted badly when he found out who we really are. I've outgrown him, as I did with those who went before him. They don't understand what the world is like. Not like you and me, Johnson. We know the kind of monsters that walk amongst us. That is why God brought you to us. Don't you see?' She brushed his cheek with her hand. 'The first time I saw you, I knew you were different. It has been so tough not to tell you the truth before now, my love, but I had to keep my true self hidden, until now. Don't you feel it too? We're destined to be together. I thought I was imagining it at first, but once I'd saved your life, God spoke to me, and told me it was meant to be.'

He coughed. 'What are you talking about?'

'Last Tuesday. Those three youths were going to rob you and leave you for dead. God spoke to me, and told me I had to save you, Johnson. He's calling to us now, Johnson. Can you hear Him?'

'Three youths? The Hatchett: that was you?'

'I saw them following you from the pub. They were mugging you when I stepped in. They thought they could take me, but they underestimated my inner strength. I couldn't tell you who I was then, as I was still in Paul's clothes. I wouldn't have been able to convince you of who I was.'

'You killed them.'

'They deserved to die. There are so many bad people out there. He spoke to you in that nightclub in London. He spoke to you again on that rooftop when you could have pulled Lennon back over. You heard Him, didn't you? You heard Him tell you to sacrifice them for the greater good. That's the only way to save their souls. If they die naturally, Satan gets to keep them. If we sacrifice them in God's name, because it is His will, He can still redeem them.'

'I can't believe this. You're fucking insane!'

She shook her head gently with an empathetic smile. 'No, I'm not, Johnson. I understand your scepticism. I've faced it all my life. I'm special, as are you. Everything I have done in my life has led me to this point. Everything you have done in your life has led you here. Our paths have been on this trajectory since we were born. This is fate, destiny, or karma, however you want to describe it.'

'You're delusional! Your name is Steven Preston. You changed your name to Kevin Lyons, and then to Paul Sanza.'

'Steven, Kevin and Paul were a part of me. They were aspects of my personality, but I am the true embodiment.'

'Multiple personalities. That's why you were in Angel Hall.'

'They tried to silence us, but I told Paul we could beat the system. I showed him how.'

'You're not well.'

'You're one to talk!'

'Have you looked in the mirror? A wig and a dress doesn't make you a woman. You need help.'

'I am one of many personalities occupying this shell. I am Kelly, and I am the one in control.'

'I want to speak to Paul.'

'Paul is gone. He won't be back. I know who I am supposed to be now. Now you have a choice to make, Johnson. You know the path God has chosen for you.' She passed him the lighter. 'Listen to my voice, Johnson. Beth needs to die. She has been taken by Satan. You need to save her soul. It is what God wants you to do. She is the only thing holding you back. When Beth dies, you and I can be together. We can give ourselves to each other in the presence of God, and then we can join Him in His kingdom. This is what He wants, Johnson. You know I'm right.'

'Listen, Paul. We need to get out of here. It won't be long until this room is on fire too, and then the whole place is going to go up. Please? Let's just get out of here, and we can talk more outside. Okay?' He stepped towards her.

'Stay back, Johnson. It is Satan who is telling you to spare Beth. You need to ignore that voice in your head and listen to mine. God is speaking through me now. He is telling you to kill Beth.'

'I can't kill Beth. I still care for her deeply. She doesn't deserve to die.'

'Do you reject Satan, and all his temptations?'

'I do.'

'Do you believe in the one true God who wants to save your soul?'

'I do.'

'Then take this lighter and touch the flame to her hair, and He will embrace you.'

He knocked Kelly's hand and the lighter hit the curtains. There was a whoosh as the flames tore up the fabric. He charged at Kelly with a roar and the two of them crashed to the floor. Kelly's wig flew off.

'What are you doing?' she spluttered. 'Don't let Satan into your soul, Johnson. He means to corrupt you.'

He punched her across the face, and then raced to the kitchen, finding a sharp knife. He lunged back to the chair and cut through the leg restraints. Kelly was back on her feet and drove her elbow into his neck. He slumped to the floor in pain. He kicked out at her, but she was retreating. He grabbed the knife again, and tore at the ropes around Beth's wrists. She was wheezing badly.

Kelly reached out and grabbed his ankle. 'Don't go, Johnson. God wants us to sacrifice ourselves in His name.'

'I'm going to get you both out of here, and then I'm going to get you the help you need, Paul.'

'There isn't time to save us both, Johnson. It's Beth or me. Who do you love the most?'

Carmichael looked from his friend to Beth, and then back again. 'I can save you both.'

He climbed unsteadily to his feet and told Beth to brace herself. He slammed his foot onto the chair, and it splintered. Beth yelped, but pulled her hand free. He put his jacket over the two of them and they charged towards the window. They crashed through the frame and onto the ground outside. His jacket was burning, and he rolled on his back until the flames were extinguished. One of the downstairs windows blew out, covering them in tiny fragments of glass. He grabbed Beth roughly around her middle and dragged her further away.

'Keep down,' he warned, as he pulled the jacket back over his head.

'Where are you going?'

'I need to get Paul out of there.'

'You can't. It's too dangerous.'

He walked unsteadily towards the window. 'I have to try. He's my friend.'

The front of the house erupted as the remaining contents of the petrol can exploded inside.

THURSDAY

55

Carmichael parked his car in a space outside of the Dewis' house. He'd missed three calls and received a text message from Tom already that morning. He rubbed his eyes and coughed.

They'd managed to call the fire brigade who arrived fifteen minutes later. By the time the blaze was out and they managed to enter the property, it was nothing more than a shell. The charred remains of Kelly were brought out on a stretcher, and Beth did her best to explain to her colleagues exactly what had happened.

Beth and Carmichael reluctantly agreed to be checked over at A&E, but both were released shortly before one a.m., and told to go home and rest. Beth agreed for him to sleep at her place, on the understanding that she wanted to ensure his health didn't take an adverse turn. She called him her knight in shining armour: he'd broken free of Sanza's influence and saved her life. They stayed awake for hours talking about it.

They eventually fell asleep on the sofas in her living room, and only woke when Melissa phoned the flat. She had seen the report of the fire at the farm on the news. Beth explained what happened while Carmichael showered. He scrubbed his skin raw in an effort to get rid of the smell of smoke, but it was like it was now ingrained in the hairs in his nostrils.

Beth was now on her way to the Angel Hall Hospital to see what else she could find out about Steven Preston. Melissa agreed to go with her.

Tom answered the door and invited him in. 'Take a seat,' he said, when they were in the living room.

'We're supposed to be seeing your mum this afternoon, but I'm glad you called. I found the man who killed your dad.'

Tom didn't answer.

'Aren't you happy? It means your mum *didn't* do it.'

'Who is this man? Did he confess?'

'Well, no, he didn't confess as such, but he had means, motive and opportunity, and given what else we *know* he's done, we're pretty certain he was the one.'

Tom walked to the bay window and stared out.

'What's wrong, Tom? What's going on?'

He continued to stare out of the window. 'I always suspected that Aunt Helen was still in touch with Annie. She'd make off-hand comments from time-to-time, say things about Annie that she couldn't know unless she'd seen her. You know, like, she'd say Annie didn't like a particular television show or something, even though the show hadn't started until long after Annie had moved away. I never questioned her about it. I figured it was good that Annie still had someone looking out for her. Helen's always been so good to us. I was disappointed Annie didn't want to get in touch with me, but I understood that I reminded her of a past she wanted to forget.' He paused. 'I knew you were keen to speak to Annie, so I lied to Helen and said you were getting closer to finding her. I knew Helen would panic and reach out to my sister, so I followed her on my motorbike. She caught a bus to town and then onto Hedge End. She finally stopped at a small café in the village. I was across the road, and saw her sit at a table outside. Ten minutes later, a woman with short brown hair sat at the table next to her. I couldn't tell until I got closer, but it was Annie.'

'She was in Southampton the whole time?'

'I waited until they'd finished and Helen had left, before I followed Annie. I caught up with her as she reached a small bungalow. She seemed anxious to see me, but reluctantly invited me into her house…I met her daughter.' Tom wiped a tear from his cheek. 'I have a niece. She's three years-old, but she's incredible. We played with her tea set. She's such a funny little girl. When I told Annie about mum's appeal, she almost threw me out of the house. She said she didn't want to know anything about mum, and wouldn't see me if I mentioned it again. I demanded to know why. I told her mum was innocent, and that she needed Annie's support as much as mine. She said mum was guilty, and that I was wasting my time in helping her.'

The living room door creaked open behind them, and in walked a young woman with a brown bob. She was the spitting image of the young Sue in the photos that adorned the living room walls.

'Mr Carmichael, this is my sister Annie,' Tom said. 'Annie, this is the private investigator I told you about. You need to tell him exactly what you said to me yesterday.'

56

The two small flower beds, and stretch of lawn, didn't make the grey structure of Angel Hall Hospital look any more welcoming. Melissa shivered as she and Beth approached the wooden doors. The dull green walls inside weren't much warmer. The stench of disinfectant, common in all hospitals, hit them as they approached the front desk. The receptionist held up a finger, as she finished her phone call, before replacing the receiver and scowling at them.

Beth held out her identification and placed a piece of paper next to it. 'I'm Detective Sergeant Beth Taylor, and this is a warrant to see the files for a patient by the name of Steven Preston. Is there a senior physician, or facility director I can speak to?'

The receptionist took the warrant and read it, before passing it back. It was clear from her puzzled expression that she hadn't understood it. She picked up the phone once more. 'They'll be here in a moment,' she confirmed a moment later. 'Please take a seat.'

Five minutes later, two men approached them. The first was tall, and wearing a bright blue suit, with a white shirt and red tie. He wore a broad smile, and extended his hand for them to shake. 'I'm the director of the hospital. This is my colleague Dr Daniel Stark.

How can we help?'

Stark was six inches taller than Beth, and wore a white coat. He looked tired, and less jovial than the man introducing him.

Beth showed them her warrant card. 'I'm with Hampshire's Major Incident Team. I'm investigating an incident that happened on a farm near Cadnam late last night. We believe the individual involved was a former patient here. I have a warrant to see and take copies of any patient records you have relating to him.'

The director smiled again. 'I have meetings to attend. I'm sure I can leave you in the capable hands of Dr Stark. He can give you access to anything you need. If you'll excuse me.'

Stark didn't look pleased to have been abandoned. 'What's the patient's name?'

'Steven Preston. He would have been resident here in the mid-eighties.'

Stark sucked air through his teeth. 'Oh, the mid-eighties? That might be an issue. There was a fire at the facility in 1992, a lot of the old paper records that had yet to be transferred onto computer were destroyed or suffered water damage.'

'Do you still have what remains?'

Stark nodded. 'There's a room in the basement where the surviving boxes live. At some point they'll be backed up, but for now, that's where they're kept. You're welcome to have a look, and see if you can find what you want, but I can't guarantee you'll find it. The files aren't in any particular order, so *if*, and that's a big if, but *if* the file is there, it's going to take you a while to find it. I'd offer to send someone to help you, but we're so short-staffed at the moment that I can't spare anyone.'

Stark led them through the security gate, and down to the basement. Beth tried to make small talk. 'Have you worked here long?'

'About five years now.'

'Has it changed much since Preston's time?'

'Oh, I'm sure it has. Half the hospital needed to be rebuilt after the fire. It had a real makeover then.'

Beth and Melissa exchanged surprised looks, but allowed him to continue.

'Back in the eighties, this place catered for individuals who were deemed unfit to stand a criminal trial, or diagnosed as insane during trial. It's different now. We haven't accepted court-charged patients in fifteen years or so. Today, the facility is privately run, relying on donations from patrons, and the occasional government handout. Patients here are either voluntary outpatients, or those sectioned by a family member.'

'What kind of conditions do you treat?'

'A broad range of mental health issues to be honest. Depression is the most common condition, but I specialise in personality disorders.' He opened the door to a tiny room, lined with stacks of cardboard boxes, some with obvious damp. The only light came from a single bulb hanging from the ceiling. 'Here it is. Best of luck with your search. I'll have some tea sent down shortly.' With that, he was gone.

Melissa stepped into the room. 'The term "needle in a haystack" springs to mind. Where do you want to start?'

Beth removed her suit jacket, and rolled up the sleeves of her blouse. 'We need to be systematic about this. Let's start with this stack nearest the door, and work around the room. We can take a box each and start a new stack when we've finished checking it.'

By the time someone appeared, carrying a tray with two mugs of tea and a small plate of digestives, they had cleared two stacks of boxes, with five to go.

It was in the fourth stack Beth found what they were looking for. 'Steven Preston, born May twenty-fourth 1976. Bingo.'

Melissa left her box, and joined Beth by the door. 'What does it say?'

Beth skim read the first couple of pages. 'It seems young Steven was sent here by his parents as they couldn't figure out how to deal with his behaviour. This is the letter they sent the then director of the facility begging him to see Steven. It seems Steven was expelled from several schools pre-adolescence. The final straw was when he was expelled from boarding school for butchering the school's dog mascot.'

'Jesus!'

Beth continued to read the psychiatric assessments in the file, and as she turned pages, a photograph fell to the floor. Melissa crouched and picked it up. It showed two young teenagers smiling, each with an arm around the other's shoulder.

'You think one of these is Preston?' Melissa asked.

Beth glanced at the photograph, and shrugged. 'Maybe. Why else would it be in the file?' She paused at the last page in the file. 'He was released from the hospital in 1991 on medication, and that's where the story ends.'

'1991? So Preston was fifteen when he left here. We know he was arrested four years later for conning the retired folks out of their pensions. Is there anything else?'

Beth closed the file. 'Nothing that I understand. Where's that Dr Stark? Let's see if he can translate this for us.'

Beth headed back to the staircase, with Melissa lagging behind. Stark's office was on the second floor of the facility. A security guard escorted them.

'Did you manage to find what you were looking for?' Stark asked, once they were seated.

Beth pushed the file across his desk. 'Can you tell me what this boy was suffering with? It wasn't obvious from the file.'

Stark opened the paperwork and read. 'By modern standards, I'd say he had anti-social behaviour issues arising from attention deficit and hyperactivity disorder. You have to remember the treatment of mental health issues has come a long way in the last ten to fifteen years. It's less of a taboo, and the exploratory advances that we've made are -'

'I'm not after your life story, Dr Stark. I want to know how the young man described in the file could develop into the cross-dressing maniac who abducted and threatened my life yesterday.'

Stark's face grew pale. 'Well…I…uh…I don't know…I'm not familiar with this case. I hadn't even joined medical school in 1991.'

Melissa slid the photograph across the desk. 'Is there any way of identifying the second boy in this picture? We found it in the file. It looks like it was taken in the grounds of the hospital.'

Stark lifted the image and turned it over in his hands. 'There is one person who might know.' He picked up his phone and asked for Nurse Dewey to be called to his office. 'Catherine Dewey was a staff nurse here in the eighties. She's due to retire this year. If anyone remembers them, it will be her.'

A knock at the door announced Dewey's arrival. Her face was wrinkled, and she had a slight frame. Stark introduced them all and explained why Beth and Melissa were there.

She sat in the remaining vacant chair, and looked at the photograph. 'I remember these two,' she smiled. 'They were thick as thieves.'

Beth pointed at the youth on the left. 'We believe this boy is Steven Preston. Can you tell us who the other boy is?'

Dewey smiled again. 'That's not him. Steven is the one on the right. Don't worry, you're not the first to have confused them. People were always muddling the two of them. If you didn't know better, you'd have thought they were brothers, such was the resemblance.'

'Who is the boy on the left then?' Beth asked.

'That's Harry Knowles,' she frowned. 'He was a wicked boy.'

'They look like good friends,' Melissa pointed out.

'Oh they were. They spent every minute of social time together. They'd play chess, they'd play cops and robbers, but they both loved orienteering.'

'Orienteering?' Beth asked. 'In a hospital?'

Dewey nodded. 'Back then we had high fences around the perimeter of the gardens. Patients would be allowed outside on good weather days. The director at the time thought it was important for patients to feel the wind on their faces. We devised treasure hunts and the like, and those that wanted to were encouraged to use a map and compass to follow the trail. Harry loved it, and Steven would always tag along.' She glanced nervously at Stark before continuing. 'Personally, I think it can be depressing being stuck inside this place. It's so dreary.'

Stark tried to interrupt, but she ignored his attempt, and continued. 'Ultimately, that's what cost the director his job here. After Harry died, all outdoor activities were cancelled.'

Beth sat up in her chair. 'Wait, what happened to Harry?'

'Oh, I thought you knew already. It was such a tragedy. Steven was never the same after that.'

57

Annie nervously extended her hand until Carmichael shook it, and then she perched on the edge of the sofa next to Tom.

Carmichael coughed to break the tension. 'You're a difficult lady to find. My assistant has been trying to trace you for days. I can't believe you've been in Southampton this whole time.'

She glanced at Tom, before responding. 'I haven't been. I lived in Edinburgh for a while, and then moved to the south of France, before settling in the Midlands. That's where I met my daughter's father. He had to move here for work, so now I'm back.'

'I'm certain your mum didn't kill your dad, Annie. Your dad didn't steal that money either. I found the men who did, so your dad's name can finally be cleared. I believe the same men ultimately killed your dad, but I need to prove it.'

Tom put his hand on hers. 'It's okay, Annie. Tell him.'

Annie nodded, and took a deep breath. 'You're wrong, Mr Carmichael. She *is* guilty. I know it in my heart.'

Carmichael's eyes narrowed. 'How can you be so certain? I'm a pretty good judge of character. What do you know that I don't?'

Annie exhaled another deep breath. 'My relationship with Sue was strained for a long time. Maybe it was my adolescent hormones, I don't know, but we'd argued more than I can remember in the months leading to that night. Tom can't remember it as well as me. It was a horrible time in our lives. Dad was drinking all the time, and would fly off the handle at the littlest thing. Mum was stressed too. I knew he was violent towards her sometimes, but then she used to provoke him some of the time too. It was like a game to her, I think. We were all under such enormous pressure. I had friends whose fathers worked at the factory, and they refused to speak to me when the allegations hit the newspapers. It was like I'd become a leper overnight. Sue tried to keep us away from the newspapers and television reports, but I wasn't stupid. I was fourteen, I was able to buy my own newspaper and read all the sordid details. It was embarrassing. I was ashamed of her for not doing more to protect us.'

'What more could your mum have done?'

'She shouldn't have allowed him to be violent. She should have sought help. She should have made him seek counselling or something. Our safety should have been her priority, but she was more interested in seeing her friends. She was out drinking the…the night it happened.'

'I know that. She's told me your dad hit her occasionally, but he was under an enormous amount of -'

'That's no excuse! It was a relief to move in with Helen, but even transferring to a new school didn't help. Tom was young enough that his new friends didn't know what had happened. He didn't see the children staring and whispering behind our backs. School was horrible. I vowed I'd get my G.C.S.E's and then I'd get away. I got a part-time job while at school and saved every penny I earned. I was seeing a guy called Marcus at the time, and his older brother helped me find somewhere to stay when I left. I've moved from town to town ever since.' She paused. 'On the night it happened…I heard mum come home from her night out with Auntie Pat. She came to check on us. I could smell the wine on her breath as she leaned in and kissed my head. She assumed I was asleep, but she was a noisy drunk. I snuck downstairs to get myself a glass of water. I was outside the kitchen door when I heard them arguing. I couldn't hear exactly what they were arguing about as they were shouting at the same time. I heard dad yelp out, and then he said "What have you done?" before clattering into the kitchen door. I hid in the cupboard under the stairs as she left the kitchen and slammed the front door behind her. I could hear my dad whimpering, so I went to see if he was okay. I saw him slumped against the wall. He was bleeding. I tried to help him. I covered my hand with my pyjama top and pulled the knife out. I didn't know it would make him bleed more. I thought I was helping. His blood seeped onto my pyjama bottoms. He opened his eyes and told me to call for an ambulance. I went upstairs to change, and when I was about to come downstairs, I heard her phoning for an ambulance. I hid my bloody clothes, and pretended to go back to sleep. I know Sue killed my father, Mr Carmichael, because I heard her do it.'

58

'How did Harry die?' Beth pressed.

There was sadness in the nurse's eyes. 'It must have been late October 1990. It was a warm day, I remember that. I also remember the boys playing in the fallen brown leaves out on the grass. They were playing cops and robbers again. Harry asked if it was okay for them to build a den out of some fallen branches at the far side of the gardens. I told them they could, but they had to be careful. They were busy building for nearly an hour. Each of us checked on them from time-to-time, but they seemed to be having so much fun. A bell always used to sound when outdoor activities were over, and I can remember hearing it ring, but Harry and Steven didn't return as they should have. I remember telling Phil – he was one of the doctors – that I would go and hurry them.' She paused. 'I could see the den from a distance, and, as I approached, I heard crying. I called out, asking if everything was okay. You know what boys can be like; I thought they'd had an argument or something. When I arrived, I saw Steven sat by the den sobbing. He had his head buried in his arms. I asked him what was wrong, and he said Harry had slipped and he couldn't wake him. I raced under the trees of their den, and found Harry on his front.

There was blood gushing from his face, and blood all over the rock he had fallen against. I pulled him out, but couldn't find a pulse. I told Steven to run to Phil and get him over straight away. I tried to resuscitate Harry in the meantime, but to no avail. We rushed him back to the hospital, but we were too late.

'Steven wouldn't speak about it for a long time after. Something changed in him that day: he became more...withdrawn than before. He'd lost his best friend: the only joy he'd ever had here. We encouraged him to mix with the other patients, but he wasn't interested. He even refused his food for a time. We persevered, and eventually he opened up. It seemed Steven had been the police officer in their roleplay and Harry had been the robber. Steven had chased him into the den, but Harry had lost his footing and had slipped, his face smacking against the jagged rock. Well, an investigation was launched into why we had allowed the boys to play under only minor supervision. The director was held accountable and made the scapegoat. Procedures were tightened as a result, and the treatment of patients became more scientific than pastoral.'

Beth asked for the photograph back. 'What was Harry here for?'

'Harry Knowles was disturbed when he arrived at Angel Hall. If anything, his passing was a kindness, as I think he was likely to spend the rest of days in treatment. I've been involved in the care of so many children over the years, but I've never met one who could be so manipulative and cruel in all my days.'

Beth frowned. 'But you said he was Steven's best friend. You described him as Steven's only joy.'

'Yes, but he moulded himself into that role. Listen, Harry was the only child of a surgeon and a former midwife. They were a loving family from all accounts, though the father worked long hours. The mother left work and chose to educate Harry at home. I'm sure that was one of the causes of his anti-social behaviour: he didn't know *how* to make friends. A neighbour visiting the property one day found an eight year-old Harry wearing bloody pyjamas. When she asked where his parents were, he told her they were sleeping in bed. When the neighbour went upstairs she found they had both had their throats cut. The police were called and as the only surviving member of the household, Harry was questioned about what had happened. He told them he didn't know but kept asking where his sister was. He was an only child. He spent time with some of the country's leading MPD specialists, and eventually he was sectioned here.'

'MPD?' Beth asked.

'Multiple Personality Disorder. Sorry, they don't call it that anymore. It's Dissociative Identity Disorder, or DID, now. Dr Stark, here, is an expert in the field.'

Beth and Melissa turned to face Stark.

There was a moment of silence, before he realised they wanted him to explain the condition. 'Dissociative Identity Disorder is a rare illness in which two or more personalities with distinct memories and behaviour patterns exist in one individual. Symptoms can include memory loss too extensive to be explained by forgetfulness. Usually, the primary identity, or host, carries the individual's given name and is passive, dependent, guilty and depressed. When in control, each personality state, or alter, may be experienced as if it has a distinct history, self-image and identity. A personality's characteristics – including name, reported age and gender, vocabulary, general knowledge, and predominant mood – contrast with those of the primary identity. Certain circumstances or stress factors can cause a particular personality to emerge. The various identities may deny knowledge of one another, be critical of one another or appear to be in open conflict.'

Beth and Melissa shot each other nervous glances.

Dewey noticed the exchange. 'In Harry's case, *he* was the primary host, but his "sister" Kelly would emerge at times of distress. During therapy, Kelly admitted Harry's father had sexually abused him from an early age, and this may have been the trigger for her emergence. Before Steven's arrival, Kelly would bully the other patients to get her own way. Steven was different though. As Harry and Steven's friendship developed, we saw less and less of Kelly. Steven seemed to give Harry the confidence to keep Kelly at bay. He was making real progress in his therapy until that autumn afternoon.'

Beth studied the photograph. 'How can you be certain it was Harry who died that day? You said yourself they were so similar that they were often muddled.'

Dewey scowled. 'I know because it was *me* that found them. Steven was wearing his favourite football shirt. You can see him wearing it in the photograph. Plus there was the plastic bracelet on his wrist, which confirmed his identity and patient number.'

Beth held up her hand passively. 'I don't mean to cause any offence, but is it not possible the two boys could have swapped clothes, and bracelets? In all the fuss that ensued, it would be easy to overlook minor differences in their appearance.'

'Nonsense!' Dewey exclaimed.

Beth tilted her head. 'What if I told you the Preston who threatened me last night also had a dominant personality he called Kelly?'

Stark coughed. 'According to this file, Steven never exhibited any of the symptoms associated with DID. There are several criteria for diagnosing someone with dissociative identity disorder, the first being the presence of two or more distinct identities. The second is: at least two personalities must take control of the person's identity at regular intervals. Then there's the amnesia I mentioned earlier. The number of alters in any given case can vary widely and can vary across gender. The physical changes that occur in a switch between alters is one of the most fascinating aspects of the illness: patients can assume whole new physical postures and voices. It's a riveting area to study.'

'So, it seems unlikely that the Steven who was treated here would later develop the disorder, right?'

Stark chewed the end of his pen. 'It's difficult to answer either way without knowing more about what happened to him after he was discharged. If he experienced a severe psychological breakdown, it might be possible he'd developed the same condition as Harry.'

'Which is more likely: that Harry stole Steven's identity so he could escape the hospital, or that Steven developed the condition?'

Stark shrugged.

Beth turned to Dewey. 'Nobody is blaming you for a potential mix-up. You said yourself that Harry was manipulative and moulded himself to become Steven's best friend. What if his plan was always to kill Steven and assume his identity? The boy who died had his face caved in with a rock, so how was he identified? Fingerprints?'

'No…it was….well…it was…the bracelet on his arm said it, and…well, it had to be him.'

'But what if it wasn't?' Beth continued. 'What if the real Harry Knowles was the one who survived and left here? The person we are investigating is cool, calm and calculating. The Kelly I met last night was paranoid, aggressive and violent. She tried to burn me to death because she thought I was getting in the way. Does that not sound like the patient you used to treat?'

Dewey put her hand to her mouth, and looked nervously at Stark.

'I think I should meet this individual and assess him,' he said.

'I'm afraid that's not going to be possible,' Beth said. 'He died last night. I think you've both told me everything I need to know about this individual. If you don't mind, we'll go and look for Harry's file downstairs.' Beth and Melissa stood and headed back downstairs.

'I'll catch you up,' Melissa said. 'I should give Johnson a call and let him know what we've discovered.'

Beth continued down the stairs to the basement.

Melissa stepped outside and put the phone to her ear. It went to voicemail, so she left a message. As she pocketed the phone she didn't notice the woman in the garden who was watching her every move.

59

Annie looked nervous as she stepped through the metal detector.

'You've got nothing to worry about,' Carmichael reassured her. 'There are plenty of prison guards inside, and I'll be there, so you don't need to worry about your mum becoming aggressive. It's important for you to confront her with what you witnessed. She's been clinging to this lie for so long that I'm sure she'll deny it at first. That's why I don't want Tom here when you tell her. She's less likely to admit the truth with him here.'

Annie nodded her understanding and allowed Carmichael to take her shaking hand. The prison guard escorted the group through to the visitors' hall and waited until all were seated before signalling for his colleague to collect the prisoners.

Annie's knees were knocking beneath the table. 'I'm not sure why I'm so nervous,' she whispered.

He put his warm hand over hers. 'It'll be alright, Annie. I'm here. You have nothing to be nervous about.'

A buzzer sounded overhead, and then the security gate at the far side of the room opened, and the prisoners were led in.

Sue's face appeared halfway down the queue. Her eyes were tearful by the time she was seated opposite them. 'I can't believe you're here. When I read your name on my list, I…I…' She moved a hand to her mouth, and a single tear rolled down her cheek. 'You don't know how long I've waited for…it's so good to see you, Annie. Gosh, my darling, you've grown into such a pretty young lady.'

Annie looked away, searching for the right words. Carmichael passed them both a tissue from a packet he'd brought with him.

Sue dabbed her eyes, and looked at him. 'You've no idea how happy you've made me. I can't believe you managed to track her down. Wait a second, where's Tom?'

'I asked him not to come,' he said. 'There's some things we need to discuss. For starters, why didn't you tell me you were a trustee for the factory's pension fund?'

'What does it matter? I didn't think it was important.'

'Not important? It could be key in proving Ben had nothing to do with the money disappearing.'

'I don't understand. What does that have to do with me?'

'I know what happened to the money. Ben knew. I found the paperwork amongst his possessions. On the night he died he was desperately trying to get the money back. That's who he was talking to when you returned from your night out with Pat.'

'Oh God! Who took the money?'

'George Murphy was involved, but the money was taken by a man you knew as Kevin Lyons.'

'Lyons? He was the office manager. *He's* the reason Pat and I had to stop working there.'

'I know. She told me.'

'Kevin took the money? You're positive?'

Annie grunted, but continued to look away.

'Murphy has confessed his involvement in the fraud to the police, and is in custody.'

'Has Lyons been arrested then?'

He shook his head. 'That's the other thing we need to talk about. At first I thought he had killed Ben, but then…'

'But whoever took the money, killed Ben. That's what you said.'

Annie slammed her hands on the table. 'Stop lying, mother!'

The room fell silent, as everyone turned to see who had shouted. The two prison guards at the exits looked over at their table. Carmichael offered an apologetic wave of his hand.

Annie lowered her voice. 'It's time to tell the truth.'

Sue frowned. 'I don't know what you're talking about. I didn't kill your father.'

Annie shook her head. 'You're unbelievable. Even after all this time you still won't admit what you did. It's not fair on me, it's not fair on dad's memory, and it's not fair on Tom. He needs to move on with his life, rather than wasting time trying to prove you didn't do something you did.'

'I don't understand where all this hostility is coming from, Annie. I *am* telling the truth. I didn't kill your dad.'

'I *heard* you do it!' Annie growled.

'What?'

'That night. I heard you come home drunk. I heard you stumble into the chest of drawers in my room. I smelt the wine on your breath as you bent to kiss me. I heard you arguing with dad in the kitchen. I heard you stab him and then run from the house. I heard you telling the neighbour you'd found him stabbed. Why didn't you admit the truth then? Why do you still deny it now?'

Sue raised both hands to her mouth. She stared in disbelief.

'It's time to tell the truth, Sue,' Carmichael interjected. 'If you admit what you did, there might still be a chance of parole, but you have to show some remorse. You've served most of your sentence already. Nobody cares about your case anymore. Admit the truth, get out of here, and make things right before…well, before it's too late.'

Sue blew her nose on the tissue. 'Do you want to know the truth? Do you want to know what really happened that night? Are you ready for this, Annie? I've kept it buried for so many years, but as you refuse to admit what *you* did, I guess I'll have to tell him for you. I don't understand why you continue to project your actions on me.' She shook her head. 'Maybe you don't remember what happened. I've read about people who are so unable to come to terms with something bad they've done, that their subconscious mind projects it onto someone else. That way, the real culprit disassociates their own guilt.'

Annie glared at her. 'Now you're trying to blame it on me? I think I've heard it all now. Why won't you admit the truth?'

'Okay, but don't say I didn't warn you!' She took a deep breath. 'I arrived home around nine. I heard Ben arguing with someone on the phone, and I tried to speak to him, but he shut the -'

'He was speaking to Murphy,' he interrupted. 'He was demanding Murphy get the pension fund back, so he could make things right for the staff at the factory.'

Sue glared at Annie. 'Anyway, he closed the door when he saw me, so I headed to bed. My head was pounding, and I was certain I was getting one of my migraines. I checked on you, Annie, and your brother, and then closed your doors. I took one of my pills and went to bed. I was out until something woke me. As I walked out to the stairs, I noticed Annie's door was ajar. I knew I'd closed it when I'd checked on her, which meant someone must have opened it after I'd gone to bed. I went downstairs and found Ben in the kitchen. The knife was on the floor next to him, and that's when I ran to get the vet next door. The last thing Ben said to me was your name, Annie. He whispered it while we tried to stem the flow of the blood. At the time I didn't know what had happened to him, or why he'd said your name, but then, when the police brought you and your brother down, I saw you were wearing different pyjamas from the ones I'd seen you in when I'd checked on you. You gave me such a look of fear, that I knew at that moment *you'd* stabbed him.'

Annie shook her head. 'I don't believe this.'

Carmichael raised his eyebrows. 'If you suspected Annie, why didn't you tell the police?'

'Do you have children, Mr Carmichael?'

He narrowed his eyes. 'No.'

'When you do, you'll understand why I've had to keep this secret for all these years. How could I tell the police my daughter killed her dad? They would have taken *her* away and she'd have spent the best part of *her* life behind bars. It was my responsibility as a parent to protect her. I assumed Ben had lost his temper with her and lashed out, as he'd done to me, and she'd reacted to defend herself. I couldn't allow her to be arrested.'

'But why accept the guilt for something you didn't do?'

'I didn't. I never have! I've maintained I didn't kill Ben, and that's the truth.'

'Granted, but by not telling the police of your suspicions, you're still here.'

'It's a small price to pay to protect a child. I'd do it again in a heartbeat.'

Annie wiped her eyes. 'After I heard you run from the house, I went to check on dad. I found him in the kitchen. He was barely breathing. I tried to help him, but he was bleeding too quickly. I went to change, and call an ambulance, but you returned. *That's* why I was in different pyjamas, and probably also why he said my name. The look of fear you saw was because I thought you'd killed him.'

Sue wiped her eyes. 'So you didn't stab him?'

Annie shook her head, as more tears filled her eyes. 'I swear on my daughter's life I didn't.'

Sue's hands fell on Annie's, and her voice cracked with emotion. 'You have a daughter. I have a granddaughter?'

Annie nodded vigorously, causing the tears to splash on the table top.

Carmichael coughed to get their attention. 'So if neither of you did it, who was the woman Annie heard Ben arguing with? Annie, can you remember anything else? Did you hear what they were arguing about?'

'I told you this morning, I couldn't make out exactly what they were saying, as they were shouting over one another…wait, I remember something…right before he yelped she said something. I can't remember exactly what…it was something like "we were peas", or she was his "little pea", or…I don't know.'

Carmichael's eyes widened as he made a connection. 'Oh my God, you're certain? I think I know who it was. I think I know who stabbed Ben. I need to go.'

Sue and Annie both stared at him, as he stood to leave. 'Wait, who?'

'I need to check something out first. I'll be in touch as soon as I can prove exactly why she did it.'

60

Beth finished drinking her tea, and put her mug on the edge of Melissa's desk. 'What time did you say Johnson would be back?'

Melissa looked at her watch. 'His appointment at the prison was at half two, but it depends what the traffic is like on the way back. It's nearly seven, and I would have expected him back by now.'

'Is his phone still switched off?'

'Yeah, his battery's probably dead. He's always forgetting to charge it.'

'Sounds like Johnson. I'm not sure how much longer to wait. I suppose we can always tell him what we learned about Harry Knowles tomorrow.' Beth yawned. 'It's been a long day. I should get something to eat.'

Melissa picked up the two mugs. 'I'll take these out and rinse them. Can you wait until I come back? I hate locking up this place on my own.'

'Sure. Can you tell me where the facilities are?'

'Of course. They're downstairs by the waiting room. I'll grab my things and meet you there.'

Beth left the office and headed down the stairs. Melissa put the mugs in the kitchen sink and then removed her coat from the back of the door. She heard the front door close and the sound of footsteps on the staircase.

'At last,' she shouted, as she made her way from the office. 'I thought you were never going to get…' She paused when she saw it wasn't him climbing the stairs. 'Oh, I'm sorry, I thought you were somebody else. Do you have an appointment to see Johnson?'

The woman was breathless when she made it to the final step. She pushed the straggly fringe away from her eyes. 'No, dear. I don't have an appointment. Would you mind if I sit while I get my breath back?'

'Of course,' Melissa said, leading the woman through to her office and helping her into a chair. 'I'll go and get you a glass of water.'

'That would be lovely, dear.'

Melissa returned a moment later, and placed the glass on the desk in front of the woman. 'Were you looking to hire an investigator for some reason?'

'Oh no, dear. I'm Helen Dewis. I'm Tom's aunt.'

Melissa smiled warmly. 'Ah, that's who you are. I thought there was something familiar about your face. I was asking myself, where have I seen that face before? If you're after an update on the progress of the case, I'm afraid I can't help. My partner, Johnson, is handling that side of things. He should be back any _'

'Oh, I'm not after an update, dear. I came to see you.'

Melissa frowned. 'Me? I don't understand.'

Helen placed her large shopping bag on the floor by her feet. 'I saw you at Angel Hall earlier today. I saw you speaking with Dr Stark. I want to know what he told you.'

'You were at the hospital earlier?'

'That's right, dear.'

'I'm sorry, it's been a long day, and I'm tired. Am I missing something?'

'I followed you back here. I want to know what Stark told you and that police woman.'

Melissa frowned again. 'About you? We weren't talking about -'

'Don't give me that!' she snapped. 'I know why you were there. Tom told you about my mood swings, didn't he? I want to know what Stark said to you.'

'I'm sorry, Helen is it? I don't know what you're talking about. My visit to Angel Hall had nothing to do with -'

'Liar! What did Stark tell you?'

Melissa stood to exert her authority. 'Excuse *me*! What I was discussing with Dr Stark has nothing to do with you. I didn't even know Tom had an aunt before you walked in here and introduced yourself. Now, either tell me what you want, or get out of my office!'

Helen snatched the glass and threw it at Melissa. It smashed on contact with the side of her forehead.

Melissa dropped to her knees, clutching her head. 'What the -'

She couldn't finish before Helen was around the desk, dragging her by the hair. 'We can do this the easy way or the hard way. It's your choice.' She was stronger than her frame suggested. She forced Melissa's face onto the desk, and grabbed a pair of scissors from the desk tidy. 'You won't look nearly as pretty with an eye patch.'

The warm blood was trickling down the side of Melissa's face. She wanted to lash out, but the blade of the scissors was precariously close to her left eye.

'What did Stark tell you? Did he tell you I'm paranoid? That I suffer from black-outs? I bet he didn't tell you I'm off my meds.' She laughed manically. 'He thinks he's so smart, that one, but he isn't as clever as he makes out. You know, he says I project things. I threatened him once apparently. I don't remember it of course. I'd blacked out when it happened. A bit too convenient if you ask me. How could I have threatened him and have no memory of it? What does he take me for? He wants to get me in there permanently so he can get his hands on my money. Well, I won't go. I don't need that place! I'll show him.'

'Please,' Melissa gasped. 'You don't have to do this. It's just a misunderstanding. I swear I wasn't speaking to him about you. I was talking to him about another patient; someone called Kevin Lyons. He used to work for your brother.'

'What about my brother? That's why you was there wasn't it? You was asking Stark whether I killed my big brother, wasn't you?'

'Wait, what? No. I -'

'You don't know what Ben was like. I loved him. He took care of me. He loved me too, until that bitch took him away from me. She stole Ben from me, and there was nothing I could do to get him back.'

'Please,' Melissa whimpered. 'Put the scissors away, and we can talk about -'

'Shut it, slut! You're just like that bitch. You think your big eyes and hair can tempt all the boys away, don't you? Well, why can't you find a man of your own? Eh? Why did you have to go after my Ben? You took away my true love.'

'Helen, I'm not Sue. I never met Ben.'

She pulled Melissa's head up and then slammed it back against the desk. 'You're as bad as each other. When we was kids, Ben used to take care of me. He showed me what it meant to be loved. He used to tell me how pretty I was. He told me there was no prettier girl in the whole world. I knew if I could get him away from that whore, he would see me that way again. That's why I went to his house that night. I told him he'd made a mistake marrying the bitch, but he could still have me. I told him we could run away and live together. We could go somewhere where nobody knew us. He said he would never leave his kids. I told him they could come with us; that I'd be a better mother to them than that whore. I kissed him, and he pushed me away. He said I was delusional to think he would lie with me again. He broke my heart. He told me to leave. Can you believe that? My own brother tried to throw me out of his house! My fingers brushed against the handle of the knife, and before I knew it, he was slumped on the floor with the knife in his gut. It wasn't me. It was that bitch. She poisoned him against me, and that's why he died. It was her fault! Don't you see?'

Melissa was panting heavily, as her fingers gripped the edge of the desk. 'Yes, I see. You're right, it was her fault.'

'That's why she has to pay for what she did. She shouldn't still be breathing after what she did. You agree, don't you?'

'Yes.'

'Good. That's why I came here to see you, you bitch. It's so you can make up for what you did. When I kill you, it'll be over. Everything will go back to normal then. I will have avenged Ben's death. It'll bring balance. That's what Stark keeps banging on about. He says the balance is wrong in my head. When I saw you talking to him earlier I knew what you was there for. I knew you was talking about Tom's crazy old aunt.'

Melissa's fingers brushed a shard of glass, and without hesitation, she grabbed it, and thrust her head back with all her might. Helen stumbled backwards into the wall, and Melissa swung round and scraped the shard down the older woman's face. Helen shrieked, and lunged at Melissa with the scissors. Melissa bolted around the desk, but her foot caught on the handle of Helen's shopping bag and she fell forward. She scrambled to her feet, but Helen was on her in no time, and the two crashed through the office door into the hallway. Melissa was on her back, her arms pinned by Helen's knees.

Helen cackled as she raised the scissors above her head. 'Tell Ben I'll see him again soon.'

Melissa closed her eyes as the blades hurtled towards her, but just as she expected intense pain, Helen was flung off her in a commotion. Melissa opened her eyes, and was relieved to see Beth lying on top of her attacker.

She showed her the scissors. 'You okay?'

Melissa nodded, but couldn't hold back the tears. She put a hand to her face.

'Don't worry. Johnson's parking the car. I heard the end of what she said. We'll take her to the station. Are you sure you're okay?'

Melissa gave her a thumbs up, so she wouldn't have to answer.

EPILOGUE

Beth laid the bunch of flowers and stepped backwards. 'What time will Sue be released?'

Carmichael lowered his head. 'In the next couple of hours I think.'

'I'm surprised you didn't want to be there.'

'It's a family affair. Tom and Annie will be there. That's all she needs.'

'You must be pleased that her conviction will be overturned?'

'I'd say I'm satisfied. An innocent woman has been released, but at what cost? She's spent sixteen years behind bars, and missed her son and daughter growing up. I just hope she has enough time left to get to know her granddaughter.'

'But that's a good thing, right? Without you, she never would have known she had a granddaughter. She owes you a lot.'

'What's the latest on Helen?'

'It's been a week since we arrested her at your office, but she refused to comment in every interview we've done. I don't think the CPS will prosecute. They believe she is guilty, but aren't convinced they will secure a sound conviction. With her continuing treatment at the Angel Hall Institute, any defence solicitor will claim she isn't fit to stand trial. Only time will tell what will happen to Helen. The important thing is that the truth is out there now.'

'It frustrates me that all this mess could have been avoided if Sue had told the truth sooner. If she'd told the police she suspected Annie, maybe they would have found the truth sooner. She's wasted her life.'

'The things parents do for their children, right?'

He stepped forward and laid his bunch of flowers next to Beth's. 'I wonder what Anita would have made of it all.'

'I think she'd have been proud that her dad pieced it all together.'

He gently rested his hand on the gravestone. The ground was still soft beneath his feet. 'Thank you for coming with me today. I'm not sure I could have come alone. Not yet anyway.'

'I'm glad you felt you could ask me.'

'Who else have I got?'

'There's Melissa.'

'She behaves more like my mother most of the time.'

'It's only because she cares about you. We both do.'

'I know. In spite of everything, I know I'm lucky to have you both in my life.'

'I do understand, you know: why you allowed Lennon to fall from that building. I hated you for it for a long time.'

'What's changed?'

She shrugged. 'When we were in the farmhouse, you risked your own life to save mine. Even when Sanza revealed his true nature, you still wanted to save him. I think you've changed. I know Sanza tried to manipulate you with religion, but maybe some good has come from it. You seem…I don't know…different somehow.'

'To be honest, for the first time in a long time, I feel different. I thought I was somehow to blame for Anita's death, but now I can see that it couldn't be helped. I don't know if I believe in heaven and hell, but I hope there is a heaven, and that Anita is there now.'

They walked slowly from the graveside.

'So what's next for you, Johnson? Have you got more work lined up?'

'Actually, I was thinking about taking a break from the P.I. work for a while. I've been burying myself in work for too long. If I've learned one thing from this whole episode, it's not to keep things bottled up.'

'That sounds sensible. What will you do instead? A holiday?'

'I've got an appointment with a counsellor in the morning. I know now I have a problem, and I need to get professional help for it. I've told Melissa to keep things ticking over with the business until I'm ready to return. Everything that happened with Anita is still raw, and I won't be able to move on properly until that's fully resolved. Coming here today is the first step on that path.'

'I'm really pleased to hear that.' She stopped and took his hands in hers. 'I meant what I said earlier. I *do* still care for you.'

'What are you saying, Beth? You want to get back together?'

'I'm saying let's take things one step at a time. Okay? A lot of water has passed under the bridge, and

I don't know if there is any coming back from that. But I'm willing to try if you are?'

He leaned in and gently kissed her cheek. 'I never stopped loving you, Beth. If there's even the slightest chance that I can win you back, I'll do everything I can to achieve it.'

She smiled. 'I'm hungry. Do you fancy taking me out for lunch?'

He led her back to the car, and they both climbed in. He started the engine, and pulled away. As they drove past the small chapel, he raised his eyes to the sky and offered a small prayer for Paul.

THE END

A MESSAGE FROM STEPHEN

First of all, I want to say a massive thank you to you for choosing to read 'Downfall'. If you did enjoy it, I would be very grateful if you could leave a review for it. It doesn't need to be long, just a few words, but it makes such a difference to unknown authors like me. It helps new readers discover one of my books for the first time.

I would also love to hear from you too. Did you like P.I. Johnson Carmichael? Would you like to see him return to investigating crimes? Do you want to know whether Beth and Carmichael will rekindle their romance?

'Downfall' is the fourth book to feature Carmichael, and I'm taking a break from writing about him for now. I am currently writing a new series, featuring a non-nonsense solicitor called Katie Matthews. The first book, 'The Accused' will be published later in 2016. It is a dark, mystery-thriller, set in modern Southampton, focusing on the conflict faced by all legal professionals: how do you ensure the guilty are punished, and the innocent walk free?

You can get in touch with me via Facebook, Twitter, Goodreads and my website www.stephenedger.com. I read every message and will always reply. If this is the first of my books you've read, I have included descriptions of my other books in the pages that follow.

ALSO BY STEPHEN EDGER

Integration

THE OFFER

Mark Baines is a Team Leader in a call centre. He dislikes his job and dreams of the day he can afford to give up his job and buy the house of his dreams. Following a terrifying burglary at his home, he is contacted by a group prepared to pay him one million pounds in return for a favour.

THE CATCH

The offer seems too good to be true, and he begins to worry about what they might expect in return. The group calls again and tells him to integrate their laundered monies through the bank he works for, but he refuses. When Mark's girlfriend Gabrielle goes missing and his brother is attacked, Mark begins to realise just how far the group will go to get what they want.

EVERYONE HAS THEIR PRICE

As the game begins and the pressure mounts, Mark finds himself risking everything he has to find Gabrielle and save his own life before the group and the police catch up with him.

INTEGRATION

Blackmail, murder, suspense, conspiracy and money laundering: **Integration** is a British crime thriller set in the murky depths of the finance industry.

ALSO BY STEPHEN EDGER

Remorse

'I didn't mean to kill her. That is the first thing you need to understand about me...'

FAIRY-TALE LIFE

John Duggan had it all: married with a beautiful four month-old daughter; Manager with a career on the up; nice house in a good area of Southampton.

BEHIND CLOSED DOORS

His wife is cheating on him; his daughter's relentless screaming deprives them of sleep; he drinks too much.

ON THE EDGE

Unable to deal with the mounting pressure, he hires a private investigator to spy on his wife. But Johnson Carmichael has troubles of his own.

As the conclusion of Duggan's trial looms, he must come to terms with what he has done and why he is facing a life behind bars. He is about to learn a valuable lesson: not every fairy-tale has a happy ending…

REMORSE

Betrayal, revenge, regret and suspense: ***Remorse*** is a gritty British thriller exploring what fathers will do when driven to desperation.

ALSO BY STEPHEN EDGER

Redemption

LAST YEAR

Mark Baines was blackmailed into integrating two hundred and fifty million pounds of laundered money through the bank he worked for. The same group framed him for murder. Now serving two life sentences in a maximum security prison, the future looks bleak.

BREAK OUT

A siege at the prison allows Mark to escape with a mysterious group who know everything about him. They are searching for a secret passage buried somewhere in the heart of London, and they believe Mark is the key to finding it.

UNDERWORLD

Ali Jacobs is undercover with a Russian mafia family in London. She is shocked when her path brings her into contact with Mark again.

Kidnap, car chases, and an uneasy union with underworld figures mean Mark is in a race against time to prove his innocence and find redemption.

REDEMPTION

Kidnap, torture, blackmail and revenge: **Redemption** is the breath-taking follow-up to the acclaimed *Integration*.

ALSO BY STEPHEN EDGER

Snatched

Approximately one hundred and fifty thousand children go missing in the U.K. every year. That's one child every three and a half minutes.

ABDUCTION

Every parent's worst nightmare: seven year-old Natalie Barrett is snatched walking home from school. The police begin a desperate hunt to find her before it is too late. They fear the worst when a body is located near a golf course.

THE FALLOUT

Sarah Jenson is Natalie's teacher. When one of the detectives on the case is suddenly killed, Sarah believes the events may be linked and begins to search for answers. She is in a race against time to discover the true identity of the perpetrator before Natalie winds up as another statistic.

UNANSWERED QUESTIONS

Where were Natalie's parents when they should have been collecting her? Why was Natalie so scared of her Uncle Jimmy? Could a convicted sexual offender from Sarah's past be involved?

Children not found within the first seventy-two hours, rarely return home alive. Sarah knows the clock is ticking…

SNATCHED

Abduction, terror, suspense and sorrow: Snatched is a breath-taking British crime thriller set in Southampton.

ALSO BY STEPHEN EDGER

Shadow Line

THURSDAY NIGHT

The pilot of a routine flight from Paris deliberately crash lands the plane at Southampton airport. Miraculously, there are no fatalities, but who is the man in the Panama hat risking his life to save all on board and who is the mystery eighty-third passenger?

FRIDAY MORNING

An insurance broker carrying an automatic gun opens fire on his colleagues before turning the gun on himself. What motivated him to take such drastic measures and where did he get the weapon?

SATURDAY MORNING

A student enters the West Quay shopping centre with a bomb strapped to his chest. He takes control of the complex and begins to preach from the Qur'an. Why is he bringing his terrorist act to Southampton and why did he choose today?

IN THE SHADOWS

Charged with leading the three investigations, D.I. Jack Vincent is under enormous pressure to deliver results.

SHADOW LINE

Murder, espionage, suspense, terrorism and a face from the past: *Shadow Line* is the thrilling follow-up to *Redemption*.

ALSO BY STEPHEN EDGER

Trespass

VICTIM

September 1989: Beth Roper is a single mother struggling to earn enough money to take care of her four year-old daughter, Lauren. One night, she is followed home by a stranger who forces his way in and brutally assaults her whilst her daughter sleeps in the next room.

ATTACKER

May 1993: Known deviant, Nathan Green is on trial for the violent assault of two women and the murder of a third. The trial forces the victims to confront the man whose eyes they will never forget. He is eventually sentenced to life in prison, but it doesn't feel like justice for one of the victims.

ACCUSER

November 2013: Following her mother's passing, a now adult Lauren Roper hires Private Investigator Johnson Carmichael to prove that it was Nathan Green who assaulted her mother back in 1989.

With no evidence, no witnesses and only the fragile memory of the client to work with, this is a case Carmichael doesn't want. However, when he begins to ask questions and his life is threatened, he learns there is more to Lauren's claims than first thought.

TRESPASS

Fear, murder, revenge, and suspense: ***Trespass*** is a gritty thriller examining the horrifying effects of sexual assault.

ALSO BY STEPHEN EDGER

Crosshairs

WARNING

This morning, Southampton MP Eve Partridge received a hand-delivered letter threatening revenge for her failure to serve the city. She contacts the police immediately but despite her protests they ignore the warning. When the terrorist later contacts D.C.I. Mercure and tells her where he's left his first bomb, the threat becomes clear.

THE GAME

Whilst the police scramble to discover who is behind the bombs, five strangers carry on their lives, unaware that they have been targeted to play a part in the bomber's endgame. D.S. Kyle Davies is on a train to meet his new D.I. when an assassin known as 'The Serpent' contacts him directly and tells him they are going to play a little game. If Kyle does what he is told, The Serpent will tell him how to stop the final bomb exploding at 7 p.m.

RELENTLESS

With no other choice, Kyle must risk everything to take on the challenge. As the deadline approaches, The Serpent reveals the bomb is on a bus. What he won't confirm is which of the six passengers on board has the detonator.
Five innocent people. One bomber. The clock is ticking…

CROSSHAIRS

Politics, conspiracy, terrorism and suspense: ***Crosshairs*** is a British crime thriller delivered minute-by-minute until its gripping finale. This is the first book in 'The Cadre' series.

ALSO BY STEPHEN EDGER

Complicit

REUNION

Connor Price is a young man meandering through life without purpose. He receives a chance phone call from Dylan Thomas, his best friend from school and they agree to meet up. Dylan offers him money if Connor will go with him to a meeting. Connor is suspicious but Dylan assures him it is nothing illegal.

ON THE RUN

Connor's world is turned upside down when he witnesses Dylan execute two Russian gangsters at the meeting, and then steal their bags full of cocaine and cash. When Dylan disappears, Connor is left to face the music alone, and becomes the target of the drug dealer, loan shark and Russian mafia who Dylan ripped off.

NO ESCAPE

The Chairman of a secret organisation known as 'The Cadre' is hunting Dylan as well. He has terrifying plans for Britain's future and will stop at nothing to achieve his goals. He uses the members of his organisation to exert the necessary pressure to get to the truth.

Connor is fighting for his freedom, his future and his life. Who do you turn to when even the police are after you?

COMPLICIT

Politics, espionage, conspiracy and finance: ***Complicit*** is the breath-taking follow-up to *Crosshairs*. This is the second book in 'The Cadre' series.

ALSO BY STEPHEN EDGER

Double Cross

LOOKING FOR ANSWERS

Aaron Cross is hunting for the men responsible the death of his uncle. He finds himself retracing his uncle's final movements in Mexico. Dylan Thomas is still running from The Cadre whilst searching for his missing girlfriend. When Aaron's and Dylan's paths collide, little do they realise how much they are going to need each other if they are to survive and finally stop The Cadre's plans for a New World Order.

IMPOSSIBLE ODDS

D.I. Tony White and D.S. Kyle Davies are also trying to prove who really masterminded the terrorist attack on Southampton. Their chief suspect is MP Eve Partridge, but with the whole country and The Cadre supporting her, their chances of building a case are remote at best. With nobody they can trust but each other, they set out on a dangerous journey to deliver justice.

NEW WORLD ORDER

It seems like nothing will stop The Cadre achieving their plans for world domination. But they didn't account for the four men with nothing to lose, who cannot be bought and will risk everything in the pursuit of freedom.

DOUBLE CROSS

Politics, terrorism, conspiracy and suspense: ***Double Cross*** is the non-stop thriller that concludes *Crosshairs* and *Complicit*. This book is the final part in 'The Cadre' series.

ALSO BY STEPHEN EDGER

Fragments

CHRISTMAS 2014

Following an argument with her parents, 15 year old Freya Coleman storms out of the house. In tears, she goes to meet the only person who understands her: Robbie, the nice guy she's been chatting to online. She doesn't return home.

ONE YEAR LATER

A teenager's body is found in a Southampton park. She is gaunt, bruised, and barely breathing. She is rushed to hospital, but has been so badly abused that doctors fear her fragmented memory may never recover. When another girl is reported missing a day later, D.I. White of the Hampshire Major Investigation Team fears Freya's attacker has struck again.

GHOST OF CHRISTMAS PAST

With White's team focused on finding the new missing teenager, Freya's parents hire Private Investigator Johnson Carmichael to find the person who abducted their daughter. The family has a secret they can't tell the police, and it might just lead Carmichael to 'Robbie'.

FRAGMENTS

Mystery, suspense, abduction, and terror...***Fragments*** is an emotive, thrilling whodunit from the author of *Snatched* and *Remorse*.

Made in the USA
Charleston, SC
09 June 2016